Praise for Broken to Whole

'We hear and read a lot about anxiety, depression and post-traumatic stress disorder. However, even extremely stressful experiences often bring positive personal growth and transformation. Dr Gifford's book *Broken to Whole*, builds on his own experience of these which became the catalyst for turning the direction of his life upwards and towards positive growth rather than downwards into a pit of despair. This highly practical book explains how to turn tragedy into triumph. It is about transforming a mindset of easily justifiable victimhood, into a mindset of personal victory over self-pity; psychologically, socially, and spiritually. This path to growth is difficult as life's darker blessings rarely feel good at the beginning. Dr Gifford explains that it is not what happens to us that determines our quality of life, but rather, with what core motive we choose to view it through—LOVE or fear. Such a choice comes upon us, not as a mere intellectual decision but as an experiential transformation.'

Dr Phil Harker, Clinical and Organisational Psychologist, Author of upcoming book; *One Degree of Freedom: Solving the Free-Will Problem*

'Everyone, whatever their circumstances, will be challenged and enriched by reading this book by Dr Gifford. From the very beginning it is patently clear that the author has walked the talk. *Broken to Whole: How to put Humpty together again* is not only an authentic account of his personal journey from deep despair to clear-eyed optimism, but offers the reader a wealth of counsel and helpful exercises for anyone seeking a way forward. There are no slick remedies but well documented strategies for achieving personal growth and optimism for one's future. I highly commend it to anyone seeking to find ultimate purpose in life in the midst of a fractured world.'

David Hayles, Former Director of Careers Service, University of Western Australia. Elected Board Member of the Graduate Careers Council of Australia (GCCA)

'*Broken to Whole: How to put Humpty together again* is both a radical self-transformation guide and one man's affecting story of what it is to rise from the ashes. Dr Edward Gifford takes the reader through a series of strategies which will shortcut your journey to wholeness, exposing the unconscious forces which might be holding you back. Anyone who needs to bust through their personal blocks and live a life of greater fulfilment and happiness would do well to read this book.'

Michalia Arathimos PhD, Multiple prize-winning author of short stories and essays and winner of the *Sunday Star Times* Short Story Competition 2016

'Dr Edward Gifford to me has always been the consummate businessman and above all a properly decent human being who has that uncanny knack of really listening to others. His generosity in assisting and encouraging entrepreneurs is extraordinary and his story will inspire you to see things differently and take action to ensure you are fully supported in everything you seek to achieve. Life is not a children's fairy tale; it is very real, and his book, *Broken to Whole* is the guiding light you need to discover your own way through.'

Lauren Clemett, The Audacious Agency; International Award Winner, Best-Selling Author

'In this ever-changing world, it is easy to disconnect from who you really are and what your unique personal purpose is. Dr Edward Gifford shares real stories, inspiring you to live your whole life 'on purpose' each day. *Broken to Whole* will bring to life and help you to put into practice some of the most valuable lessons that will transform your personal and business path. If you are at a crossroads and looking for greater purpose and meaning in your life, this powerful book is one you will want to read again and again.'

Annette Stanton, Author, *The Power of Vision*; International Speaker & Master Coach

'Do you wish at times that you could have a more fulfilled, aligned life at a higher level of satisfaction? In *Broken to Whole: How to put Humpty together again*, Dr Gifford has brought together essentials of a change in a very readable, helpful, and grounded way. If this is you, reading this book will provide you insights and more than that, actual ways of implementing change in your own life. Having benefited from Edward Gifford's teaching personally, I know that accessing his wisdom and clarity will be so helpful for so many.'

Dr John Warlow, MBChB, FRANZCP.
Psychiatrist, Author, and Founder
of *Living Wholeness*

'Dr Gifford's book *Broken to Whole: How to put Humpty together again* picks the eyes out of abundant, yet often challenging areas of human achievements, with his goals being to enhance optimal personal, business and professional behaviours and outcomes. It is unique in that it simplifies and is thus ideal for the lay reader, yet at the same time challenges the exploring and the adventurous. His presentation is authoritative yet simple, and each section is beautifully summarised and referenced. Readers will find the book a delightful and informative read.'

Dr John Ryan, MBBS(Qld), MSc Lon
(Distinction), FRACGP, MRCGP
(UK), DCH (Irel), FICAN (Nutrition
USA), FAMAC, FACNEM

'Edward Gifford weaves his personal reflections and stories gained through many years of coaching with his academic writing flair; frequently sharing principles and metaphors from authors widely accepted as leaders in their fields. *Broken to Whole: How to put Humpty together again* is designed to offer the reader a chance to work through strategies using various 'lenses' to come up with answers to their own spiritual and life approaches. It is a valuable read for coaches who work tirelessly to engage their clients in the deeper elements of life expectations.'

Arlene Quinn, R.N. M.Comm,
Professional Certified Coach
(International Coach Federation)

'Stop procrastinating! Follow Edward Gifford's process and achieve those long-coveted goals.'
Paul Hewish, CEO, Oceanic Controls Pty Ltd

'Finding purpose takes time and introspection. With the help of Broken to Whole's probing questions and insights, I came up with my purpose statement: I exist to serve by Encouraging Growth. I love that Purpose is more encompassing than your job title, your business, or your talent. The wider wisdom Edward Gifford draws into this book will help readers understand and live in alignment with their true self. If you're your own worst critic, down on yourself or ready to quit, then be prepared to open the window and let some fresh and challenging ideas in.'
Jennifer Lancaster, author of
Creative Ways with Money

'I have known Dr Edward Gifford for over 25 years. He is a man of compassion, courage and integrity. His new book, *Broken to Whole: How to put Humpty together again*, which builds on his personal recovery from adversity, is an inspirational story. He insightfully explores his recovery in this intensely personal book and the processes and lessons that he outlines should provide useful learnings for many of his readers, helping them to attain more fulfilment in their lives.'
Ted Scott AM, former CEO of Stanwell
Corporation; Author of *Augustus Finds Serenity;*
***Yu the Dragon Tamer; Froth and Goblets* and**
co-author of *The Myth of Nine to Five*

'*Broken to Whole* is a timely self-guide book for these chaotic and uncertain times, where it is more common than not, to get off track or lose direction. It is a rich resource for taking stock of life, finding your anchor, enriching your career and along the way, being aligned with your true self. Supported by an array of reflective exercises, Dr Gifford gently guides the reader, step by step, on how to secure and live a meaningful and purposeful life, challenging us to make paradigm shifts in the way we live and work. He shares with you decades of experience and knowledge as a career and life coach. But what makes it a powerful read, is that he shares of himself. You learn from his mistakes, his struggles his experiences, his wisdom. This is a "dig deep, reach down into the depths of your soul and spirit" type of book. Not for the fainthearted but richly rewarding for those who take seriously what they will find within. It could change your life.'

Rob Ware, Workplace and Career Coach;
Director – WorkWare Solutions

'This is an inspiring and educational book full of empowering and life changing strategies to guide you to map out a purposeful life and yet made simple and elegant by the masterful work of Dr Edward Gifford. The book's depth and detail are impressive, a sound prescription based on research and evidence-based information for anyone wanting to improve their life, business, relationships and wellbeing. *Broken to Whole: How to put Humpty together again* is a game changing book which gives guidance and at the same time exposes the limitations of the status quo.'

John Hebrard, Head of Commercial Sales &
Small Business Solutions - TAFE Queensland

'The furnace of personal adversity honestly reflected on and grown through, combined with the intellect of the author, Dr Edward Gifford, results in a work with some gold nuggets to be mined by almost every reader. Thank you Edward.'

Andrew Lind, Chairman & Director
- Corney & Lind Lawyers

'In this captivating and inspirational book *Broken to Whole: How to put Humpty together again*, Dr Edward Gifford gives profound insights into the things that can hold us back or impede us in life and provides powerful, practical strategies to overcome these. The timeless principles and wisdom in this book are a brilliant roadmap and resource for anyone wishing to reach their potential and live a life of purpose and meaning. I have been thoroughly inspired to take action and apply these strategies in my own work and personal life!'

Bryan Barclay, Senior State Manager -
Opportunity International Australia

'Dr Edward Gifford's book, is a gift that awakens your soul in such a gentle manner that can only be written by someone who has walked the path from broken to whole. There is no over-the-top fanfare. Rather a practical, doable, step-by-step roadmap to awareness, choice and purpose. You will love this book and love the ending. Thank you for writing such a relevant book Edward.'

**Tess Brook, Director, 1st Call Consulting,
Founder of: Cohesive Conversation
Professional Development Portal &
Confident Conversations Method**

'A riveting personal story of triumph over adversity expertly woven into a formula for finding satisfaction, fulfilment and happiness in life - this book fits into the "read it once every year" category. Don't open this book without a box of tissues, a full day (it's a genuine page turner) and your own note book - which you will fill. Prepare to be inspired.'

**Paul Blackburn, Founder of
Global Success Academy**

'Dr Edward Gifford's book offers deep insights into his life journey and includes numerous tips, approaches and strategies to help us overcome the everyday 'demons' that we all face. The influence of knowing your Purpose and being On Purpose, has been a beacon for my personal life as well as my business and it is a constant reminder that this unique and simple tool can be life changing. And so too can this book - filled with easy to use techniques backed by inspirational examples from his clients and his personal story. The book *Broken to Whole: How to put Humpty together again* reflects the heart of who Edward is: courageous, inspiring, caring and just downright honest. Love the book, a good read for anyone ready to embark on a journey of self-discovery.'

**Kristine Berry, Director, People
Connexion Recruitment**

BROKEN TO WHOLE

HOW TO PUT HUMPTY TOGETHER AGAIN...

EDWARD GIFFORD PhD

First Published in Australia in 2020 by Edward Gifford
On-Purpose Partners® Pty Ltd – 101 642 497
4 Pinehurst Crescent
Dunsborough Western Australia 6281
Email: edward@on-purposepartners.com
www.onpurposepartners.com.au

Prepublication Data Services available from the National Library of Australia
Author: Gifford, Edward F.
Title: Broken to Whole: how to put Humpty together again / Dr Edward Gifford.
Edition: 1st ed.
Copyright © Edward Gifford 2020
ISBN: 978-0-9925331-1-3 (pbk)
ISBN: 978-0-9925331-2-0 (ebk)
Subjects: Life skills, Leadership Skills, Purpose, Spirituality, Self-actualisation

Typesetting and layout design by Publicious Book Publishing
Published with the assistance of Publicious Pty Ltd
www.publicious.com.au

While every care has been taken in researching and compiling the information in this book, it is not intended to replace professional advice and counselling. Readers are encouraged to seek professional help and advice with due regard to their own circumstances and as they think is appropriate. The author and the publisher expressly disclaim any liability and responsibility arising from the application of information in this book.

Every effort has been made to contact and or acknowledge copyright holders of material where relevant. Should any infringements have unwittingly occurred, both the author and publisher offer their apologies and will be happy to rectify this in any future editions.

Dedication

To my lifelong friend and best man, the late John Edwin McDiven. When John passed away in March 2018 from pancreatic cancer, I and countless others experienced a great loss. John inspired us all through his resilience, optimism, creativity and humour. John got Mack-Trucked countless times – he'd had encephalitis, was the miraculous survivor of a plane crash and a victim of shocking sexual abuse, had his jewellery business robbed multiple times and had epilepsy.

Through all this John remained determined, diligent and dignified. He would not allow life to defeat him. He was not just a survivor; he was a spiritual giant – a superhero. He was an unforgettable character. In any encounter with John you could only say: 'What a truly amazing man!'

Contents

Foreword   *i*

Author's Note   *ii*

Chapter 1: Finding Purpose   1

Chapter 2: Shifting Paradigms   27

Chapter 3: Understanding Goals   67

Chapter 4: Optimising Growth   105

Chapter 5: Beating Procrastination   165

Chapter 6: Busting Stress   197

Chapter 7: Developing Resilience   223

Putting Humpty Together Again   *247*

Acknowledgements   *248*

Meet the Author   *251*

Humpty Dumpty sat on the wall,
Humpty Dumpty had a great fall.
All the king's horses
And all the king's men,
Couldn't put Humpty together again.

Foreword

Are you, like Humpty, 'sitting on the wall', mostly content with your life and career, but not wanting to push the boundaries of your comfort zone too hard? Deep down – and I think many of us have deep down thoughts and feelings about 'sitting on the wall' – do you yearn for something different? Or is the fear of change greater than the fear of staying the same? If so, have you decided not to challenge the status quo and to let life roll on the same way?

When you are at this point in your life, my observation is that the universe, God or a higher power, whatever you understand that to be, has a way of dealing with us. Some of us just need a prod or push, but others need a Mack Truck. I got *Mack-Trucked!* I not only hit the wall but 'had a great fall'. And when you hit rock bottom you feel shattered, broken and in pieces.

At this point most of us rely on 'all the king's horses and all the king's men' to help us to recover and to 'put us together again'. We rely on the medical system, including psychiatrists, psychologists, psychotherapists, and general practitioners, as well as medication to magically 'heal' us, thereby transforming our brokenness to wholeness.

While we might want the 'silver bullet' or the 'magic pills' to miraculously heal us, despite the good care medical specialists provide and the love and support of family and friends, ultimately we have to do the work *ourselves*. Maybe 'Humpty' has to fall in order to 'rise again' with a renewed mind. This is not about being less broken but about becoming more whole. We are all inherently capable of wholeness despite our circumstances.

This book, *Broken to Whole,* describes how Humpty *can* be put together again, piece by piece, and how to create a new, whole, eternally transformed being.

Author's Note

This is a self-help book with a difference. It's different because it authentically weaves my story around transformative strategies that helped me to piece my life together when 'I had a great fall' and when 'all the king's horses and all the king's men' couldn't put me together again.

My intention was always to write a book that would help people get unblocked so that they could live successful, fulfilling and meaningful lives. Having written nearly five chapters of this work, I sensed a restlessness in my spirit. What I had written was helpful, but it was missing something important. It needed to be more authentic.

I desperately wanted to help my clients and others who were stuck in their lives, businesses and careers. People like me who had 'hit a wall', been *Mack-Trucked* or had their worlds turned upside down. Our company's Purpose is *Inspiring Transformation*. That was the outcome I wanted for my clients and readers: transformation from lives of quiet desperation to lives of wholeness, transformative renewal after depression, after life-changing curve balls, after being stuck in their businesses or careers, after plateauing, after feeling trapped, after hopelessness.

I wanted readers to understand what holds them back and why this happens; to gain clarity around the things that matter most in their lives and how to achieve better in these areas; to set goals for personal and business growth knowing that they will rarely fail. I wanted my readers to understand and apply self-awareness in such a way that they would move from self-absorption to self-observation.

Most importantly I wanted to help my clients and readers to understand who they *really* are and how the One Choice they have can set them free!

Another name for my spiritual DNA is *Igniting Enthusiasm*. That is my personal Purpose statement. So, it's no surprise that through this book I also wanted to revitalise, re-energise and re-motivate readers to live lives that are On Purpose.

Having written several chapters, my spirit was saying: 'Be authentic and tell your story…people don't want to read sermons'. Shortly after this happened, I was having lunch with Angela, my wife and my sounding board. I asked her if she was willing to have a conversation around my reservations about what I had written and my intended title. As always, she readily agreed.

We explored many of the usual questions about target audience, key messages, and the 'golden thread' that would link the content of the manuscript. At that point, I was not happy with my title. After explaining the why, who, what and how of the book to her, Angela said: 'That sounds like 'From Fucked Up to Flourishing'. I was shocked, not only at what she had said but at the fact that she'd even used that terminology! My Judeo-Christian upbringing and values screamed at me, saying: '*You can't call it that – what will people think of you?*' But I decided to sit with it and think about it, and so I did. Later that afternoon while I was walking, something 'clicked' for me. And here's why: This was my story! This was my journey! I went from fucked up to flourishing.

Here's what happened.

Back in 1998, as a Senior Lecturer at university, my life and career fell apart. Apparently I was only a year away from becoming an Associate Professor, when an event (or maybe a series of events) happened. Relating the details would be inappropriate. I'll just say that I was professionally and medically abused under anaesthetic. A week later, not feeling well, I took leave. Two weeks later, attempting to open my office at work, I could not get the key into the lock. My whole body was shaking uncontrollably. It was a scary new experience and sensation. Even now, writing about it, I have goose bumps and my breathing has acutely escalated.

While undertaking the mandatory medical route, I was told by one medical professional: 'You are totally fucked mate'. Later in his report he wrote: 'This man will never work again'.

I left that appointment broken. Tears streamed down my face. I called my wife and got her to come and pick me up. I could hardly speak. I have never cried so much or felt as hopeless as I did that day.

iii

While that incident did snuff out a 20 year academic career, I'm here to tell you that he was wrong. Certainly, I may have been in a dark place at that time, but I still clung to a place called *hope*, knowing my reason for being. I knew that my Purpose and my life were not going to be defined by what others said about me, or by my circumstances. I refused to be a victim.

Together with Angela (who also experienced a life and career-changing event two years after me), I have been running my own business since the year 2000. Having been a salaried worker to suddenly having to find clients who would support us so that we could live and pay the bills was confronting, challenging and scary. It was exciting too, but I'm not sure if I felt that emotion at the time.

The first few years can be described in one word: I was in a *fog*, plain and simple. It was hard to concentrate and focus, and my confidence was at rock bottom. I had to learn a whole new knowledge base, skill set and vocabulary. Sometimes I would be talking but really I had no idea what was happening. Attending networking events in order to meet new people and create brand awareness was scary and difficult. It was a period of reinvention: going from being a Senior Lecturer in Music Education to being a business entrepreneur. Suddenly I was creating, selling and facilitating personal leadership and business development services.

At the time of writing, it is some twenty years since being told I was fucked up and would never work again. However, Humpty has been put back together again. I'm flourishing and living out my Purpose. I have done this through retraining myself to be an internationally recognised professional coach, developing proprietary training programs and workshops for businesses, developing personal leadership, career and coach training and delivering keynote addresses at conferences and for industry-based groups. All in all, I have reached thousands of people, assisting them in transforming their personal lives, businesses and careers.

I want to point out that the title suggested by my wife became a very helpful working title, keeping the 'golden thread' of the themes and chapters together. In the end, I needed a different one for the final publication. But I didn't know what it would be.

The title appeared unexpectedly with the assistance of my daughter Susie. When hearing of my frustration during the finishing stages of the book and how I wanted to move away from my working title, she invited me to a 'walk and talk', which resulted in the current title. It was such a relief! The real title was there all the way through my book, but I couldn't see it on my own!

This book is about my journey from brokenness back to wholeness. The strategies I used 'to put Humpty together again', and that I suggest you may use include:

- Finding my Purpose and learning to live it as a constant presence.
- Living my life from a new paradigm when my old one had failed me and run its course.
- Learning who 'I' really was and that I only had one big choice to make if I wanted true peace of mind.
- Having a growth mindset and learning how to set goals for growth and not for glory.
- Understanding and successfully dealing with my conditioned thinking patterns and outdated stories that had negatively impacted my life and usually resulted in self-sabotage.
- Learning about procrastination, including why I procrastinated and how to overcome procrastination.
- Understanding why I 'had a great fall' and then learning how to handle stress, depression and anxiety.
- How developing my Emotional Intelligence was such an important factor in my journey to wholeness, significance and success.

There are countless other strategies and anecdotes woven throughout each chapter. I'm very mindful that there are so many more powerful stories than this one. But this is mine, I have written it, and I thank you for reading it and journeying with me. My hope and desire is that you will find it helpful. Above all, I hope my story has relevance and meaning for you and that you can take from it what you are ready to take. I hope that you will be able to implement these changes into your own life, as I have in mine, so that you in turn help transform the lives of others.

Humpty Dumpty had a great fall,
Life's curve balls seem to hit us all,
Discovering our Purpose deep in our soul,
Starts our journey from broken to whole.

Chapter 1 – Finding Purpose

'Without purpose we would not exist...
It is purpose that created us...
Purpose that connects us...
Purpose that pulls us...
Purpose that guides us, that drives us, that defines us....
Purpose that binds us.'

Agent Smith, Matrix Reloaded

The Power of Purpose in my Life

It is said that everything happens for a reason. Little did I know that reading a book over 30 years ago was to have such an important and positive impact on me, especially in successfully journeying through and out of depression and ultimately shaping my new career. It was as if this book had been written just for me. Perhaps you too have been touched and impacted at some time in your life by reading a book or listening to a speaker. Timing is everything! Nevertheless, what might be life changing and transformational for some passes others by. The book I refer to is *The On-Purpose Person* by Kevin W. McCarthy[1]. This chapter has been inspired and informed by this book, together with my own experience.

At the end of this chapter, I share how finding and living my Purpose contributed so significantly to my personal transformation from someone experiencing post-traumatic stress to someone experiencing post-traumatic growth.

But first I want to unravel the mystery and confusion around the concept of Purpose, including why you need a Purpose, and how to find your Purpose in your life, business or career. I hold the view that each person and business has a unique Purpose. It follows that we are

1

required to make a contribution to life while we are alive, and this, in turn, unconsciously becomes the key dimension of our legacy.

I will also explain how you can live out your Purpose regardless of your circumstances and conditions, and have it flowing through all aspects of your life, as well as explaining that Purpose is a state of *being*, which helps to keep you in the present. You will also discover that your Purpose has power – more power than you could possibly believe in or imagine. I believe that it is present with you whether you are conscious of it or not.

Finding your Purpose and living it out seven days a week is transformational. If you are stuck or blocked in your life right now, the chances are that you have not found the answer to this deep, fundamental life question: What is my Purpose?

Being Off Purpose

Many people I have met often describe the symptoms of being Off Purpose well before they learn about Purpose, or being On Purpose, so it is worth exploring. When we are 'blocked' or 'stuck' in our life or work we feel Off Purpose. We lack energy, feel depressed, stressed, confused and unmotivated; we can't seem to focus, and our mojo has gone out the door.

Most of us know when we are Off Purpose. Our energy is drained, we regret the past, and we are unfocussed and unfulfilled in the present and anxious about the future.

> Most of us know when we are Off Purpose. Our energy is drained, we regret the past, and we are unfocussed and unfulfilled in the present and anxious about the future.

The personal and professional cost of being Off Purpose is more costly than we can imagine. It drains us of peace of mind, rich and meaningful relationships, confidence, clarity and the deep satisfaction of experiencing life in the present moment. It costs us money too!

I think we have all been there on occasions, as this is part of going through the different seasons of our lives and part of the lived human experience. But being Off Purpose for an extended period means we are in danger of living a diminished life, one lacking in hope and meaning. It's OK to be Off Purpose for a while but it's not OK to stay Off Purpose if we want to live a rich, full and meaningful life.

Could you be going through an Off Purpose period in your life? Inspired by the back cover of The On-Purpose Person[1], here are some questions for you to ask yourself and explore:

- ❑ Are your days and weeks so busy you can hardly think about what is important in your life?
- ❑ Have you got that *empty* feeling deep inside that tells you there is more to life than what you are doing and what you have?
- ❑ Have you been trying to live up to other people's expectations while your own plans and dreams go unfulfilled?
- ❑ Is your life filled yet unfulfilled?
- ❑ Do you feel pulled in a thousand different directions?
- ❑ Is your schedule out of control?
- ❑ Has all the fun and adventure gone out of your life?
- ❑ Are you stuck doing meaningless work – work that has little sense of meaning or fulfilment?
- ❑ Are you unhappy with your career path or present position?
- ❑ Do you feel that you are just exchanging your life for a pay cheque?
- ❑ Do you feel that you are just going through the motions in life or work without being able to make a difference?
- ❑ Is your relationship with your spouse or partner at a crossroad?
- ❑ Do you feel overwhelmed with 'busyness' or business?
- ❑ Is hopelessness gaining a foothold in your life?
- ❑ Do you feel alone, lonely and unloved?
- ❑ Are you wanting to make plans but can't see a clear path ahead?

If you have answered *yes* to a number of these questions, it is likely that you are living a life that is Off Purpose. You may use other words like being 'stuck', 'blocked', 'plateauing', 'depressed' and so on.

Perhaps you know this but can't see a way through to turn your life around because it seems too overwhelming. Thankfully, life can be different, and filled with energy and hope again.

Being On Purpose

Deep down, most of us know what we want from life. We generally seek peace of mind, fulfilment, happiness and love. If you are like the people I work with, you also want to be appreciated and valued for who you are, to have meaningful and happy relationships, to earn a good income, to be physically, emotionally, spiritually and mentally healthy, to make good choices and to have a successful career. You also want to make a difference as you live out your life in service to yourself and others (and maybe to God or a higher power; whatever you understand that to be).

> When people are asked what being On Purpose means to them, typically they use words such as being fulfilled, energised, having a high mojo, being in the flow, focused, feeling whole, hope, meaningfulness, purposeful, and significance.

In other words, you want to be On Purpose. You know when you are because, in addition to the above, you experience high energy and focus and have a sense of purpose and meaning in your life. You have clear goals and are purposefully working towards them, thereby achieving your heart's desires. You are living your life with intention and by design.

When people are asked what being On Purpose means to them, typically they use words such as being fulfilled, energised, having a high mojo, being in the flow, focused, feeling whole, meaningfulness, hope, purposeful, and significance.

In summary, there are numerous benefits to having a clear Purpose and being On Purpose. These include:

- Having a sense of deep satisfaction and accomplishment in achieving the things that are important to you.
- Being motivated and energised internally, thereby giving you confidence and a sense of positive self-worth.
- Gaining clarity and focus which helps you jettison the unimportant, and which keeps you on track and stops you wasting time.
- Giving you peace of mind, knowing that you are making a difference and are involved in meaningful work.

- Having a clear sense of Purpose so that you are not pulled in a thousand different directions.
- Being more able and confident in what you say 'yes' or 'no' to, so you are not dancing to the beat of other drummers.
- Being more able to make informed choices and confident decisions because you have a clear plumbline and homing beacon.
- Living a life of intention and design with the side benefit of reducing your stress.
- Ensuring that you act proactively and stop reacting and living from crisis to crisis.
- Setting worthwhile goals and strategies, enabling you to be more productive at work and in other areas of your life. This ensures a sense of accomplishment and achievement.
- Being able to exchange *burnout* for *balance* thereby reducing your stress and living more at peace with yourself and others.
- Assisting you to plan and prioritise more effectively, thereby replacing *confusion* with *clarity* and confidence.
- Growing intentionally as a person and shortening your learning curves, thus giving you more time to concentrate on things that matter most in your life.
- Being On Purpose may mean you respond more out of love in life situations rather than out of fear.
- I have observed in my coaching that when you respond to all the stimuli that come your way from your Purpose, you will unconsciously attract people into your life and dramatically increase your leadership capacity and capability.

Phew! It's no wonder then that in books, articles and research around the topic of Purpose, that Purpose appears to be so essential to being able to live a fulfilling life. Psychiatrists, psychologists, leadership authors and coaches, university lecturers, counsellors, career and life coaches, and mental health workers to name a few, extol the importance and benefits of having a Purpose. A quick internet search will throw up multiple pages of organisations and experts who work in the field of Purpose. Check it out for yourself.

Defining Purpose

Having taught and coached in this area since 1997, I have found that many people are unclear as to what Purpose really is. Mostly, Purpose is used synonymously and confused with mission and mission statements. Herein lies a major difficulty. Purpose is about 'being'; about who you are, whereas mission is about 'doing'. Purpose is your 'Why' while Mission is how you live out your Purpose and accomplish your Vision.

Mission statements were popular in the manufacturing and Industrial Age. This was the age of *doing*, when goal setting gained prominence. We sent a manned spacecraft to the moon. The Industrial Age was the age of 'hands and feet': the age of achievements and accomplishments. 'I'm on a mission' or 'let's make this a mission' are common phrases that are associated with mission or mission statements. In the armed forces, a combat is often referred to as a mission and the phrase 'mission accomplished' is commonly associated with the result. And we all remember the *Mission Impossible* movies that captured our attention and imagination (if we like fiction, action movies and Tom Cruise).

So often people think that their Purpose is what they do: the one job or position that gives them purpose and meaning in life. We know that is nonsensical. We only have to go back one generation to know people who had a job for life. Nowadays this is unheard of!

To add to the confusion, when we moved from the manufacturing age to the Information and Knowledge Age, vision statements became a focus in order to lend future direction and focus to individuals and organisations. This was the age of the head, so vision was generally about future direction or where we were headed. These statements painted a picture of the future in our mind's eye. Vision statements became the focus for corporations and businesses to align and energise their people.

Today, we recognise that while we are still fully immersed in the Knowledge and Information age, the Age of Purpose and Consciousness has been gaining traction for years. Abraham Maslow stated that people are motivated to achieve certain needs and that some needs take precedence over others. From a Maslow's Hierarchy of Needs perspective, those of us who are fortunate enough to have our lower order needs met are seeking self-actualisation, purpose and meaning in life. No longer are we satisfied to just exchange our lives for money. In my experience, some professionals are even seeking to downshift and forgo their incomes in order to engage in more meaningful and fulfilling work.

It's as if there is a corporate 'Tower of Babel' that encourages confusion over the meaning of the words: Purpose, vision, mission and values. In some instances, these are used interchangeably.

In order to be able to move forward in this area, here are the definitions I will use. In doing so, I acknowledge and draw on the work of Kevin W. McCarthy, the author of The On-Purpose Person[1] and The On-Purpose Business Person[2].

Purpose is your *reason for being*. It is Why you or your organisation exists. It is defined by knowing *why* and *how* you serve others. The others you serve include your customers, society, and yourself. Metaphorically, Purpose comes from the heart. It is the spiritual DNA of the individual or organisation.

Vision is your *picture of the future*. It encompasses your dreams and possibilities. It inspires you and others. Metaphorically, vision resides in the head and eyes. We see an internal picture of the future we want and bring that into fruition.

Mission is the *expression of your purpose in action*. It is about what you are doing or performing now or in the near future in measurable terms. Metaphorically missions are our hands and feet. It's how we bring about our vision.

Values are the things *that are important to you*. They help you govern and choose what is right and wrong for you. They serve as your conscience and boundaries. Metaphorically, values are represented by our stomach and throat. When you violate your values, you will notice the discomfort in these body parts.

**Purpose: Reason for being
– Your Why? (Being)
Vision: Picture of the future
– Your Where? (Seeing)
Mission: Expression of Purpose
in action – Your How? (Doing)
Values: Things that are important
– Your What? (Choosing)**

These words have very different meanings. Your Purpose is not the same as your mission, even though many leading management consultants and authors still refer to mission statements as your 'Why?' I'm advocating for a common use of these terms. As we have long moved past the 'Doing Age', we should scrap our mission statements and replace them with crystal-clear Purpose statements which include Purpose, Visions, Missions and Values.

I'm mindful that together with my previous mentor Kevin W. McCarthy, I'm one of few advocates in this regard. Mission statements are so entrenched in our research, speaking events, self help books and organisational psychological literatures that change is slow. I hope you can see why it's important to understand the difference in these terms.

One Purpose! That's big! I'm saying that we are born with our Spiritual DNA and many of us unconsciously live it out throughout our lives. But making the unconscious conscious is powerful.

What may be confronting to some is that Purpose, (from my perspective) is singular. We only have one Purpose, but our visions, missions and even our values will change over a lifetime. One Purpose! That's big! I'm saying that we are born with our spiritual DNA and that many of us unconsciously live it out throughout our lives. But making the unconscious conscious is powerful.

Discovering your Purpose and living it out seven days a week is life transforming. Purpose is the 'golden thread' and the one constant that links together the seasons of your life, the different roles you fulfil (spouse, parent, father, mother, grandparent, sibling, co-worker, uncle, aunt, business owner, manager etc.), and the different occupations you undertake. It is who you are 'being' regardless of what you do. To repeat, Purpose is about 'being', Visions are about 'seeing', Missions are about 'doing', and Values are about 'choosing'.

> **Purpose is the golden thread and the one constant that links together the seasons of your life, the different roles you fulfil and the different occupations you undertake. It is who you are 'being' regardless of what you do.**

Think of it this way. Electricity has always latently existed, but it needed to be discovered. Once it was discovered, it had to be harnessed. Only then did it have power. It was given more life by naming it – in English we call it 'electricity'. There is something special about giving a name to a child. So too, it is special and powerful to name our unique DNA. Our parents named us, and most of us continue to use those names. What is the name of your Purpose? It's there – latent and permanent – wanting to be harnessed in the service of doing good and given a name.

Finding and Naming your Purpose

Once you understand that your Purpose is your spiritual DNA which exists over your lifetime, and that it is powerful and meaningful for it to have a name, you may wonder how that might look and sound.

'What? How could something as complex and important as my life's Purpose be just two powerful words?' I hear you ask, and 'Why just two words?' Let's find out! You can undertake this process for yourself through a tool developed by Kevin W. McCarthy[4] where you will come up with your two-word Purpose Statement.

In my one-on-one and group coaching, these words are tested, discussed, and refined. The advantage of having only two words is that you will never forget them. They will become your written constitution. There is no need to remember a paragraph or even a sentence, though there is nothing wrong with that if you can easily recall it.

Your Purpose Statement conveys Purpose in a memorable and meaningful way. The two words have a structure to them – the first word is an action gerund ending in …'ing', and the second word is a noun or the object of your purpose. You can look at these as representing the X and Y chromosomes of your spiritual DNA.

Because the essence of Purpose is service, each Purpose Statement has a generic beginning or stem such as such as 'I exist to serve by...' or 'My reason for being is...' or simply 'My purpose in life is...'

> **Purpose is eternal – in our past, present and future – it's been, being and becoming. More importantly, it brings mindfulness and meaning to the present – as 'now' is all we have. It isn't a single defining event; it's expressed and defined moment by moment over a lifetime.**

The purpose statement concludes with two unique and powerful words, such as: Optimising Potential; Awakening Freedom; Announcing Freedom; Inspiring Greatness; Enriching Community; Radiating Love; Sparking Joy; Creating Meaning; Rejuvenating Spirit; Igniting Enthusiasm; Inspiring Transformation; Nourishing Growth, Maximising Opportunity, Releasing Potential and so on.

Notice again how the first word of the purpose statement ends with 'ing'. This implies that you are *always in the process* of 'being' your Purpose. It shows us that Purpose is eternal – in our past, present and future – it's *been, being* and *becoming*. More importantly, Purpose brings mindfulness and meaning to the present – as 'now' is all we have. It isn't a single defining event; it's expressed and defined over a lifetime.

The second word is the *object* of the action gerund. It is the more important of the two words. It brings laser focus and depth to your 'reason for being'. Your Purpose does not change, however, as you come to better understand your Purpose, your Purpose Statement may be refined over time.

A sample personal purpose statement using three different stems might read like these:

I exist to serve by Liberating Greatness
My reason for being is Lifting Spirit
My purpose in life is Maximising Potential

How does knowing your own personal Purpose Statement help you in your career and your life?

These two words help keep you On Purpose. They are a powerful reminder of why you exist. Your Purpose is like a homing beacon that keeps you on track and prevents you from being distracted –

especially when life throws you 'curve balls', which it inevitably will do. In fact, you would not be reading this if that were not the case.

Goals are stepping stones that lead you to your Purpose. That's why Purpose is unending. To reiterate, Purpose is not something you 'do'. Purpose is something you 'are'. With a clear, articulated Purpose, no matter what comes up in your life, you won't stray. Every choice and decision you make will be aligned with your Purpose.

Here is what one of my workshop participants said about finding her two-word purpose statement after a defining moment in her life. I'll call it 'Bet's Story.'

> I have spent the last 30 years of my life trying to discover who I am. During this time, I have experienced the depths of depression and the daily struggle to come out of darkness into the light. I have attended numerous workshops on personal development, read and continue to read a variety of books related to personal growth, and even run my own workshops… Throughout this journey there have been moments of true enlightenment that have helped put me on 'fast forward'. One of these was when I attended an On Purpose Workshop run by Dr Edward Gifford.
>
> At the start of the workshop I thought 'I've done this all before, why am I here?' but little did I know! As I listened and did the exercises, I started to get a feeling of anticipation but then experienced a block as I tried to uncover the true Purpose of my life. With sensitive and insightful questioning, Edward came alongside me and suddenly, there it was! My life's Purpose! Not a long mission and vision statement! No lengthy text! Just two words! As I spoke them out my spirit soared and I knew it was right.
>
> Since then, these two words: Lifting Spirit, have helped keep me on track at home, within my family and especially at work. Knowing my life's Purpose has been really

important in the workplace where, at times negativity, uncertainty and power plays exist. Sometimes at meetings I find myself getting 'sucked in' to the games and when I do, I repeat and 'be' those two special words and everything changes for me and those around me. And... as I have come to learn, lifting my own spirit and the spirit of my husband, children, grandchildren and friends has brought meaning, fulfilment and purpose to my life.

What a difference a day can make!

How to write your Purpose Statement

To commence this process, you will need a period of quiet reflection time to answer several questions. These questions will help you to go deep within to uncover your True Self, your spiritual DNA – in essence, your true identity or who you really are when you live from your sense of a 'higher Self'. Your two words attempt to name your 'spirit', as challenging as that may seem or sound. Take some time to reflect and write down your answers.

1. What are your passions in life – things that give you a real sense of meaning, significance, and contribution?
2. What are some of the talents and strengths for which you are recognised?
3. When people ask for your help, how do they want you to help them?
4. Think about the times in your work that have been extremely fulfilling and meaningful for you – where you knew you were making a difference, resulting in a rich, fulfilling and meaningful life for you and others. List some of them here.
5. Consider each of the experiences you listed. Why was each of these a peak experience? How did you feel in that moment? What was meaningful?
6. What are some of the outcomes of these peak experiences? How did you and others benefit as a result?
7. What would you say truly motivates your life?

8. When do you know that your 'life compass' is pointing North?
9. What are your core values? (Your guiding principles that you choose to live by.)

Further questions to dig deep and use to look within

If you come to a point where your responses dry up or slow down, reflect on these questions[3]:

10. If I were told that I would die in five years and that I would be healthy and active until that moment, I would...
11. If I had no possibility of failing and therefore were guaranteed of success, I would...
12. If I had three messages to give to the world, the three most important guidelines I would give them to live by would be...
13. What talents, abilities or character traits would I like to develop further at this point in my life?
14. If I had nothing to prove and achieve and I had all that I needed, what would I love to invest my time in?
15. Given my talents, passions and values, how could I use these resources to serve, help and contribute?
16. What would I like said about me at my funeral or in my eulogy?

Looking back over your responses, what do you notice? From where did your responses emanate? My encouragement to you is to recognise the responses and words that come from the heart and gut rather than from the head. This is not an exercise in logic, but in deep introspection. As we are conditioned to think and use our 'heads', our 'heart' responses often go unnoticed or are dismissed.

Now reflect on the responses you have given to these questions. Start listing phrases and words that give you clues as to your significance. From these can you identify some of your 'ing' words such as Empowering, Sparking, Influencing, Maximising, Nurturing and so on? Next find words that capture the object of your purpose that organically emerged from your brainstorming – words such as Joy, Wisdom, Growth, Potential, Opportunity and so on.

Keep digging. The answers will emerge – not suddenly but slowly.

The more you get into this zone of deep reflection, the more self-aware you will become.

From undertaking this process, you have come up with your first draft of your two-word Purpose Statement. If the winner of your X Chromosome was *Optimising* and the winner of the Y Chromosome was *Success* then when placed together, your Purpose Statement would read:

(I exist to serve by) Optimising Success or (My reason for being is) Optimising Success.

If your two word combination rings true, great! You have a personal Purpose Statement! If it doesn't quite sound and feel like 'you', play with other words that might refine it. Write down different words and combinations. This process can take some time, so don't give up! A Thesaurus may help. Better still, access the online tool by Kevin McCarthy.[4]

Your Purpose is Reflected in your Whole Life

Every dimension of your life is infused with your Purpose. Therefore, the real test of a meaningful Purpose Statement is that it should translate into each area of your life – physical, spiritual, mental, familial, social, financial and career.

Example 1 – Tata's story

I would like to share 'Tata's story' to illustrate how these two 'word seeds' infuse and work across all of our life areas. Tata is my wife's father. He passed away some years ago but the story I'm about to share is indelibly imprinted on my memory.

We resided interstate a lot because of my work at universities, but no matter where we were located, my parents-in-law came to visit us each year from the other side of Australia.

One evening, Tata and I were walking, quite slowly as he was well into his eighties, and at the time he had a limp. We got to talking as we usually did about life, and important things as older people tend to do when they know that the years are ticking by fast. On this occasion, we somehow got onto the subject of Purpose and legacy.

Here's how the story went as best I can remember.

'Well,' he said, 'I'm old man... I have no Purpose... soon I die.' (Tata came to Australia from an Eastern European Country after the war and still had his accent despite speaking pretty good English).

I couldn't resist.

'But Tata, even though you are old, you still have a Purpose, you have always had a Purpose and it will always be with you.'

There was silence for a while, the slow limping walk continuing and us both pondering... deep in contemplation and introspection. Finally, I recommenced the conversation.

'Tata, tell me about the times when you are most satisfied, when you have a deep sense of fulfilment and feel most at peace... when your life really makes sense and when you are truly happy.'

Again, silence...but out of the silence came his response. It cut right through me.

'To tell you the truth, I have had long, good life but I'm most contented when cultivating my garden.' He went on, 'This is when I am most happy.'

I quickly picked up on two words he had spoken – 'cultivating garden(s).'

'Tata,' I said, 'You have shared something very meaningful and important and have given me a truly wonderful metaphor of your life – 'cultivating my garden.' May I share something with you about what you said?'

'Of course,' he agreed.

'Do you realise you have been 'cultivating your garden' and not just literally, when growing your amazing tomatoes, capsicums, watermelons, and pumpkins? Look how you have always cultivated your spiritual, family and physical garden.'

He looked at me enquiringly and willed me to continue.

I went on to gently (but enthusiastically) explain how each day he cultivated his spiritual garden by practising yoga and meditation; how he walked daily and hung from monkey bars to cultivate his physical garden. I pointed out that he took great care of his physical body through the food he consumed. (My mother-in-law was so careful about what went into their mouths.) Tata cultivated his intellectual and mental garden by reading extensively every day from a variety of sources like newspapers, to books on the history of Europe and could engage in so many interesting conversations. He joined the local chess club and loved the intellectual stimulus chess provided. He also attended night school in his twilight years to do woodwork and made furniture for the family.

Never a week went by without him ringing us and our children and he always asked after our welfare and updated us on the rest of the family. Cultivating his 'family garden' was so important to Tata and he was so happy when he could have his whole family together and when he could stand up, smile and cry at the same time, and give his speech to and about everyone seated around him. Today, the closeness which we all share as a family and the respect we offer to each other is a legacy Tata has left.

Tata also cultivated his financial garden. He worked hard, kept careful track of family spending and savings (always looking for the best deal) and invested wisely in property for security and retirement funds – something which stood them in sound financial stead in their retirement.

When I had finished explaining to him how Cultivating Garden was his Purpose, his unique DNA, and how he had always been doing it and continued to do so, he stopped, looked up at me and said:

'You have given me new hope and reason for long life.'

Tears welled in his eyes as he embraced me in the middle of the quiet suburban street… and they well in mine too as I recall and write this story. The emotion was intense, and his legacy clear. I always loved Tata but the special bond between us at that moment was indescribable.

I retold this story at his funeral. Tata passed away aged 90, more than 20 years ago, and in the retelling of this story, his legacy continues to a far wider audience and 'family' than he could ever have envisaged. He would be delighted!

I'm sure you have the idea about the power of Purpose and how you 'be' these words no matter how old you are, what you do or what your circumstances are.

Example 2 – 'Shining light'

I have been given permission to use the following example to illustrate the potential power of Purpose. In this case, this was written by my wife Angela to a special young person in her life:

> Dear _____,
>
> This morning I was lying in bed thinking of you and the words 'shining light' popped into my mind, so I reached for my phone to see where those thoughts might lead me.
>
> Your name means 'light' or 'illumination'. When I think of you in that context, the words that come to me that uniquely and deeply describe who you are, are 'shining brightly'.
>
> When I think of things that shine brightly, my mind goes to stars.
>
> So, how do stars shining brightly connect with you? I believe that your name accurately reflects your character and who you are becoming as a person. You were born into this world to shine brightly – to shine light. **This brings amazing life-giving and life-affirming light into the lives of those you touch with your presence.**
>
> However, this is a big calling – to live out your name of shining brightly, because light cannot flourish in darkness. It either dims or sputters out. (You can blame your parents for the name, but seeing you as you have been growing up, that name is totally appropriate…and so too is shining brightly).
>
> In life, as you are already discovering at your age, there are things that will try to obscure that light. One of these for you is the feeling of anxiety that I know overtakes you from time to time. Although it may try to fool you into thinking otherwise – because that is what our thoughts and minds do with the aim of protecting us, anxiety is really just a cloud passing across the light.

You, as a shining light, cannot suffer from anxiety, because you are not your anxiety. However, you can observe it passing by. 'Ah... I notice anxiety... there it goes floating past again.' A cloud can never put out light, although it can temporarily obscure it. Anxiety is the same. It can temporarily obscure our purpose, direction and focus, but **above the cloud of anxiety there is the shining light, immeasurably more powerful, energising and life giving than we can possibly imagine.**

This does not mean that anxiety will never overtake you, but it cannot ever define you, because at the level of the spirit you are not anxiety but light...and love...and hope!

I am curious to know how you relate to this metaphor of anxiety being a cloud passing by the shining light.

Love _____

I hope you can begin to glimpse the power of Purpose. Imagine the positive impact a two-word Purpose statement would have on the millions of people around the world living with depression and anxiety?

The Power of your Purpose

Having a two-word Purpose Statement is not a gimmick, a slogan or a word-smithing exercise. It is your energy source, reason for being – a road map that inspires you and gives you confidence and clarity each moment of the day. It's your spiritual DNA.

> **Having a two-word Purpose Statement is not a gimmick, a slogan or a word-smithing exercise. It is your energy source, reason for being – a road map that inspires you and gives you confidence and clarity each moment of the day. It's your spiritual DNA.**

I invite you to get in touch with that two-word Purpose Statement you developed for yourself or with your organisation. Notice the **POWER** it has!

Precision – It is precise, detailed, and specific and your laser beam. It provides a context for the content of your life; it gives you your unique identity and precisely names your spiritual DNA. It is who you 'are' and 'be'. You can write it on a T-shirt, a business card or a gravestone!

Oneness – Not only do you have one Purpose, but this one Purpose is shared by all (but in different ways). Purpose connects and integrates us all at the deepest level. In any organisation (family, business, club and so on) it brings people together, aligns them to a common goal and gets everyone on the same page. This results in shared interests, shared solutions and shared outcomes. As individuals it gives us one clear authentic reason for 'being'!

Written – Like written goals, when you write your Purpose it brings the unconscious to consciousness. You write it and 'be' it. It's your written constitution. It's not just a couple of fluffy words which drift around like clouds. There is something very powerful about writing these two words down and displaying them visually. They name the 'real' you or the heart of your business (your True Self and identity) not the family name which was given to you by your parents or your business name. Your written Purpose becomes your map. It is your homing beacon or your lighthouse – your 'true North'. It helps you to make sense of your life and business – your 'been' 'being' and 'becoming'.

Energy – When you are connected and aligned with your heart and spiritual DNA and with the oneness of the 'true life' in which we all share, the energy is transformational. Being On Purpose and living with one Purpose, you are energised, confident, and have clarity and focus. You live your life by design. You make decisions which are in alignment with your Purpose. You tap into your talents, strengths and unique gifts. You say 'yes' to your heart's desires and 'no' to the beat of others' drums. Feel the energy when you are set free!

Relationships – Living in alignment with your Purpose transforms relationships. You no longer focus on the conditioned and egoic self, which seeks separateness, protection and self-centred relationships. Purpose is by definition 'good'. It comes from a place of 'Godness' and 'goodness'. It seeks relationships with the Universe, others and self through a core motive of Love and not fear. When you respond to all relationships from your 'being', (your Purpose) you respond in Love and seek relationships that focus on shared interest rather than self interest and shared outcomes and shared solutions rather than separate outcomes and solutions. Relationships at the trans-personal (self with higher power); intra-personal (self with self) and inter-personal (self with others) are transformed and enriched.

The Power of Being On Purpose

Notice that when you know your Purpose, and live On Purpose, you are fully awake to life and live in the present. You live 'above the line' regardless of what life throws at you at any moment. You are proactive, not reactive; you choose to be better, not bitter; and live life as a victor, not a victim.

> **Purpose is where Love resides and is manifested outwardly though a shared life.**

In the space between stimulus and response (a concept further explored in the next chapter), resides your big choice, the only true Choice you ever have! The real you or True Self chooses to respond to life either through a core motive of Love or react from a core motive of fear. Purpose is where Love resides and is manifested outwardly though a shared life.

Imagine if your Purpose were 'Releasing Potential'. Your response to every situation would be from this core motive and state of being. You would be consciously and unconsciously responding in such a way that you were releasing the potential in you, those you serve and the community at large. That's powerful!

And powerful for one of these three stonecutters too who clearly understood his 'Why'. The *Parable of the Three Stonecutters* is widely used in personal and business training courses and was made famous by Peter F. Drucker, the writer and management consultant in his 1954 book, *The Practice of Management*[5]:

The story of three stonecutters building a medieval cathedral, goes something like this:

When a passer-by asks the first stonecutter what he is doing, he replies angrily, 'Can't you see? I'm cutting stones!' Moving onto a second stonecutter, the observer asks the question again, to be told, 'I am earning a living for myself and my family.' When the passer-by asks a third stonecutter, he receives a joyous and enthusiastic response: 'I'm building a great cathedral, for our community and all of the world to worship in.'

What we need to note is that each of the three stonecutters was doing identical work.

It's not hard to see that the first stonecutter worked with a sense of meaninglessness and futility. His work was dull and boring. He knew what he did but had no understanding or comprehension of his macro 'Why'. The second stonecutter was exchanging his life for money – earning a living to pay the bills and look after his family (and there's nothing intrinsically wrong with that). The third stonecutter, doing identical work to the other two, infused his work with joy, meaning and Purpose. He was able to identify a larger more transcendent Purpose for what he was doing which permeated his being. He wasn't just laying stones – he was *Building Magnificence.*

Reflections: The Power of Purpose in my Life

It's one thing to write with passion about Purpose from a teaching perspective, but another to share meaningfully how using Purpose has played out in my own life.

At the time of writing, it's some 20 years since I left an academic position. As explained in the Author's Note, sometimes in life we get a gentle push in another direction. Other times we get hit by a Mack Truck!

I got *Mack-Trucked!*

Despite this unexpected event, I continued with my university work as best I could, but I noticed something was not quite right. I had prepared for the semester, organised all the sessional staff that were required, put all the programs in place and given one group lecture to some 250 students. At the end of the first week of semester, I went to the Dean and asked for a week's leave.

I didn't know what was wrong, but I knew I was not right!

Two weeks later, after some medical intervention, I returned to my office. I could not get the key into the lock due to my hand shaking so much. I felt extremely stressed to the point of having a panic attack. I went back to my car and sobbed. Returning home, I explained to my supportive wife what happened.

I never went back to university life. My academic career was cut short prematurely. The *Mack Truck* had the last say. My professorship was purported to be some 18 months away, but that would never happen.

With that began two years of journeying through the wilderness.

During this period, I had the mandatory medical appointments with specialists. One said in his report: 'This man will never work again', and also said to my face: 'You are totally fucked, mate!'

So, from there, what got me through to the point where I set up my own leadership and management consultancy and became a successful coach, mentor, trainer and speaker? What helped me reinvent myself completely from being a music educator to being a professional leadership and business coach?

The answer is a lot of things, including my supportive and loving wife and kids, my determination to get well, and my inner calling to continue to make a difference. I knew that I was unemployable because back then, the stigma of having to resign because of a major depression and anxiety condition was the death sentence for re-employment. Sadly, I believe this is still the case!

I have to say that what got me through to this point was also my sense of Purpose and my own Purpose Statement of 'Igniting Enthusiasm'.

Back in 1994 I came across the book by Kevin W. McCarthy called *The On-Purpose Person.*[1] The same year I took a trip to the US to meet the author, spent a day with him and returned three months later with my wife to undertake a one-week intensive training course on 'The Power of Your Purpose'. In that program I wrestled to find my Purpose. At that stage, I mistakenly thought that Purpose was what I did – my 'What'.

It took over three months to come up with these two words that named my spiritual DNA. It was soul-searchingly agonising on some days but ultimately transformational, when I discovered I could 'be' my Purpose, regardless of my circumstances or conditions.

My work as an academic had given me clues to my Purpose. At the end of each semester, students mandatorily completed feedback forms about the unit they had studied and about the lecturer – his or her strengths and weaknesses. Over a 15 year period, 99% of the students spoke about my passion and enthusiasm as my greatest strengths. It was obviously deep within my DNA. Even today, my wife, family, grandkids and friends see it as an expression of who I am.

There was something else at play that helped me get through my *Mack Truck* period. Another specialist remarked to me:

'Edward, you are not like the countless people I treat with a major depressive illness…despite losing your career and being unwell, you are optimistic and positive about the future.'

For me, those two special words – 'Igniting Enthusiasm' shone a gentle ray of hope through the dark tunnel of depression.

It was transformational, when I discovered I could 'be' my Purpose, regardless of my circumstances or conditions. For me, those two special words - 'Igniting Enthusiasm' shone a gentle ray of hope through the dark tunnel of depression.

As you have learned by reading this chapter, Purpose serves the individual as well as others. This was an invitation for my Purpose to serve me. Many days I experienced the depths of frustration, disappointment and despair, yet those two words were like a homing beacon or lighthouse for me. They gave me peace and hope and kept me on track in my desire to return to normality. I asked myself daily: 'How have I ignited enthusiasm today?' Some days there were no answers, other days just an imaginary whisper, but over time I could answer this question in relation to myself, my family, my spiritual life, and my physical well-being. At that point, meeting anyone socially was a challenge.

Today, when I arise in the morning, and when I retire at night, I ask myself: 'To what extent have I lived out my Purpose today?' That question brings me back to the present, keeps me mindful, and more than anything else, reminds me to live in the now, because that is all we have.

Are you ready to harness the power of your Purpose? How are your life, career and business going right now? Is your life filled yet unfulfilled? Are you pulled in a thousand different directions, which take you away from what is truly meaningful and important to you? Are you saying 'yes' to other people's projects and activities while neglecting the things that matter most at your core? Are you in touch with your heart and your spiritual DNA? Have you aligned your life to your Purpose, or do you feel you are still living a 'life of quiet desperation', squandering your talents and living a life of regret?

The Eagle Fable

I'd like to close this chapter with the Eagle Fable, a story I came across over 20 years ago and which I often use in my training sessions about Purpose:

> A man found an eagle's egg and put it in a nest of a barnyard hen. The eaglet hatched with the brood of chicks and grew up with them.
>
> All his life the eagle did what the barnyard chicks did, thinking he was a barnyard chicken. He scratched the earth for worms and insects. He clucked and cackled. And he would thrash his wings and fly a few feet into the air.
>
> Years passed and the eagle grew very old. One day he saw a magnificent bird above him in the cloudless sky. It glided in graceful majesty among the powerful wind currents, with scarcely a beat of its strong golden wings.
>
> The old eagle looked up in awe. "Who's that?" he asked.
>
> "That's the eagle, the king of the birds," said his neighbour. "He belongs to the sky. We belong to the earth – we're chickens." So, the eagle lived and died a chicken, for that's what he thought he was.

And so, it is with us. You are born for a Purpose and created by design. Yet sadly, like the eagle, many of us never discover our Purpose and therefore are unable to align our lives to our spiritual DNA. You are no accident. You won the sperm race! You were born to win! You were the winner of 250-400 million sperm. Despite living in an imperfect world, you are significant and because there is a place called hope, you can choose to meaningfully contribute to life.

What I have hoped to convey in this chapter is to increase your understanding of how to find your Purpose and how to harness its power in your life, career and business. There will be seasons or periods in your life where you feel stuck, lost and are overcome by a sense of meaninglessness. Taking the time to bring your spiritual DNA to consciousness is powerful. Discovering and naming your 'reason for being' or your 'Why?' and learning to align your life to it, will be transformational.

References and Notes – Chapter 1

1. McCarthy, K.W. (1992). *The on-purpose person: Making your life make sense.* Colorado Springs CO: Pinon Press. Second Edition: McCarthy, K.W. (2009). Winter Park, Fl: On-Purpose Publishing.

2. McCarthy, K.W. (1998). *The on-purpose business person: Doing more of what you do best more profitably.* Colorado Springs CO: NavPress. Updated edition, 2012 Published and distributed by On-Purpose Publishing, Winter Park, Florida.

3. Blackburn, Paul (2019). These questions were used in a workshop I participated in facilitated by Paul Blackburn from Global Success Academy.

4. McCarthy, K.W. The online tool from www.ONPURPOSE.com is where you can discover your two-word purpose statement.

5. Drucker, P.F. (1954). *The practice of management.* New York, NY: HarperCollins.

6. The Eagle Fable is a remake of *The Ugly Duckling* by Hans Christian Andersen.

Humpty Dumpty had a great fall,
Our old life paradigm fails us all,
When the True Self rises from the ashes,
It's only Love that truly matters.

Chapter 2 – Shifting Paradigms

'Everyone has two choices.
We are either full of love or full of fear.'

Albert Einstein

The Coffee Shop

Mostly, conversations in coffee shops are ordinary enough and often commonplace. Others may be interesting, memorable and helpful. And some may be life-changing!

Although over 20 years ago now, I still recall quite vividly one conversation I had with my friend and spiritual mentor, Dr Phil Harker. This was the beginning of an ongoing transformational journey for me.

We met in a small coffee shop in Brisbane for one of our many conversations about life. We always seem to return to discussions around philosophy, spirituality and psychology. These may not be the normal conversations of the typical Aussie male, but for me, these are the best!

In the course of one conversation he asked, 'Edward, what do you think is the greatest question you ever have to answer?'

Shifting on my chair I replied, 'Well maybe it's 'Is there a God?' or 'is there life after death?' (On reflection now, perhaps it should have been: 'Is there life *before* death?'). I thought a moment longer. 'Maybe the biggest question is: 'What do I want my life to stand for and how do I wish to be remembered when I die?" Remembering a talk I had presented some years earlier, I threw in for good measure: 'What do you want to do with your 'dash'?' (i.e. The dash on the grave headstone between Born _____ and Died_____)

'Yes,' he replied, 'all good questions, but have you ever thought about the question: 'Who am I?' How would you answer that?'

I shifted again, this time in a more pronounced way. I could sense my neck reddening and I noticed feeling uncomfortable and challenged by this question.

Finally, after a lengthy silence I responded. 'Well Phil, I'm Edward Gifford, a Senior Lecturer in Education, married to Angela, with two children and, well...you can see who I am...not quite the body of my youth!'

'Yes,' he agreed with the last part of my offering with a smile, commenting: 'How the mighty have fallen! But you can't be your body as all the cells of your body change every seven years and you can lose part of it in an accident. You can lose or change your job tomorrow, so you aren't your job or career. You are not your name either, Edward, as you can very easily change it. And, you could change your partner, or she could be killed in an accident, so you are not your partner or your relationships.'

That made sense, but I was certainly starting to feel I was being 'put through the wringer'.

More tentatively I offered. 'I'm what I think...I'm my thoughts, my beliefs, philosophy and attitudes.' This was sounding a bit more promising and convincing, I thought.

'OK,' he replied. 'Let's think about that. Your thoughts are like the weather. Like the rain, clouds, wind and sunshine, they come and go – possibly some 60 to 80 thousand every day. If you were your thoughts, you would be changing every moment of the day. Even your beliefs, attitudes and values change throughout life. And our thinking affects our behaviour so that will keep changing too.'

Whilst these were not exactly Phil's words as this conversation took place many years ago, they do reflect the gist of the conversation and the points he was trying to make.

Well, I wasn't going so well. I had realised to this point that I was not my material world (body, relationships, career, position) and I was not my thoughts (thinking, feelings, attitudes, beliefs, values and manifested behaviours), so who was I? Obviously, I was more than my physical and mental self.

'Come on, Edward, think about it. You've been in education for 25 years and you teach your students about metacognition!'

> **The question of 'Who am I'? was the beginning of a journey of greater self-awareness, self-understanding and personal transformation which played an enormous part in my rejuvenation and has profoundly impacted my life and business since.**

That I did know about. Metacognition is about how we have the capacity to watch over, observe and think about our thinking and our thoughts. When I explained that to Phil he replied:

'OK, if you can watch your thinking, who or what is doing the watching?'

He pointed out that this was not a trick question but he was simply asking to help me understand that what I was observing or watching was not my *true* identity but rather, as he explained, 'a decision making-function that had no more freedom than that of any other animal.' I didn't fully understand this last statement at the time.

But what I did understand was that he was talking about the third dimension or aspect of what it means to be human – Our unseen higher dimensional Self, and that I had not even thought about in answer to the question. So, I reflected, if I could observe my thoughts and my body, who or what was doing the observing?

This question was the beginning of a journey of greater self-awareness, self-understanding and personal transformation. This played an enormous part in my rejuvenation and post-traumatic growth as well as profoundly impacting my life and business ever since.

Chapter Overview

The first part of this chapter unpacks my understanding and developing awareness of my dual identity: that of my body-based identity involving my body and mind, and the other dimension of what it means to be human – my Higher or True Self.

As I continue to ponder the answer to this, the greatest of life's big questions – *Who am 'I'?* I am learning to see the world differently. I am coming to understand what is real and what is an illusion, including what part of me represents my *ego* and what is the True Self, beyond the fragile mortal body that I identified with previously.

After answering the first question of 'Who am I?' I will explore a related second question: 'What choice do I have?' This second question links to and expands the first question. The first question profoundly determines the nature of the answer to the second question regarding what Choice 'I' really has, in influencing the daily decision-making processes taking place in this body I call 'myself'.

My understanding of these concepts and paradigms has been growing over time. There has been no blinding flash of the obvious or sudden illumination.

In the second part of this chapter, my growing understanding and explanation of the nature of 'human choice' reflects my developing awareness of what happens in the space between 'stimulus' and 'response' and how we can choose to be reactive or proactive in how we respond to our thoughts, experiences and circumstances.

This naturally led to the idea of living 'above or below the line' and the difference between choosing responsibility for our lives or claiming victimhood. The final part of this chapter explores the deep implications of responding to and living our lives through a core motive of Love or fear and shows how that plays out in every decision we make.

> **The deepening realisation of my dual identity and what it means to be human, together with my new understanding of how I could choose my response to any situation or circumstance, was central to my journey of recovery after having been *Mack-Trucked*! I could either choose to 'wake up' or 'break up'.**

I will also explore how understanding these great questions represents the difference between those who seem to fail and live 'lives of quiet desperation', as Henry David Thoreau[1] aptly phrases it – desperate to protect their body-based identities, contrasting with those who wake up to life by understanding more deeply what it means to be human.

The deepening realisation of my dual identity and what it means to be human, together with my new understanding of how I could choose my response to any situation or circumstance, was central to my journey of recovery after having been *Mack-Trucked*! I could either choose to 'wake up' or 'break up'.

Use of capitalisation in Chapter Two

Before continuing, I want to explain the use of capitalisation with certain words. You may have noticed that some words in this chapter (and throughout the book) have been capitalised, e.g. 'True Self.' I have also used inverted commas with words and phrases for certain emphasis and meaning. For example, when I refer to the 'I' in relation to my True Self I use single inverted commas for 'I'.

The reason for this is to clarify which 'reality' or 'identity' I am referring to. To reiterate, I have used capitalisation when using terms which relate to Our unseen and therefore unfamiliar suprapersonal Identity. This differentiation is critical to an understanding of the 'choice' that forms the foundation of my main point in the second part of the chapter: namely the 'choice' between the two contrasting 'states of being' which are Love and fear. These in turn correlate with our two contrasting 'identities'—the physical human identity that we most readily identify with ('me') versus the unseen and timeless Identity of our Higher or True Self ('I'). I have demonstrated this with some examples in the table below.[2]

Individual body-based identity (me or false self)	Unseen suprapersonal Identity ('I' or True Self)
self: an individual's body-based personal identity.	Self: The unseen suprapersonal identity common to all sentient beings.
I, me – e.g., Edward – a temporary *homo sapiens sapiens*. The personal 'me' including my body, thoughts, feelings, emotions, and everything to do with my material world.	'I': that unseen, unseparated, suprapersonal Life. My True 'I'dentity or True Self.

You/our/us/we: an individual's body-based identity, bounded by a name and taught its characteristics.	You/Our/Us/We: That shared Identity that sits behind or 'watches' the observed temporal self.
mind: the generally accepted concept of a personal body-based decision-making function.	Mind: Suprapersonal Non-local source of the Light of Life that enlightens the unseen core of the human psyche. It enables the uniquely human capacity for cognitive self-awareness, and a personal self-concept. It is the one Mind which we all share.
life: that which has the appearance of self-animating existence.	Life: The unseen agency that enlightens and animates existence.
local: pertaining to this physical, individual body-based life.	Non-local: pertaining to Mind and Life.
love: the feeling of deep affection which we associate with the local mind or the personal self. All the common ways we use this terminology associated with the 'me'.	Love: Unconditional Oneness at the unconscious level of Mind (Love). The dissolution of separateness at the level of Real Life.
fear: biological and psychological feelings and emotions associated with self-preservation of the personal self when faced with threatening danger ('flight', 'fight', 'freeze' or 'flop').	fear remains in lower case throughout this manuscript as fear does not exist in Our suprapersonal Identity.

I will explain these terms more fully and provide a context for them throughout this chapter.

Who am I?

After the coffee shop conversation, it became evident to me that 'I' was not just my body, thoughts, feelings, attitudes, career, religion and so on. So, who am I? You might be asking yourself the same question by now. For me, understanding the answer to this question was and still is the Holy Grail in my quest for peace.

If, as humans, we can watch over our thoughts and observe our own thinking, feelings and behaviours, who is doing the 'seeing' or the observing?

I was first introduced to the dualistic concept of 'two minds' by my good friend Phil Harker in our many conversations and through the book *Awareness* written by the Jesuit teacher Anthony de Mello[3]. In this book, de Mello differentiated the *subjective* self and the *self as object* by referring to them as 'I' and 'me' respectively. It's not that we have two minds, but these are two aspects of 'one being'. The 'I' is the unseen but constantly present-perceiving Subject, an extension of the eternal Mind, whereas 'me' is our body-based identity, which we associate with our name.

When we make this differentiation, we see ourselves and the world quite differently. We no longer assume our identity only as an unchosen consequence of our fate at birth, but that there is another level or dimension which is unseen of itself, and unique to sentient human existence.

Think about it for a moment. If we are more than our body and our thoughts, why do we frequently allow our thinking to paralyse us in our lives? We get fused with and attached to our thoughts when mostly they cause us anxiety, stress, depression and ultimately rob us of our peace of mind. The old paradigm in which we are no more than our bodies and thoughts becomes unworkable, as it did for me. Staying stuck or tethered to something that is unworkable is, I believe, why so many people sink into depression and anxiety, or even worse, end up taking their own lives.

The discussion of what it means to be human and the confusion over the concept of the 'I' and the 'me' has been exacerbated in Western society by Descartes.[4] His famous statement, *'Cogito ergo sum'* (I think, therefore I am) suggested that the identity of the essential self (the 'I') was somehow its thoughts.

Phil Harker challenged this view of what it means to be human and questioned how different the Western world might have been if Descartes had said: 'I am aware of my thinking therefore I must be more than my thoughts!'[4]

It's easy to describe 'me' as this identifies all the ways we traditionally define ourselves – our bodies, our thoughts, our feelings, our names, our occupations, our nationalities, our religious beliefs, our political leanings, and so on. In other words, 'me' in de Mello's terms is our body-based entity comprised of our physical body and mind. The tragedy for most of us is that we can't get beyond this concept of who we think we are. We become inordinately attached to these trappings of our physical existence.

In de Mello's[6] terms such people are 'asleep' – they lack awareness of the way the universe really is. They believe that they are no more than their separate, body-based personal identities. Conversely, those who are 'awake' understand who they *really* are – with an unseen supra-personal identity which is shared by all sentient beings through self-awareness.

Later in this chapter I will explore the concept of our dual identity in more detail – especially noting that these twin sides of our present being represent two aspects of mind: Love and fear.

Learning how to handle depression and anxiety through awareness

In terms of dealing with the negative impact of unhelpful thoughts, (anxiety, depression, failure, lack of confidence, feeling that 'I'm not good enough', guilt, jealousy and so on), it was Anthony de Mello's four-step process for dealing with 'suffering' that first impacted my ability to see the world differently and to deal with my own depression proactively. This process is underpinned by clearly understanding the difference between the 'me' and 'I'.

His first step is to 'Identify your negative feelings'. This requires a certain capacity for Emotional Intelligence. Not everyone finds it easy to get in touch with their feelings and emotions. I think men of my generation have had to learn how to do this. We were conditioned to supress them and to show our toughness and resilience. 'Big boys don't cry' was the mainstream masculine mantra of my upbringing. Although now a cliché, it was a powerful message and to unlearn this to the point of being able to identify, sit with and become in touch with my emotions has been an ongoing journey.

We only have to witness the amount of physical domestic violence today to see that many can't even master this first step. We see men, and dare I say, some women, who rage when anger becomes overwhelming. It takes self-awareness – an essential component of Emotional Intelligence, to step back and utilise the space between *stimulus* and *response*. Some people are not even aware that they are shouting, that their body is tense and that their heart is thumping. They are too busy *being* their anger to observe or even to notice it.

His second step is to 'Understand that the negative feelings are in you, not in the world, not in external reality.' Our negative feelings therefore are a personal construct. The same stimulus that produces a particular feeling in me may well result in a completely different feeling in you.

With respect to feelings, the world doesn't generate them or bring them to us. Our feelings are our unconscious choices about how we respond to the world. Many of these responses are learned because they rewarded us in the past. We got what we wanted and therefore our behaviour was reinforced. As a result, when our environment elicits a certain stimulus, we react (not respond) as we have always done in the unconscious hope that we will be rewarded accordingly.

His third step is, 'Do not see the negative feelings as an essential part of 'I' – these things come and go.' Like the wind, rain and clouds, our thoughts and feelings come and go. Even our bodies are changing, with our cells being replaced regularly. Knowing that the egoic or conditioned self (the 'me' in de Mello's terms) will do anything to protect itself, has helped me to understand that it's natural for us to have negative emotions and feelings. I dare say that even the most enlightened have their equanimity challenged. It's part of being human. In fact, the pursuit of and attachment to being constantly happy is unrealistic. We only need to observe nature to see that there is not a tree that flowers continuously, a river that flows placidly in all its reaches, or an ocean without tides.

To assist further in understanding that our negative feelings are not part of the essential nature of who 'I' really 'is', I'll share a common metaphor I first encountered through the work of Dr Russ Harris[7] in one of his ACT (Acceptance and Commitment Therapy) workshops.

This is my recollection of his message: Our True Self, the 'observing mind' (which ACT labels 'self as context') is like the blue sky. Above the clouds, the blue sky stretches unendingly as far as the East is from the West. It is ever-constant in its oneness. Sometimes for some and frequently for others, the clouds, rain and weather partly or totally obscure it. Those clouds are like our thoughts and emotions, part of the conditioned 'me' or 'thinking mind' (which ACT labels as 'self as content'). They come and they go. But we know that they are not the sky as neither our thoughts, feelings and emotions are the True Self or the essential 'I'.

> **I think we were born happy but have been conditioned to be unhappy!**

Sometimes we get so obsessed by the clouds that we forget about the blue sky altogether. We forget who we really are. We search for what is already there! I think we were born happy but have been conditioned to be unhappy! It's easy to forget that what we are looking for is already there! In other words, the thoughts, feelings and emotions behind what I'm physically experiencing are just clouds obscuring my own blue sky.

I have learned to implement de Mello's third step: to detach from or to not fuse to the frequent negative thoughts and feelings, which are often crippling! Like the clouds, I know these thoughts will come and pass. I know I can't stop them, or press *delete*, because my thinking or personal mind will always have thoughts. But I can watch and observe them and detach from them. Otherwise, I end up becoming my anger, depression, sadness, frustration, shame or guilt and fuse with all my 'not good enough stories'.

It's what I often explain to others in my workshops or coaching as being the difference between self-observation and self-absorption. This heightened self-awareness of knowing my true Identity has been healing, life-changing and liberating. Having this helicopter metacognitive view of ourselves, we can notice and observe what is going on in, through and around us.

> **This heightened self-awareness of knowing my true Identity has been healing, life-changing and liberating.**

There are days when my negative thoughts, feelings and emotions can still be debilitating. Having these 'black dog' days is like being in the thick dark clouds, but I have learned to dis-identify or detach from these. I am conscious of them, get in touch with them, detach from them and observe them, watching them pass. I get on with my day, taking small steps to begin with, and soon the blue sky re-emerges. I return to my oneness and wholeness again. I come home!

In step four de Mello says we must 'understand that when you change, everything changes'. For me, this fundamental change meant that I understood that I was no longer the manifestation of the objective state 'me' but that I was the embodiment of the subjective state 'I'.

When I realised who 'I' really was – the essential third dimension of our humanity – I gradually learned not to identify immediately with my feelings, emotions and thoughts. I began to see the world and what was happening around me differently.

> **Through detachment, de-fusion or disidentification, I can observe or notice my negative thoughts and feelings come and go, knowing that they don't define me.**

Knowing that my True Self is the observer or watcher (the blue sky or what others call and the Collective Unconscious or the Shared Mind) has dramatically changed my worldview. Through detachment, de-fusion or disidentification I can observe or notice my negative thoughts and feelings come and go, knowing that they don't define me. I now watch my thoughts enter my awareness and pass by just like the black clouds travelling across the blue sky.

As Anais Nin[8] insightfully wrote, 'We don't see things as they are, we see things as we are.' Seeing the world from this new awareness changes everything. It has for me, on most days!

I'd like to conclude this section by sharing a poem written by my good friend and mentor, Phil Harker, which encapsulates what I have been sharing with you as to the nature of our true 'I'dentity!

THE ONE-NESS OF LIFE
Across the sweep of human history
Life has always been a mystery
Where it comes from, where it goes
No one ever really knows
But this one thing must surely be
Real Life is not just what we see
We are the 'See-er' not the seen
We are as we have always been
We are the 'Knower' not the known
The unseen 'Watcher' on the inner throne
One Life of Love unites us all
But Life unshared feels separate and small
And in its 'dreams' of separation
Causes strife in every nation
Till once again it comes to see
It's just One Life not 'you & me'
This mortal 'self' is but a 'tent'
To which attachment must be rent
So that the 'Knower' can be known
And sit again upon Its throne
Real life is Spirit, it is not flesh
It's always living, it's always fresh
And grief will therefore fleeting be
For those who really clearly 'see'

© Dr Phil Harker (Used by permission from the author)

In this section I have shared how my greater understanding and awareness of my true Identity has played such an important part in my rehabilitation from brokenness to wholeness. I had to change my mind about my mind and my understanding of who 'I' really was.

The diagram below is the summation of a journey that began many years ago which includes the answer to the first question posed in this Chapter: Who am I? This is partly encapsulated in the space between stimulus and response. It is encouraging to know that when you change your thinking about who 'You' really are, your whole being, and life will change too.

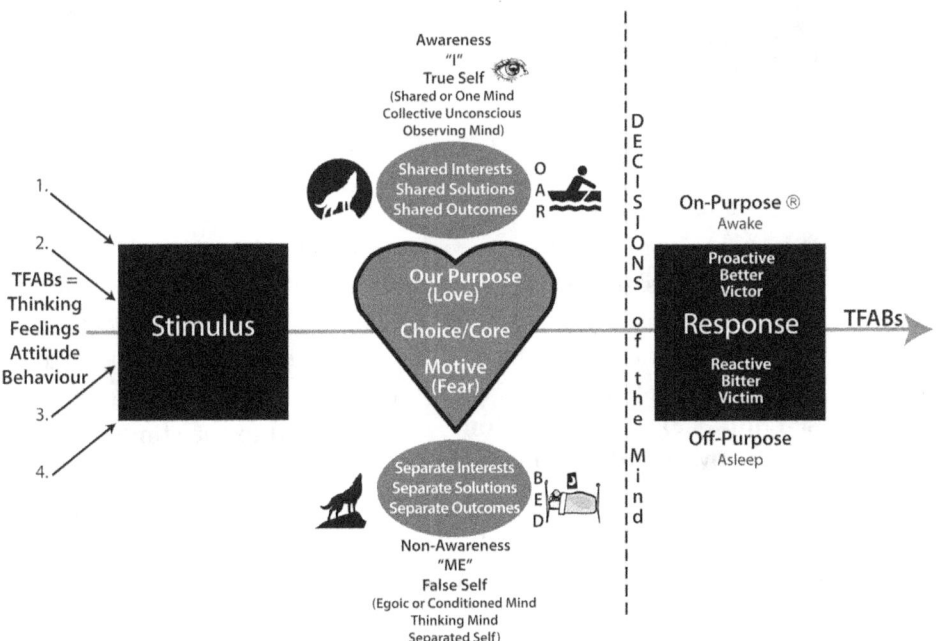

To help you understand this diagram more clearly, I would like to back track on my journey to answer the second question: 'And what choice do I have?'

What Choice Do I Have? – Understanding the astonishing truth of only having one choice in life and how that changes everything

Stimulus and Response

I think most of us understand that the quality of our lives, including our success, peace of mind and happiness, is not dependent upon *what happens to us* but rather, *how we respond to what happens to us.*

Figure 1

> Within the space between stimulus and response resides both free will and our core motive, and thus the freedom to choose our responses, and in these 'choices' lies the invitation for our growth and happiness.

What was new for me was my understanding of the *significance* of humans having a *space* between stimulus and response. We can choose how we respond to the stimuli that impact on our lives day by day. Within this space reside both free will and our core motive, and thus the freedom to choose our responses, and in these 'choices' lies the invitation for our growth and happiness.

Animals have no such space – only sentient beings have this capacity. For example, my Chocolate Brown Labrador (who loves food, walks and pats), immediately salivates when I even mention the word 'dinner'. By the time the food is in the bowl she is positively drooling. For Poppy, there is no space to choose her response to the stimulus of food or food sounds.

The ability to choose one's response was also a philosophy espoused by Victor Frankl in his book *Man's Search for Meaning.*[9]

Frankl clearly moved away from accepted social mirrors of genetic determinism, (your grandparents did it to you); psychic determinism (your parents did it to you); and environmental determinism (your boss, spouse, government, neighbour, economic situation is doing it to you).

In developing a proactive model, Frankl believed that there was a space between stimulus and response for humans, and that therefore, as a human, he could decide for himself how any stimulus was going to affect him. (We will talk more about the nature of choice and this decision-making process later in the chapter). That might not sound very profound, but Viktor Frankl was a Jewish psychiatrist living in Vienna in the Nazi era. Rather than fleeing to America, which he could have done, he chose to remain in his own country. He, his pregnant wife, his brother, and his parents were all imprisoned in concentration camps. All died except for Frankl.

After enduring the suffering in these camps, Frankl concluded that even in the most absurd, painful, and dehumanising situation, life potentially has meaning. Even when he was stripped bare of everything that most of us would hold as basic, he chose his response and did not allow others to dictate it for him.

Basically, Frankl felt that a person was primarily driven by a 'striving to find meaning in one's life'. Although his work is usually referred to in the context of finding meaning and purpose, his life is an example of someone who chose to be proactive and who lived in the present whilst looking to the future in order to live life fully, rather than reliving the past. He also clearly demonstrated that feeling peace even in the middle of devastation is possible, and that no circumstance can overwhelm us unless we allow it to.

Proactive or Reactive

At the time of my being *Mack-Trucked*, I **did** know that I had a choice of how I handled my newfound situation thanks largely to my having read the writing of Frankl and Stephen Covey's book: *The Seven Habits of Highly Effective People*.[10] Especially relevant was Covey's Habit 1: *Be Proactive*. I could react by claiming **victimhood or respond with a victor mindset**. I understood that I did not have to be defined by my circumstances. Whilst at the beginning stage of my 'awakening' I did not fully understand the nature of this 'choice', namely the developing understanding that in the space between stimulus and response lay the potential of seeing the world and life through a new paradigm.

Looking back, I'm convinced that this new self-awareness about our freedom to choose and to direct our lives was a life-changing gift for me. I have had life throw me many curve balls since that time, two life-threatening, others career-threatening and another, resulting in facing bankruptcy as a result of the Global Financial Crisis (GFC). Almost daily, I kept coming back to this simple but power-filled principle: my freedom to choose in the space between stimulus and response.

At a personal level, I still struggle with the temptation of clinging to victim status, especially after facing financial ruin as an outcome of the GFC and the behaviour of others. Even today, in the course of many conversations and in answer to some 'difficult' questions, I am conscious that victimhood did impair my ability to forgive and that clinging to my past wounds justified my thoughts and behaviours. I have learned that forgiveness is not necessarily an act of generosity on the part of the forgiver as people behave in the best way they know how. Instead of seeing the negative, I remind myself about how supportive people were through this time, especially some family members, without whose generosity, my family and myself would have been holed up in a caravan for the rest of our lives!

In summary, as we see in Figure 2, as human beings we can choose to be proactive or reactive. And correspondingly we can be better or bitter or have either a victor or a victim mindset.

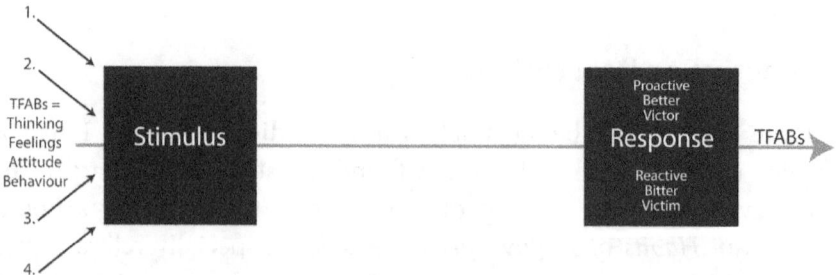

Figure 2

Take a moment to think about your life and how you respond to all the things that happen to you moment by moment and day by day. Think of a time when you have behaved in a reactive way, perhaps, where after the event, you wished you had never said, thought or done that particular thing.

> **Regardless of what has happened to me and what has happened in your past; what people might do or say; what happens when you hope for something else to happen; what goes on that is out of your control – whatever happens, how it happens, who or where it comes from – you can choose your response.**

In a nutshell, regardless of what has happened to me and what has happened in your past; what people might do or say; what happens when you hope for something else to happen; what goes on that is out of your control – whatever happens, how it happens, who or where it comes from – you can choose your response. If we want joy and peace in our lives, we choose or create it. No one else can do it for us.

While I have not consciously explained which 'you' is being referred to in the paragraph above (when 'you' can choose your response) I will clarify that part of our dual identity that makes the 'choice' of being proactive or reactive – (responding 'above the line' or reacting 'below the line'), later in this chapter under the section Love and Fear. (You can probably already guess that it is the 'I' metaphorically residing above the line and **not** the egoic 'me' or our body-based identity, that makes this one 'real' choice).

Living Above the Line or Below the Line

Notice in Figures 2 and 3 there is a line running through the space between stimulus and response. Many of you will have seen something similar where you are asked to observe whether you are living 'above' or 'below' the line. I have defined the line as your thinking, feelings, attitudes and behaviours or TFAB's.

So now you can ask yourself: 'Am I proactively taking control of my responses where 'I' choose to be better, not bitter, to be a victor

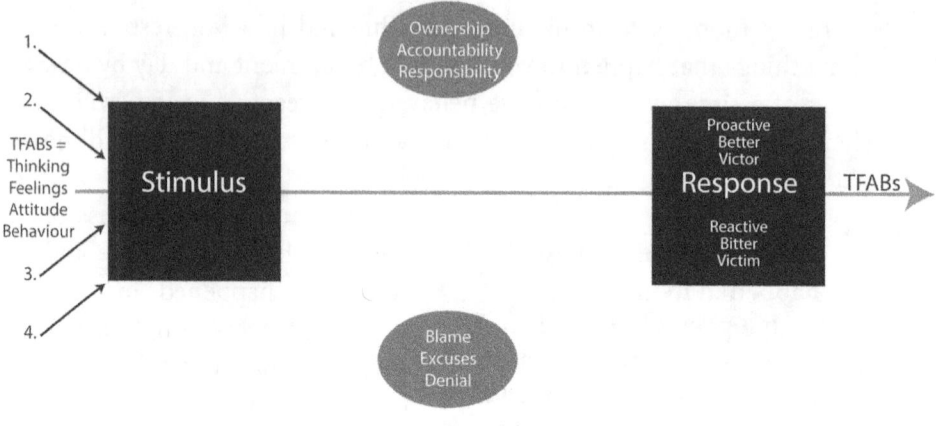

Figure 3

regardless of my circumstances and not see myself as a victim or having a victim mindset?'

> **'You' have a choice to be a prisoner of the past or a pioneer of the future. Either we give voice to our True Self which sets us free or allow the false self to keep us in bondage.**

Remember the old saying: 'If you don't bury the past, the past will bury you!' 'You' have a choice to be a prisoner of the past or a pioneer of the future. Either we give voice to our True Self which sets us free or allow the false self to keep us in bondage.

Living above the line also means 'You' have the choice of taking ownership, being accountable and taking responsibility for your thoughts, feelings, attitudes and behaviours. This is easily remembered by the use of the acronym OAR. (Ownership, Accountability, Responsibility.)

Like Victor Frankl, Nelson Mandela is another great example to consider. His life under the South African apartheid led him to question the injustices and inequalities that Black Africans had to endure. Joining the African National Congress (ANC), Mandela was an activist in many demonstrations against the White dominated government. Unable to deal with him any longer, and frightened of the support he was gaining, in 1964 the South African Government sentenced him to life imprisonment.

Even in prison on isolated, austere, cold Robben Island, he was a symbol of hope for Black Africans, and found ways of continuing his mission.

In 1990, after 27 years of imprisonment, he was finally freed and within five years, had been awarded the Nobel Peace Prize and was elected President of South Africa. His book *Long Walk to Freedom* tells his amazing story.

Both Frankl and Mandela had adversity thrown at them in a huge way. Both realised that they could choose their response to it and that they had ownership of and were responsible and accountable for their thoughts, feelings, attitudes and behaviour.

But what about somebody more 'everyday?'

You probably know somebody more 'everyday' yourself if you stop and think about it. Perhaps this is someone who has stayed the course through amazing adversity and still has a smile on their face. Perhaps it is someone who, despite what has happened to them, still radiates hope. Perhaps it is someone who lost their home and belongings in a flood or a fire. Perhaps it is even someone who, having lost their battle with cancer, has left a legacy that has been an encouragement to others. I acknowledge the work of my wife Angela in the examples that follow.

One such person is Belinda Emmett, actor, recording star and former wife of TV personality, Rove McManus. Emmet was first diagnosed with breast cancer when she was 24, and then several years later she found she had bone cancer. She was just 32 when she passed away. Her story was told on *Australian Story* on ABC TV and was called 'Some Meaning in this Life'. Belinda refused to give in to the cancer that was killing her. 'I am not going to let [the cancer] kill my spirit', she said. Even though she wanted the chemotherapy to be over, she was still determined to enjoy every single day.

Her family and friends testified to this and her attitude helped them through the trauma of watching her slowly succumb to her illness. She sang in concerts, recorded music, and made the best of her situation by choosing to get as much fun and enjoyment as she could out of the time she had left.

Her death prompted many Australians to donate to breast cancer research. (This is a similar story to that of Jane McGrath, wife of

Aussie Test Cricket great, Glen McGrath and in this way, as well as through her TV appearances, CDs and her friends and family's memories, her legacy lives on. The cancer might have killed her body, but she chose not to let it kill her spirit.)

The flip side of OAR and 'below the line' is BED. This acronym stands for Blame, Excuses and Denial. It is the exact opposite to OAR. Instead of responding proactively to everyday life events you are choosing to respond in 'BED'. This means you are asleep!

We have lots of good examples of this. Look no further than the daily news. Our politicians are always blaming the other party or person, making excuses as to why they have broken their election promises and often refusing to admit responsibility by denying that there is a problem of local and national importance.

It is not hard to find other people who are in BED, asleep. Our homes and workplaces are full of them. Listen to the conversations around you. 'It's not my fault he walked out on me. He wasn't really capable of loving anyone anyway. It's his fault. He should go and see a shrink and get himself sorted out.' (Blame). 'I did my best. I couldn't help it if I was late for the exam. I had to study until very late last night.' (Excuses). 'Just because six boyfriends have left me, doesn't mean that there is something wrong with me. They should just get real!' (Denial).

Such people are not much fun to be around and do not end up having much fun. Most of us would prefer to be with positive, energetic, inspirational people, and we soon tire of trying to help those who won't help themselves. People like this expect everything and everyone to change but don't realise that they are the problem. They usually end up as being VDPs (Very Draining Persons) and eventually they find themselves left to their own misery.

As you become more aware of your responses and reactions, notice where your energy is directed. When you are 'living' below the line, not taking responsibility and acting out of self-interest, you will undoubtedly take in and give out negative energy. This will result in stress and anxiety, as well as negative thoughts and behaviours. This doesn't make for a happy home or workplace.

Perhaps check out where you see yourself operating in your life. Which 'you' are you putting in charge? Are you responding well and navigating proactively '*above* the line' or reacting negatively to your circumstances and events '*below* the line?' OAR or BED? The choice you make will have a profound impact on your life and those around you.

Love and Fear and the Nature of 'Choice'

In this section I want to explain in more detail how the choice between stimulus and response is made and what part of our Identity is making the 'choice'. The answer to these questions is vital, as it underpins every decision we make.

> **More importantly, embedded in this choice is a core motive for life and living – we either live a life of Love or a life of fear. The 'choice' between Love and fear is not in the decision itself but in the *motive* that such a decision will serve.**

It explains why we can choose to be proactive or reactive. It also explains how we choose to live 'above' or 'below' the line. More importantly, embedded in this 'choice' is a core motive for life and living – we either live a life of Love or a life of fear. I will explain that all decisions of the mind are made either through a core motive of Love or fear. This represents a paradigm shift that when made, will naturally influence every consequent decision that our natural mind makes. Hopefully you will come to understand that the 'choice' between Love and fear is not in the decision itself but in the *motive* that such a decision will serve.

Previously in discussing our dual identity, I explained how it seems that we have two minds. The first is the one with which we most commonly identify; what de Mello called the 'me', is our natural, body-based personal mind. The 'me' is also referred to in literature as self-as-content, conditioned mind, local mind, egoic mind, thinking mind, separate mind or false self – in other words, our 'known self' having a personal body-based decision-making function.

The second, what de Mello referred to as our 'I' has been called many names. For example, some refer to it as the Christos Mind,

I Am, Observing Mind[11], Watcher[12], Shared Mind[13], True Self[14], Higher Self, Buddha nature, Mind at large[15], the supra-personal non-local source of light and life that enlightens the unseen core of the human psyche[16], or what Carl Jung[17] calls the Collective Unconscious. Anthony de Mello simply calls it the Mind of Love or the eternal 'I'.[18]

I need to explain that the words Love and fear are used differently here to how these words are used more commonly in everyday conversations. I'm not referring to 'falling in love', loving my kids, spouse, family and friends, loving my food, holiday, car and so on. Nor am I referring to the fear from the biological and psychological bases in terms of 'flight', 'fight', 'freeze' or 'flop'.

Love and fear, (when viewed non-possessively as opposite states of being), represent the two contrasting identities: the 'I' and the 'me' with whom the 'choosing capable 'I'' can identify.

In the context of this discussion, the word Love is being used as a criterion for choice and as a core motive for action. It represents a fundamental paradigm shift and motive for action at the core of our being at the level of the 'I' or True Self.

Fear on the other hand is used to define the core motive of self-preservation of the known or egoic self – sometimes called the false self. (The ego will go to no end to protect itself. I'm constantly amazed at how much time, energy, stress, worry and anxiety I have spent trying to protect that which is not real!)

Black wolf – white wolf illustration

The fable I share here is one of my very earliest encounters of how we may choose between Love and fear. It is a very helpful reminder about which of our core motives we choose to give voice to. The answer is clearly indicated in Figure 4 below.

> One evening an old Cherokee told his grandson about a battle that goes on inside people. He said, "My son, the battle is between two 'wolves' inside us all. One is EVIL. It is anger, envy, jealousy, sorrow, regret, greed, arrogance, self-pity, guilt, resentment, inferiority, lies, false pride, superiority and ego. The other is GOOD. It is joy, peace,

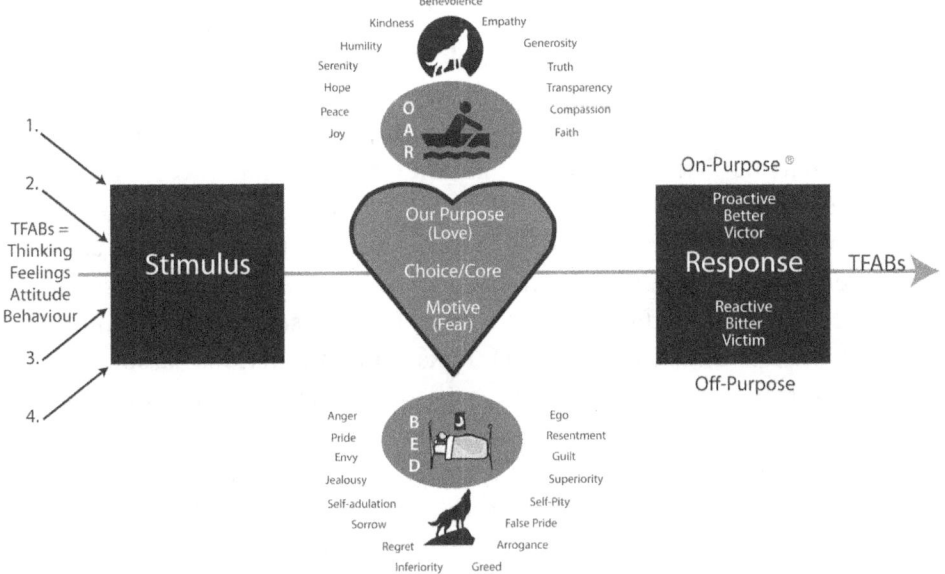

Figure 4

love, hope, serenity, humility, kindness, benevolence, empathy, generosity, truth, compassion and faith." The grandson thought about it for a minute and then asked his grandfather: "Which one wins?" The old Cherokee simply replied, "The one you feed."

As you noticed when reading the fable, Love and fear have many faces. This story provides a helpful starting point for understanding the fundamental choice we have in life. It is the 'one choice' influencing every conscious and unconscious decision. It is the choice between Love and fear.

Taking this idea further, Albert Einstein[19] made the comment that 'Everyone has two choices. We are either full of Love or full of fear.' My understanding of this comment is that he was inferring that at some level of our present being, these two 'states of being-itself', Love and fear, are incompatible and are mutually exclusive ways of looking at and living life.

It is our capacity to choose our moral direction that separates sentient self-aware human existence from its animal beginnings in un-self-aware infancy. A new baby does not have a body-based sense of self-concept and thus has no existential fear. What is essential to understand here is that our 'separation' and identification with our body-based identity (our false identity or what de Mello refers to as the 'me'), commences around three months of age and is largely completed by age three. From this point onwards, the fear we talk about here is the ego's determination to preserve the 'me' or the egoic self at all costs. And with our attachment to this body-based identity comes a growing awareness of the risks and limitations associated with our 'separated selves', which is the possibility of the death of this new identity.

We need to be careful and not assume that the thinking and decision-making mechanism we call 'me' can choose between the two as circumstances arise. As Einstein said, we are either one or the other. The 'choice' we make between stimulus and response is a choice that is made at the level of the unseen spirit – by 'I' or the True Self and not a decision of the body-based thinking or conditioned mind. *The 'choice' is not in the decision itself but only in the motive that such a decision will serve.*

Michael Leunig[20] echoes the sentiments of Einstein when he wrote:

There are only two feelings: Love and fear.
There are only two languages: Love and fear.
There are only two activities: Love and fear.
There are only two motives, two procedures, two frameworks, two results:
Love and fear.
Love and fear.

I think by now you are starting to understand that 'one choice' is all we ever have. I reiterate, all decisions of our personal decision-making mind are made through a filter of fear or Love.

> **Who do you put in charge: LOVE or FEAR? This single 'choice' at the core or ground of our being (a fundamental paradigm shift) provides the foundation criteria for all our subsequent decisions, actions and reactions. So, although we make many conscious intellectual decisions of the mind, the choice for which we are ultimately responsible (our core motive) is always the same and answers the question: are we acting to fulfil the purposes of Love (shared interests) or fear (separate interests).**

So, how do you find yourself responding to your circumstances? Out of Love or out of fear who do you put in charge: Love or fear?

This single 'Choice' at the core of our being (a fundamental paradigm shift) provides the foundation criteria for all our subsequent decisions, actions and reactions. So, although we make many conscious intellectual decisions of the mind, the choice for which we are ultimately responsible (our core motive) is always the same and answers the question: are we acting to fulfil the purposes of Love (shared interests) or fear (separate interests).

When we see the world through the eyes of Love, we know that our deepest well-being is enhanced by furthering the well-being of humanity.

In their book *The Myth of Nine to Five*[21] Ted Scott and Phil Harker explain this well. They assert that this moral choice between Love and fear is ultimately the only way any human being can influence the direction of his or her own life, forming the foundation criteria for all our decisions, actions and reactions. This can be a great shock to the human ego or the natural mind that imagines that it is making all its decisions as an independent entity.

Choice versus Decisions

I would like to clarify further the difference between the nature of human choice and how we make decisions filtered through the 'one Choice' available to us. To do this I will draw on many discussions I have had over the years with my friend Phil Harker. By doing so, I

51

hope to show further how the two questions posed at the beginning of this chapter: 'Who am I' and 'what choice do I have?' are linked. The second follows naturally from the first.

The personal mind is a decision-making function that is common to both animals and human beings. For example, when I call our dog Poppy, she comes to me straight away. Why? Because I feed her more often than my wife does. The dog has no 'choice' regarding the motive, hidden from its view that determined the outcome of her decision-making process. For her, the unchosen motive is simply species-specific genetic self-preservation. Human beings on the other hand have an element in their structure of being that provides a single degree of freedom in terms of the motive, hidden from the conscious view, in their decision-making process.

Every decision we make will serve an unconscious motive, and this is true for both animals and humans. However, human beings have another aspect or 'compartment' to their structure of 'being': namely our 'divine core' and this is where our spiritual dimension resides. Hence, it is through this divine Gnosis, that the dynamic relationship between 'good' and 'evil' exists. This means that every human being contains the potential to stay in identification with an individuated personal 'self' or awaken to their shared Identity.

The decision made in the personal mind (that we also have in common with animals) will serve one of two 'masters' – the egoic illusion of fear-driven competitive animal existence always seeming to 'save its own life' or the Love 'Master' that is willing to share fully in the common benefit of all humanity. This 'Choice' is not conscious even though it is being made in every timeless moment of now.

In corporate life, these two contrasting thought systems will be manifested as 'separated interests → separated solutions → separated outcomes' vs. 'shared interests → shared solutions → shared outcomes'.

I hope you have a deeper insight into what Einstein was referring to when he said we are either full of Love or full of fear. The Love referred to in this chapter is unconditional and unseparated. Conversely, fear is the protection of our 'separated' body-based identity.[5]

The widespread disharmony in families, businesses, and society in general (pride, guilt, adulation or blame and all that the black wolf stands for in the previous black wolf/white wolf illustration), shows us how few people function from this fundamental paradigm.

As previously mentioned, we must remember that our histories and ongoing circumstances are largely unchosen (i.e. our biological histories, our genetic histories and our early social histories). They are assigned at our births. We did not choose our gender, or our parents or the environment in which we were raised. Mostly we react in certain ways because that is how we have learned to react in response to our core motive, which once we have fully 'separated', (usually by age three) is the fear-driven preservation of our vulnerable body-based identity.

> When we come to the end of our tether, we can either experience post-traumatic stress or post-traumatic growth. When we choose post-traumatic growth, we do so through the realisation that our old unworkable paradigm needs discarding and that we are not victims of our circumstances. We can view the world through a different interpretive filter that sets us free! We can either 'wake up' or 'break up'!

Perhaps you have got to a point in your life, like I did, where you realise that your old paradigm is not working? Possibly you no longer wish to continue identifying with your fear-driven identity but want to 'awaken' to the realisation of a shared identity at the level of being which we call 'I' or Love.

Have you been trapped living a life of frustration, anxiety, and quiet desperation, hoping that one day things will change? Have you come to the end of your tether like me, realising that my old paradigm of what it meant to be human was failing and unworkable?

When we come to the end of our tether, we can either experience post-traumatic stress or post-traumatic growth. When we choose post-traumatic growth, we do so through the realisation that our old unworkable paradigm needs discarding and that we are not victims of our circumstances. We can view the world through a different interpretive filter that sets us free! We can either 'wake up' or 'break up'!

Perhaps we need to examine our relationships at home and work, notice how we handle rejection and criticism, question why we won't step out of our comfort zones, why we won't set and keep goals, why we won't believe in ourselves, and why we won't put ourselves in challenging situations and take risks.

How have we attempted to preserve the fear driven temporary body-based 'self'? Have we spent our lives attempting to preserve it, when all the time there is a timeless invulnerable self looking out from the core of our very being, inviting us to Life?

How do we bring about this fundamental paradigm shift at the unseen core of our very being?

How do we make this paradigm shift or awaken to this new life? We can read about it, talk about it, desire it, but we cannot bring it about simply by conscious deliberation or choice. Ultimately, the choice to Love unconditionally is an awakening, a deep paradigm shift that comes upon us without warning, like 'scales falling from the eyes.' This is like an 'ah ha' moment that occurs in the famous 'old lady' - 'young lady' visual illusion. Most people can see only one face and are surprised when the other is revealed.

Anthony de Mello suggests we do nothing at all, just watch, notice, observe, and be fully aware. For him it was 'awareness, awareness, awareness'. Watching and noticing what was going on in, around and through me was a key starting point for me.

Changing my perception and understanding who 'I' really was, was also an important contribution to my paradigm shift. Being aware of my different and contrasting identities, and seeing what was my false self and what was my unseen, eternal True Self and understanding that at some level of our present being, these two 'states of being' are incompatible and mutually exclusive ways of looking at and living life also helped me to awaken.

The gradual illumination of how fear holds us captive explained why my old paradigm brought me to the end of my tether. I opened my heart to my 'true voice', which was always with me, but I had forgotten to listen to it in the busyness of my egoic, separated, self-centred journey.

Thomas Kuhn, when describing the nature of all paradigm shifts, maintained that such paradigm shifts do not come about by 'deliberation of choice'.[22] The transition is not one that individuals make or refrain from making, however good our reasons for doing so may be. Instead, at some point in the process, we slip into a new paradigm without a decision having been made. He wrote:

> To translate a theory or worldview into one's own language is not to make it one's own. For that one must go native, discover that one is thinking and working in, not simply translating out of, a language that was previously foreign. That transition is not, however, one that an individual may make or refrain from making by deliberation and choice, however good his reasons for wishing to do so. *Instead, at some point in the process of learning to translate, he finds that the transition has occurred, that he has slipped into the new language without a decision having been made.*

If you are still wondering how this 'hidden choice' is made, it cannot be made directly, but it can be desired and that will be enough.

And now back to Love. As I write this, I cannot help but recall the quote in the Bible that has almost become a mantra – 'Perfect Love casts out all fear.'[23] There is no fear in Love because fear involves torment and punishment. Love is unconditional. There are no strings attached to it. It is indiscriminate, unconditional and gratuitous; it is unselfconscious; and it is free.

The aspects of Love and what it looks like when we 'be' Love

With the help of Anthony de Mello,[24] I would like to paint a picture of what Love looks like, sounds like and feels like when we awaken to the spiritual dimension of our higher self.

Love is indiscriminate

Love is indiscriminate. Nature helps us understand and demonstrates this quality of Love beautifully. It's so easy for a rose or tree or lamp or the moon to be Love. The rose gives its fragrance to us indiscriminately, regardless of our race, religion, or circumstances, whether we are good or bad, rich or poor, or saints or sinners. It doesn't say 'I will give my fragrance to you because you are such a kind and generous person, but I will not share it with your brother because he is selfish and self-centred.'

Notice how a tree does not discriminate between who it gives its shade to. It doesn't matter whether we are good or bad, young or old, hot or cold, whether we are humans or animals, or even if we have a chainsaw in our hand ready to cut it down.

The same can be said for a lamp, torch or light. They are like the moon which shines its rays on anyone seeking to walk in its light. Like the tree and the rose, the lamp or a light, Love is indiscriminate.

That's a hard call when we look at people who wrong us, are not our type, and who are 'takers' and not 'givers'.

When we Love like this, we treat others with a core motive of good will. There might be those you don't like very much such as difficult co-workers or someone who you are trying to forgive. You don't have to be bosom buddies, but you can choose to treat them well. A smile, greeting, compliment or hug may be a good way to start demonstrating this quality of Love. These are unlimited natural resources with which we can be generous. Whatever we give to another, we give to ourselves.

Love is unconditional and gratuitous

Love is unconditional and gratuitous. We have heard this so many times, but I think it is the hardest aspect of Love to live out or 'be'. It's easy to love someone who provides us with emotional, intellectual, financial, sexual and spiritual gratification and to avoid or be less loving to those who don't. When we are positively disposed to someone who gives us what we want, and who lives up to our expectations, love is easily reciprocated or given. Notice how easy it is to withdraw love or how we behave negatively or indifferently to those who don't reciprocate.

Taking the time to stop and observe how love plays out in your business as well as your personal relationships is important. For example, in your relationships, do you believe that love should be earned, or do you recognise that true Love is a gift and not a reward? Do you manipulate relationships by giving or withholding love to fulfil expectations or do you give Love and positive regard as a gift, without expectation and therefore wanting the other to be free and under no obligation? Do you love others only to the degree that your expectations are fulfilled?

Therefore, it's important that we create emotional environments or behave in such a way so our partners and friends have opportunities to give their Love as a gift. The moment coercion, control or conflict arise, Love dies. Think of the tree: it doesn't drag you into its shade. The rose doesn't force its fragrance on you.

Life and relationships change remarkably when we apply this kind of Love. Where Love is gratuitous and unconditional, there will be absolute equality, absolute trust, willingness to risk, absolute freedom, no condemnation, no expectations and no obligations. That's pretty positive, isn't it?

'How do I do this?' I hear you ask. Perhaps we need to stop trying to 'do' love, to force it or cultivate it. If we do, we run the risk of love being phony. When we stop trying to 'do' love and just 'be' Love, we just let Love unselfconsciously 'happen' – just like the rose, the tree and the moon let it happen. They offer their fragrance, shade and light regardless of whether there is someone there to enjoy it or not. Like these things, Love also exists independently of others – Love simply 'is'. It has no object.

On the journey of 'being' Love, we can practice Emotional Intelligence, especially in being self-aware and empathetic. Tapping in to our higher or True Self means that we can observe our thoughts and behaviours and those of others. With this helicopter metacognitive view, we can notice our body-based personal identity with all its conditioning and selfish behaviours. When we are fully present and aware, we can watch and observe our Love for what it really is: either it's unconditional or it is a camouflage for selfishness.

Love yourself first

I understand that many people are without partners or live alone and that for some people this may mean feeling alone or lonely. They may be conscious of the intimacy they are missing out on. If you are in this situation, remember that your circumstances don't define your self-worth. Love starts with loving ourselves. Love is unconditional so it means we can be kind and generous to ourselves, to self-soothe and to understand that we are fully whole and complete without depending on a relationship with another. You, as an individual are enough and you can Love yourself indiscriminately, unconditionally, unselfconsciously and with complete freedom because unconditional Love is unconditional freedom.

Shared Interests vs. Separate Interests – the Other Faces of Love and Fear

I have found that in some settings, people find it more accessible to think about Love as shared interests, shared outcomes and shared solutions. When we respond to our material and cognitive world out of fear we are operating out of our separate interests, solutions and outcomes. I have shown this in the diagram below in Figure 5.

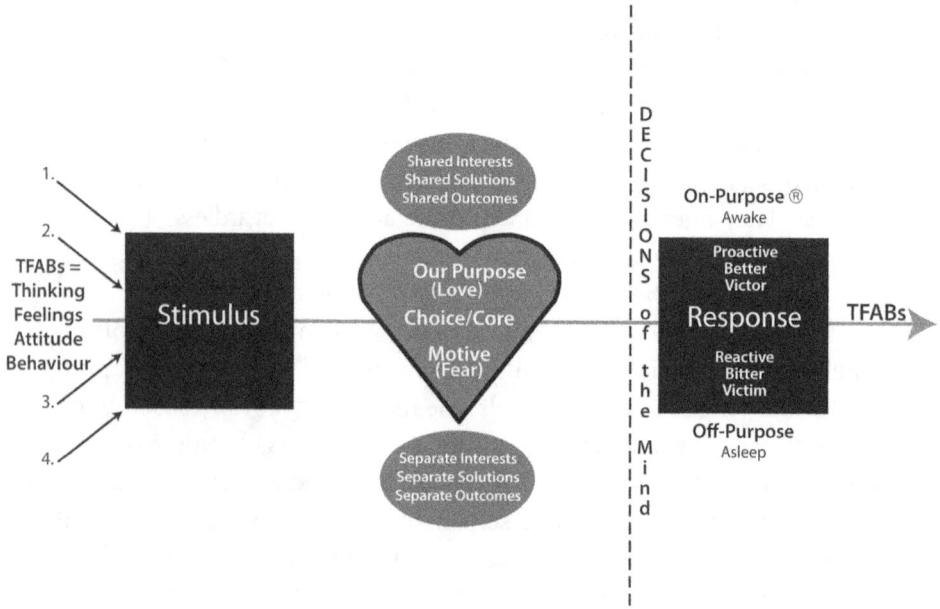

Figure 5

What about relationships in the workplace? Would you say most people operate out of a core motive of shared interests, solutions and outcomes or is this sabotaged by the ego which thrives on self-interest? Have you noticed how much time and effort is spent in workplaces by people trying to protect their own backs?

Stop and observe how this plays out in your personal life. For example, in your relationships with other people, do you believe that love should not be given as a gift but that it must be earned, or do you share Love unconditionally as a gift and not as a reward?

The energy and effort that we endlessly expend to protect that which is temporary and hence not real is enormous.

As Ted Scott and Phil Harker point out in their previously mentioned book *The Myth of Nine to Five,* 'Love is the dissolution of separateness'. When we are motivated and respond to our circumstances out of *self* or *separate interests*, we have a 'give a little, take a lot' mindset and attitude. We put our own goals and gratification ahead of those affected by our self-centred behaviour. For any relationship to really last, there must be unconditional Love.

Finally, by way of summary, I would like to return to the diagram I presented at the beginning of this chapter.

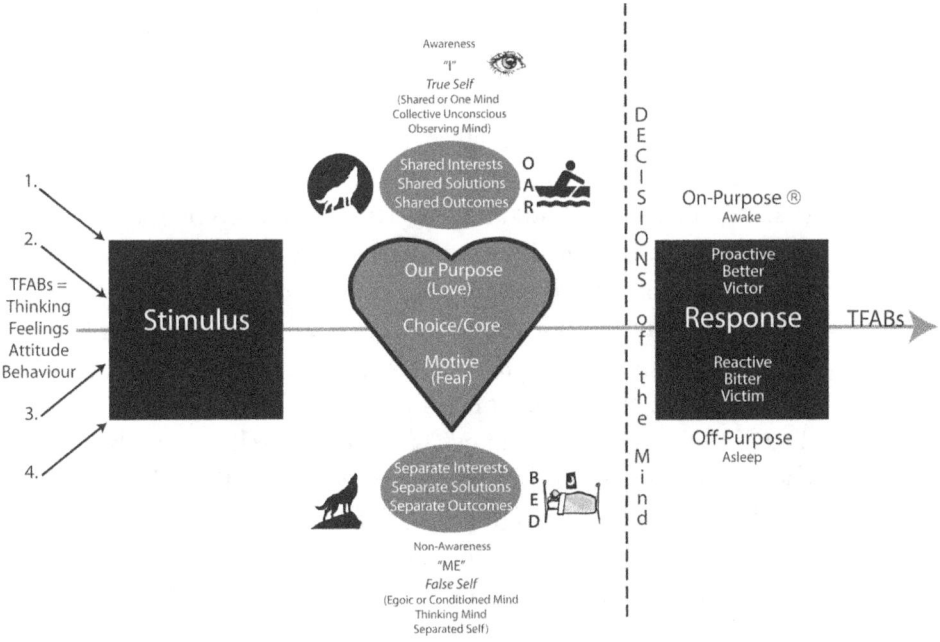

Figure 6

Summary

- Many of us live out our lives not fully understanding that as the unseen, but constantly-present perceiving Self, we are more than both the ever-changing image of our body and the ever-changing thoughts and feelings we perceive and experience.
- Most of us identify with our separate, 'self' as we have been conditioned to understand that this is who we are: just another

vulnerable and mortal human being constrained within the boundaries of a name.

- de Mello's 'I' is the third, and now for me, most important dimension of what it means to be human. It has been given many names, such as: I am, True Self, Higher Self, Watcher, Spirit, Observer, Shared Mind, the Christos Mind, Collective Unconscious or simply the Mind of Love. Regardless of what you call it, most spiritual writers, philosophers, mystics and an increasing number of psychologists, claim that this dimension of our being is who we 'really' are.

- The work of de Mello referred to these twin sides of our present being as the 'I' and the 'me'. These are two aspects of one being. It's not that we have two minds, but that 'I' is an integral extension of an eternal Mind. It is at this deeper level of 'knowing' that the dynamic tension between 'good' (harmonious shared life) and 'evil' (the chaotic, competitive and destructive nature of life) is understood. When this 'knowing' (or Gnosis) is fully gained, the awakened 'I' is matured in humility and grateful for being granted the wonder-filled opportunity to gain the real meaning of unconditional Love. I think that this is the great macro Purpose of Life!

- The 'I' (just like the human eye) cannot see itself. It can observe and watch our separated body-based egoic identity. This is the starting point for becoming self-aware and realising that we are more than our body, thoughts, feelings, attitudes, career, religion and so on. It is the difference between self-observation and self-absorption.

- Once we fully grasp the essence of our spiritual nature and know that our True Self is the Observer or Watcher, and not merely the observed and watched, this dramatically changes our worldview and the way we see ourselves.

- Having this helicopter metacognitive view of ourselves, we can observe or notice what is going on in, through and around us. When we drop our temporal attachment, we can notice our thoughts, feelings, attitudes and behaviours (including all negative thoughts and feelings) watch these enter our awareness and pass by like the black clouds travelling across the blue sky.

- Being able to detach, dis-identify or diffuse from the thoughts that we incorrectly perceive as the cause of our suffering, means we are no longer defined by are negative thinking or by our circumstances.
- Einstein is said to have made the comment that we are either *full* of Love or *full* of fear. By this he is inferring that at some level of our present being, these two incompatible 'states of Being-Itself' will determine how our unique genetic and sociological upbringing and circumstances will be shaped into and impact on our ongoing manifest thoughts and behaviours.
- Love and fear when viewed non-possessively as opposite 'states of being', represent the two contrasting identities, the 'I' and the 'me' with whom the 'choosing-capable' 'I' can identify. When we increasingly understand who we 'really' are as the unseen and all seeing 'I' behind the body-based 'me', we also experience mortal life with an increasingly peaceful state of mind.
- This process is gradual, and every threatening experience that would once have disturbed our peace of mind, becomes an opportunity to remember again this core choice. This provides us with the opportunity to further embed and strengthen this state of inner peace. Every time we seek to defend the vulnerable 'me' against unfairness or loss, we disturb our inner peace of mind and must remember the superordinate Purpose of our earthly existence: to let Love transcend fear.
- When our core motive is one of Love our identification with competitive self-interest no longer drives us. We seek to make life better for those around us and in so doing, we enhance the well-being of all. We understand that what ever we give to another, we give to ourselves.
- We need to be careful and not assume that the thinking and decision-making mechanism we call 'me' can choose between Love and fear as circumstances arise. As Einstein said, we are either one or the other. Ultimately, the choice to Love unconditionally is an awakening – a deep paradigm shift that comes upon us without warning, like 'scales falling from the eyes.'
- To bring about this fundamental paradigm shift at the unseen core of our very Being-Itself is a key question. We can read

about it, talk about it, desire it but we cannot bring it about simply by conscious deliberation or choice. de Mello suggests we do nothing at all; just watch, notice, observe and be fully aware.

Reflections

I believe this chapter to be the most important, both in this book and as part of my own journey of spiritual transformation, which had hitherto largely been limited by the boundaries of a fundamentalist religious belief system.

At the time of being *Mack-Trucked,* I thought that this was the worst period of my life. It was like being stranded in the prime of my life, drained of joy, self-confidence, clarity and mojo. Life could have continued to be bleak, but it wasn't. I was able to find peace in the midst of what I initially thought was personal devastation.

Looking back, I now realise it was the best thing that ever happened to me. My old failing paradigm of what it meant to be human would never have been replaced by a new awakening paradigm if it had not come to the end of its natural life. I could have either experienced post-traumatic breakdown or post-traumatic growth. Unquestionably, from my perspective, I experienced the latter.

I believe that post-traumatic breakdown comes from the **denial** that the old unworkable paradigm needs to be discarded. On the other hand, post-traumatic growth is the realisation that we are not a victim of circumstances but rather a victim of those circumstances through an old interpretive filter that keeps us in a state of continuing victimhood. This old interpretive filter is when we make all decisions of the mind through a core motive of fear.

In other words, at the end of a nightmare which I, like many others have experienced, you may 'wake up' or 'break up'. And for me this was a totally unexpected but gradual wake up to the realisation of another way of life and living: an unshakable sense of the transcendence of life. One of the main reasons for writing this chapter was to encourage others and let them know that such a life is available to all without exception, should they come to realising as I did that their old sense of life was insecure and unsustainable.

The realisation that I wasn't who I thought I was changed everything for me. I was hitherto conditioned into identifying with and protecting that part of my identity which was not 'real'. Understanding that my True Self was not just my body, my thoughts, my feelings, my attitudes and my career and so on, was the starting point of my journey of awareness and realisation as to who this unchanging, unseen observing 'I' really was. This realisation has allowed me to continue this temporal journey with increasing peace of mind.

I have come to understand that although we have a dualistic identity – the 'I' and the 'me' – we don't have two minds, but that 'I' am an integral extension of an eternal mind. It is as if this part of our true 'I'dentity has been placed into a deep sleep, waiting to be awakened. At this deeper level of knowing, the dynamic tension between 'good' (harmonious shared life) and 'evil' (the chaotic, competitive and destructive nature of life) is understood.

The four-step process to awareness that de Mello writes of, (happiness, peace, love; call it what you like!) has had a profound influence on my life and work. No effort other than sheer awareness and observation is necessary to make this transformation.

Why we have missed this fundamental truth for so long in the West is baffling. But we are beginning to 'wake up'. There is daily evidence of this in my coaching clients in leadership, careers and personal areas. Inevitably conversations come back to the spiritual, as this uniquely human search for meaning is sparked at certain critical points and phases in our lives. I believe no meaningful discussions on leadership and life can fully ignore or escape this uniquely human question: what are we doing here really? Are we just passing time till it ends for us all or is there something more?

I'm convinced that most people who experience the kind of anxiety and depression that I went through, do so because of unwittingly unhelpful thinking patterns, mostly unconsciously, and through no fault of their own. As mentioned previously, our biological and early social histories have had such a powerful impact on our attitudes, beliefs, behaviours and values that we almost never question them until they fail like they did for me. Dig deep and there will be fear there somewhere.

References and Notes – Chapter 2

1. Thoreau, D.T. AZ Quotes: https://www.azquotes.com/quote/345853
2. I acknowledge that this table concept and content has been developed in consultation with Dr Phil Harker and will appear in an expanded version in his upcoming book: *One Degree of Freedom: Solving the free-will problem.*
3. de Mello, A. (1992). *Awareness: the perils and opportunities of reality.* With J.F. Stroud (Ed.), *A de Mello spirituality conference in his own words.* New York, NY: Doubleday, a division of Bantam, Doubleday Dell Publishing Group, Inc.
4. Descartes, R. (1637). *Discourse on method.* Cited in Newman, Lex, "Descartes' Epistemology", The stanford encyclopedia of philosophy (Spring 2019 Edition), Edward N. Zalta (ed.), <https://plato.stanford.edu/archives/spr2019/entries/descartes-epistemology/>.
5. Harker, P.J. Conversations both spoken and written with Phil over 20 years. His poems are included and used with the permission of the author.
6. de Mello, A. (1992). *Awareness: the perils and opportunities of reality.* With J.F. Stroud (Ed.), *A de Mello spirituality conference in his own words.* New York, NY: Doubleday, a division of Bantam, Doubleday Dell Publishing Group, Inc.
7. Harris, R. (2019). *Act made simple.* 2nd Edition, Oakland, CA: New Harbinger Publications, Inc.
8. Nin, A. (1961). *Seduction of a minotaur.* Chicago, Illinois: The Swallow Press. (Afterword added in 1969; sixth printing in 1972) (Verified on paper in sixth printing 1972). When Nin wrote the adage she did not take credit for the notion. Instead, she pointed to a major religious text: Rabbi Shemuel ben Nachmani, as quoted in the Talmudic tractate Berakhot (55b.) https://quoteinvestigator.com/2014/03/09/as-we-are/
9. Frankl, V.E. (2004). *Man's search for meaning.* London, UK: Rider – The Random House Group.
10. Covey, S. R. (1990). *The seven habits of highly effective people.* New York, NY: Simon and Schuster.
11. Harris, R. (2019). *Act made simple.* 2nd Edition, Oakland, CA: New Harbinger Publications, Inc.

12. Scott, T., & Harker, P. (2002). *The myth of nine to five.* North Sydney, NSW: Richmond Ventures.

13. Schucman, H. (1976). *A course in miracles* (ACIM). Mill Valley, CA: Foundations for Inner Peace.

14. Merton, T (2007). *New seeds of contemplation.* New York, US: New Directions Publishing Corporation.

15. Kastrup, B. (2019). *The idea of the world: A multi-disciplinary argument for the mental nature of reality.* Winchester, UK: Iff Books.

16. Harker, P. (2019). *From fundamentalism to freedom: The search for the true Holy Grail.* Unpublished manuscript.

17. Jung, C.G., & Read, H. (Editor) (1969). *The archetypes and the collective unconscious.* Collected works, NJ: Princeton University Press.

18. de Mello, A. (1992). *Awareness: the perils and opportunities of reality.* With J.F. Stroud (Ed.), *A de Mello spirituality conference in his own words.* New York, NY: Doubleday, a division of Bantam, Doubleday Dell Publishing Group, Inc.

19. Einstein, A. Albert Einstein Quotes https://www.azquotes.com/author/562876-Albert_Einstein - <a href="https://www.azquotes.com/quote/562876" title="Albert Einstein quote"><img src="//www.azquotes.com/p

20. Leunig, M. (2006). *When I talk to you: A cartoonist talks to God,* p. 45. Sydney Australia: Andrews McMeel Publishing.

21. Scott, T., & Harker, P. (2002). *The myth of nine to five.* North Sydney, NSW: Richmond Ventures.

22. Kuhn, T.S. (1996). *The structure of scientific revolutions.* Chicago, IL: University of Chicago Press.

23. John 4:18

24. de Mello, A. (1992). *The way to love – meditations for life.* Melbourne, Australia: Angus and Robertson.

Humpty Dumpty had a great fall,
Being *Mack-Trucked* doesn't end it all,
Learning how to realise your goals,
Continues our journey from broken to whole.

Chapter 3 – Understanding Goals

When I was *Mack-Trucked* and in other times when life has thrown me curve balls, setting and keeping goals have helped me get back on track.

For me, goals were the difference between floundering and flourishing.

For as long as I can remember, I have always been a goal-setter. Being the youngest of five children and having two older brothers and sisters who were high achievers in different life areas, may have subconsciously fostered this. I'm sure I tried hard to keep up with and emulate the achievements of my brothers. Even today, my wife Angela says: 'Still trying to make a hundred fruit boxes a day?'

The story behind this was that my eldest brother Ray could knock up a hundred fruit boxes by lunch time (this was prior to bulk bins being used in orchards). Dad was impressed by this, and so I learned at a very young age what I needed to do to gain admiration, love and acceptance. My Dad was a farmer in the Southwest of Western Australia, born in Bridgetown in 1907. Whether he was conscious of it or not, he always spoke about results and achievements: striving for top quality, wanting to have the best produce and stock in the district. His mantra was: 'Whatever you do, do it with all your might!' This was followed closely by another mantra which was: 'If a job's worth doing, it's worth doing well!' In reflection, I think his life Purpose was *Producing Top Quality*!

All my siblings were great at sport and we were also a very musical family. All of us were prefects and all but one were School Captains at our local Junior High School.

At that time, both my brothers excelled in athletics, cricket and AFL (just called 'Footy' in those days). Clearly, I grew up in an environment of high achievers and I wanted to be at least as good as my older siblings. I just had to be Captain of everything and excel in everything; even at schoolwork, despite not being gifted academically at that point in my life.

Looking back now, I can see where the seeds of perfectionism and the birthplace of burnout originated.

This book is not intended to be my memoir but in terms of being a goal-setter, there are a few memories worth sharing.

I'm ashamed now to admit that in Year Nine, I was a teacher's nightmare, both badly behaved in the classroom and disrespectful to my teachers. I was doing very poorly at academic work also. Halfway through the year, I 'flicked a switch'. I knew that in term three the Head boy and girl for the following year were to be appointed by the staff. My goal, like that of my two brothers before me, was to be Head boy, but that was never going to happen the way I was carrying on. I learned something then, which only became conscious later in goal-setting. Goals need to be emotionally charged, and if you have a strong enough reason to achieve your goal, you'll achieve it.

As another example, in Year Ten, I wanted to use my AMEB piano exams as a subject for my Junior Certificate. Up until then, I did not practice, and Dad was wasting money on my music tuition with the local Pastor in town. Again, I wanted to achieve my goal: and I mean *really wanted to*. To do that I went to the local convent after school to learn from one of the nuns. I practiced for at least an hour daily on school days and on weekends, and I was successful.

One important factor in achieving your goals is having milestones and being persistent. As I lived some 12 kilometres out of town, my only way of getting home was hitch-hiking. My school case was usually laden with books. Most days I was lucky, as travelling salespeople would be returning to their homes at that time of day. Some days I was not, and after walking for hours late in the winter evenings I would call into one of the neighbours' houses to make a phone call home. Dad would be quite sheepish with the neighbours who never understood why he wouldn't pick me up on those weeknights. I never complained, as that was just what happened in those days. I was prepared to do whatever it took. Persistence and commitment paid off (and my milestones and stepping stones were certainly real!).

I later went on in Year Twelve to gain a High Distinction in Music through the AMEB, as I knew I could not matriculate if I did not have maths, a language or music. Languages were not on the curriculum in Junior High schools at that time and I was really struggling with maths. So, passing music was an extremely strong motivation for me.

I could recount numerous other examples of setting and attaining goals in sport (playing A grade cricket), in academic achievements and in other areas of my life. It's important to note that I didn't always achieve my goals and I will explain why goal setting seldom works for most people.

In the early stages of my recovery from being *Mack-Trucked*, my goals were small. But despite feeling that my whole world had fallen apart, I set small daily targets. Walking, meditation and prayer, learning to cook for the family, and being part of a men's group were just small steps that provided some sense of meaning and fulfilment at that time.

The remainder of this chapter will explore how to set and achieve meaningful goals that work. The key reason we fail to achieve our goals will also be discussed.

Why are Goals Important?

At some point, most of us have set goals of some sort. These may have been related to our career, personal life, business or even all three.

Typically, January is a time where we make New Year's resolutions as we want to make a fresh start and a new beginning. For example, we resolve to reach a certain weight, go to the gym, walk 10,000 steps per day, practice mindfulness and meditation daily, not eat dessert, drink less alcohol, generate a certain income, find a new career and so on. For most of us, these aspirations are toast by the end of January. And with that often comes disappointment, a sense of failure and a loss of personal trust or integrity. We may also rationalise (or rational lies) about why our goals weren't important anyway.

If you are like me, you will have had mixed successes over the years. As previously shared, I have had success in pursuing sporting, career and personal goals and in passing music exams and attaining academic qualifications including two Master's degrees and a PhD.

The secret for me has been not just setting SMART goals (Specific, Measurable, Achievable, Realistic/Relevant and Time-Bound) but more importantly, clearly identifying and articulating the emotional 'buy in' and impact in setting and achieving the goal. Family goals have also been important for me and as I got older, goals in spiritual growth, health and fitness.

I have also failed to achieve some important goals in my life and as a result have been disappointed with myself for not persevering. However, I am learning to understand why I have not always been successful and more importantly, not to be so hard on myself for missing goals.

Regardless of how successful you have been, I strongly believe that goals are important if we want to grow as human beings. Most of us have some inbuilt motivation to better ourselves and to make a difference in the world. We can set goals for glory, but ultimately I encourage you to set goals for growth: growth in the important areas of your life such as:

- Fitness/Physical Health
- Faith/Spiritual, Family
- Fun/Recreation/Adventure
- Finance/Wealth
- Mental Health
- Relationships
- Learning/ Intellectual
- Vocation/Business/Career
- Relationships
- Contribution/Giving and so on.

In my experience, these are areas where many people have identified a deep desire for growth.

So, why do we set goals anyway?

The underlying assumption here is that when we set and achieve goals that result in meaningful growth in our lives, careers or businesses, we feel a sense of purpose, fulfilment and achievement. Our self-worth soars, our energy increases and our outlook on life becomes more positive. We get unblocked, feel successful and enjoy a sense of well-being.

Reportedly, two nearly identical studies on the importance of goal-setting were carried out in the US at Yale University in 1953 and at Harvard in 1979. The 1979 Harvard MBA study on goal-setting analysed the graduating class to determine how many had set goals and had a plan for their futures. Interestingly, the results of the 1979 Harvard MBA study were identical to the 1953 Yale study.[1]

In the Harvard Business School MBA study on goal setting, the graduating class was asked a single question about their goals in life. The question was this:

Have you set written goals and created a plan for their attainment?

Prior to graduation, it was determined that:

84% of the entire class had set no goals at all;
13% of the class had set written goals but had no concrete plans;
3% of the class had both written goals and concrete plans.

The results?

20 years later, the 13% of the class that had set written goals but had not created plans, were making twice as much money as the 84% of the class that had set no goals at all.

However, the apparent kicker is that the 3% of the class that had both written goals and a plan, were making ten times as much as the rest of the 97% of the class.

If this study were true, and most people believe it is not, then it would be saying a lot.

If you have been interested in goal-setting literature and research, you may have come across the widespread mention of these studies by motivational speakers such as Zig Ziglar, Brian Tracy, Tony Robins and Tom Bay.[2] According to Mike Morrison, 'unfortunately none of these are true!'[3]

I must confess, that prior to researching these studies, as a business mentor, coach, speaker and trainer, I too, had often quoted from these secondary sources, thus unconsciously perpetuating the myth or urban legend.

However, one study that I did discover, undertaken at Dominican University of California in 2007 by Gail Matthews[4] PhD, provided empirical evidence of the significance of having written goals, a commitment plan and accountability. Her conclusions were as follows:

- The positive effect of accountability was supported. Those who sent *weekly progress reports* to their friend accomplished *significantly more* than those who had unwritten goals, wrote their goals, formulated action commitments or sent those action commitments to a friend.
- There was support for the role of public commitment: those who sent their commitments to a friend accomplished *significantly more* than those who wrote action commitments or did not write their goals.
- The positive effect of written goals was supported: Those who wrote their goals *accomplished significantly more* than those who did not write their goals.

With the proliferation of business and personal coaching and the often-anecdotal reports of coaching success, it is important that this growing profession be founded on sound scientific research.

This study provides empirical evidence for the effectiveness of three coaching tools: *accountability, commitment* and *writing down one's goals*. From my perspective and experience, clear written goals keep us On Purpose, thereby giving us focus, clarity, energy and a sense of meaning.

The key reasons we fail to achieve our goals

As already mentioned, despite the best of intentions in our New Year's resolutions, we all know that our goals are usually out the window by the end of January or earlier. There may be many reasons for this, including procrastination, poor goal setting strategies and other reasons discussed below.

Thanks to these reasons, we are often frustrated and disappointed at not being able to move forward in the direction we want. Often our head says one thing, our heart says something else and our hands and our feet never get into action. It seems that what we want to do we don't, and the things we hate doing and want to change, we do nothing about. No wonder we feel confused…and disappointed!

Here are some of the reasons why I believe we rarely achieve our goals.

We don't write our goals down and plan for their attainment

The study I previously referred to by Gail Matthews (2007) indicated that those who wrote their goals down achieved significantly more than those who had no written goals. There were three other groups in the study. As well as writing their goals down, group three was asked to formulate action commitments, group four was asked to formulate action commitments and send their goals and action commitments to a supportive friend and group five was asked to formulate action commitments and send their action commitments and weekly reports to a supportive friend.

Group five outperformed all other groups while groups two-five significantly outperformed Group one, which did not write their goals down at all.[5]

I think there is just some good old-fashioned common sense here as well. From my experience, there seems to be special magic in taking thoughts out of our head and committing them to paper. The mind does not judge whether what we write is true or not. The process clarifies our thinking and embeds our ideas in the subconscious.

Our goals are not specific and measurable

Apart from not writing our goals down, a major reason for New Year's resolutions and other goals invariably failing, is that they are not specific. Instead of merely *saying* 'I'm going to get a new job/ career, or lose weight, or get fit, or make new friends, or earn more income,' we need to *write down exactly what we want to achieve and be able to measure it when we achieve it*. Write the number, amount or percentage and put a date on when you will accomplish your goal. I have offered several examples in the next chapter. You will never accomplish a goal that is vague. Having it be specific, measurable and time-based means you can track your progress. And don't forget to write down the day and date of when you want to achieve the goal. If you want to achieve the goal by December, you must put which day in December!

Our goals are not important enough and don't have strong enough motivations

Looking back over my life and observing where I have been successful in achieving my goals, it becomes clear that having a strong reason was vital. I mean a *deep down reason*, beyond the superficial or materialistic. You need to ask why you want it and repeat this question as you drill down to the core. A great way I have found of testing this is to write down all the reasons why the goal is important to me. I then ask a friend to perform a simple Kinesiology test by pressing down on my arm as I read out each of the reasons I have written down. It's amazing. My arm stays strong only on the 'real' reasons and collapses for any that are not. I have come to learn that our bodies don't lie. (You may need assistance with this practice from an experienced kinesiologist).

For example, when I set a goal to write this book, I asked myself the simple question: 'Why are you writing this book, Edward?' I had to think hard about this. At the time, I came up with these reasons. I am writing this book because:

1. I wanted to beat procrastination and 'get off the nail' that I'd been sitting on for six years.
2. I wanted to inspire transformation in myself, others and the wider community.
3. I had a deep desire to help others get their lives back on track after they too had been hit by a Mack Truck.
4. I wanted to make a positive difference in the lives of others.
5. I wanted to help others achieve their dreams, visions and hearts desires.
6. I wanted to build trust and authority in order to further develop my online business.

When I tested these through Kinesiology, two of these emerged as the 'real' reasons.

We often set goals for the wrong reasons. When the reasons are deep and they really mean something to you and for you, you'll more likely push through to achieve them. Always ask yourself why you want to achieve the goal and keep digging with the 'because' answer. For example, if your goal is to increase your net worth by $500k in twelve months from now, why do you want this? Your written conversation to yourself might go something like this.

'I want to increase my net worth by $500k in twelve months from now because…I'm worried about not having enough money when I retire.'

'I'm worried about not having enough money when I retire because…I want to have financial security.'

'I want to have financial security because… I don't want to have to struggle so much in my retirement.'

'I don't want to have to struggle so much because…I want the freedom to have choices.'

'I want the freedom to have choices in my retirement because…I don't want to feel trapped.'

If I were coaching this person, I would keep drilling down. Security, freedom, and choices are some deeper reasons for wanting the goal but if we kept drilling down, we would get to the real reason for wanting the goal and that is *fear of the future*. Interestingly, the more we keep exploring the reasons for our goal, a very different goal usually emerges. And this becomes the 'real' reason.

It's great to have deep reasons for your goals but these reasons, like your goals, must be written to give you more confidence, clarity and courage.

We march to the beat of another drummer

This is closely related to the above. Often we try to live up to the expectations of others and 'march to the beat of other drummers' rather than listening to the music deep within us. Our goal is set for the wrong reason. What matters most to us is overshadowed by our desire to please others. I believe this results in our self-worth being compromised.

I think that deep within us, we hear or unconsciously sense the gap between what is realistic and unrealistic. You may have gone to a seminar or workshop where emotions run high and you are challenged to 'climb your Everest'. You set goals that will stretch you way outside of your comfort zone.

I'm not suggesting at all that 'stretch' goals and high aspirations are not worthy. But have you questioned if this is what you really want? Have you set a goal to please someone else without it having any intrinsic meaning for you? Furthermore, if your goal is being set and kept in the face of others' expectations, of what value is that ultimately? Your gut and heart may even recognise this as forced or passive compliance and we understand that anything given or worked on in the face of expectation is ultimately of little value, or meaningless.

We fuse to or attach to our negative thoughts and beliefs

This is all about fusing to or attaching to our self-limiting beliefs or unhelpful thinking patterns. As humans, we have a 'thinking mind' and an 'observing mind' as discussed in Chapter Two.

Relevant at this point is to understand that it has been estimated that the 'thinking mind' has somewhere between 12,000 – 60,000 thoughts per day and that 80% of these are negative. So, learning how to manage up to 40,000 negative thoughts per day may seem daunting. Most of us don't know how to do it and this powerfully impacts on our ability to achieve our goals. Also, we are creatures of habit because as many as 95% of our thoughts are the same as we had the day before.[6]

Whether these numbers are accurate or not (there are varying estimates reported), the point is that the 'thinking mind' produces an enormous number of thoughts each day and the majority of these are negative.

Negative thoughts are particularly draining. They diminish our self-worth, deplete our energy and produce corresponding chemicals that weaken our physiology. No wonder we feel exhausted at the end of the day! More than anything, they rob us of confidence and the belief that we can achieve our goals and heart's desires.

So, what do some of these negative thoughts and self-talk look like? Here's a typical list I get from my clients.

- I'm going to fail anyway.
- I should be more disciplined.
- I never meet deadlines.
- I don't deserve to be successful.
- There's no point in trying, look at all the times I've failed in the past.
- I'm just too busy.
- I never complete what I set out to do.
- I can't do it.
- How will I live if it doesn't work?
- I'm not good enough.
- No one in my family has ever been successful.
- Who do I think I am?
- It's just not me!
- What will people think of me (if I fail…or succeed?)
- They should treat me better.

I could add a lot more but I'm sure you get the point. When we fuse to these negative thoughts, we become them. Our bodies respond to the way we think, feel and act, which is often known as the mind, body, spirit connection. There's an old proverb which goes like this: 'As a person thinks in their heart, they so become'. So, you are or become what you think. When we fuse to our negative thoughts, they blind us to engaging purposefully, proactively and productively with life. All we can think, see and feel are the limitations that the 'buying in' to these thoughts brings.

Learning how to defuse or detach from these negative thoughts was explored in the previous chapter.

We set conflicting goals

In our desire to develop, grow and change we sometimes unknowingly set conflicting goals. It is as if we have one foot on the accelerator and another on the brake. We end up stationary, unable to proactively move forward with the change we are seeking.

I think there are two types of goals that conflict: one type I'll call objective, extrinsic or technical and the other subjective, intrinsic or what Lisa Lahey[7] refers to as adaptive. Both can be conscious or unconscious, though it is more likely that many of our conflicting goals are unconscious – initially anyway, until we become acutely self-aware as to what is causing this self-sabotage.

For example, at the more obvious technical or behavioural goal level, my goal to write a book and have it completed by a certain date may conflict with my business cash flow goals for the same period. If I were to be uncompromising on both, these in turn will deleteriously impact on each other and on another goal of implementing a daily success routine of exercise, meditation, and planning. Furthermore, these conflicting goals could end up being excuses for not implementing any goals at all. One thing is for certain, conflicting goals increase our anxiety on many levels. With this goal-setting perspective, we need to be aware of the 'red flags' that caution and warn us of goal conflict.

At a deeper level, when we are striving for self-improvement, to make adaptive or internal changes in our lives, careers or businesses, conflicting goals manifest themselves in a much more subtle way. For example, we may have goals such as to become a highly sought-after keynote speaker, to be better at time management, to lose weight and to keep it off, to be a more engaging leader, or even something as broad as building a successful business. In all of these, there are many behavioural or technical changes we can learn and apply. At this level, the goal can seem simple: we just learn the knowledge and skills and then implement them, right? Wrong! Of course, if it were that simple, we would never have trouble achieving our goals.

Conflicting goals arise subconsciously within our 'inner landscape'[7] and until we understand what is going on at this level, we will find adaptive change or transformative growth nearly impossible.

For example, I have worked with hundreds of small business owners and managers who deeply desire to leverage and grow their businesses and to have more time to work *on* their business rather than remain stuck working *in* it. Many have been facing burnout, are enormously stressed, and have no work-life integration. By their own admission, their situation is non-sustainable. Invariably, after further exploration, the goal of becoming better at time management emerges and part of this goal is to improve prioritising and delegation skills. They can see that delegation is one way of bringing sanity back into their situation but when they do so, they end up defaulting to micromanagement. Probing deeper, we find that beneath all of this is a latent need for control. And that's not the end of it!

So what's going on here? What is causing the counterproductive behaviours that arise from inner goal conflict? In this case, when we dig deeper still, we end up with the usual suspect: fear. Fear of losing control, fear of someone else 'stuffing up', fear of losing income, fear of loss of reputation, fear of not being useful or of being dispensable or fear of loss of identity.

The presenting issue is never or very rarely the problem. The problem that we need to solve is much different from the one we thought we were trying to solve. In this example, while the presenting problem may have been stress, anxiety and overwhelm and the goal was to become better at time management, there are unconscious 'inner self-protective goals' in play. These include not to lose control, not to lose status and power, not to damage relationships, not to lose identity, not to be reduced to meaninglessness and so on. And the scariest of all is the unconscious and underlying assumption that 'I won't be needed around here anymore' and that is an extremely stressful self-realisation. So we have come full circle to stress and anxiety again.

From the above, we can see that the forces acting against learning better time management strategies such as delegation are enormous and may seem insurmountable. It's as if we have an inbuilt immunity to change. Biologically, the emotional part of our brain which we know as the amygdala is part of our body's self-protecting mechanism which always responds to keep us safe and protect us from difficult emotions and uncomfortable feelings. In this case, we end up staying in our comfort zones, remaining in the slow lane where the best way of offering value and making a difference is to always do what we have always done…and we end up always getting what we've always got!

We all have unconscious 'stuff' going on deep down inside us, which tries to counteract self-transformation. It can be quite a shock when we first become aware of how strongly our limiting beliefs, underlying assumptions and 'old stories' hold us back. Being aware of and uncovering these is an important first step. It takes courage to look deep within ourselves to see what's there and what is actually going on. But it's also a great relief when we discover that others we know experience similar human frailties.

When we understand that our brain is biologically wired to keep us safe and out of danger, we can see that our self-protective mechanism is just doing its job. For me, understanding this and thanking my brain for wanting to keep me safe was a huge breakthrough. It's at this point of self-awareness that we can acknowledge that we no longer need our self-protective mechanism to keep us safe from the perceived fears of lack of control and contribution.

Dealing with these conflicting goals requires a contemplative practice. This enables us to identify and get in touch with those challenging emotions that we try so hard to avoid and which act so powerfully against the change, growth and transformation we are seeking. Once we have identified these (e.g. humiliation, embarrassment, guilt, unworthiness, shame, frustration, disappointment, disgust, regret, frustration, anxiety and so on) one technique is to sit with them, as uncomfortable as they might be, and visualise their colour, size, and position in our bodies and breathe into them. This makes space around them, lets them be and then lets them pass. They will certainly return but over time through mindfulness, self-awareness and meditation, they will fade as the brain learns that these emotions are no longer a threat.

Initially, you may need assistance with this practice from an experienced personal coach or counsellor. As your awareness increases in relation to the feelings and emotions associated with your goals, you will be so much better equipped to deal with conflicting goals.

The good news in relation to the example I cited above is that when those business owners and managers I worked with overcame their fear and understood the inner forces that conflicted with their goals, they transitioned from micromanager to mentor; from control freak to coach – and often with the same team members to whom they were so frightened to delegate in the first place!

Our goals are often written without strong emotion or meaning around them

Most of us have been taught to set SMART goals: Specific, Measurable, Achievable, Realistic/Relevant and Time-Bound. Typical SMART goals, while helpful, tend to be left brain, rational and pragmatic. Without clearly articulating the emotional benefits of the goal, we give up when life gets in the way. We all know that people buy on benefits and not features. So too, we will enthusiastically buy into our goals if the emotional benefits are inspiring. Ask yourself: as a result of achieving your goal how will you feel and what difference will it make to you and others? Achieving your goal needs to impact you and others positively.

Goals that are set purely based on logic and rationality may never be realised. Both history and experience show us that where people are passionate and committed, they are more likely to achieve their goals.

For this reason, I like to extend the traditional idea of SMART goals to SMARTIE Goals. The 'I' is for Inspiration and the 'E' for enthusiasm and emotion. Your goals need to **inspire** you and you need to be **enthusiastic** about them. So, as well as logical SMART goals you need SMARTIE goals that come from the heart and are embodied with **emotion**. There needs to be a whole brain approach to goal setting to allow for emotion to *infuse* as well as *enthuse* the goal. I'll have of examples of these later.

We set too many goals in too many areas often resulting in overwhelm, anxiety and confusion

I know I have been guilty of this in the past. Maybe it's a personality style thing or relates back to the learned thinking and behaviour of my upbringing, which emphasised that my worthiness was dependent on my achievements. Or maybe it's to do with FOMO: the fear of missing out! We want all of life's advantages at once! As a result, we end up being pulled in a thousand different directions and are not able to focus on what matters most in our lives. Our brains can only focus on one thing at a time and having too many goals, results in overwhelm, anxiety and confusion. This means we don't follow through and we give up. The downward spiral continues until we reach a state of failure, unworthiness and ultimately anxiety and depression. Setting goals correctly is a serious process and needs to be done with sensitivity, understanding and insight.

We don't have an implementation process or procedure to achieve our goals

No matter how worthwhile, lofty, meaningful or challenging our goals might be, and regardless of what the goal is and why we want it, without an implementation and execution plan, our goal is dead in the water. We need to create a plan, a roadmap or have milestones with dates for each action step and be as thorough as possible. A goal without an implementation plan is a goal that will fail.

We don't schedule our big rocks!

Having an implementation or execution plan is meaningless if we don't prioritise our goals and the things that are really important in our lives.

I'm reminded of the story about priorities by Stephen Covey[8] in *First Things First*, relevant to prioritising and goal-setting. Jim Collins, in his book *Good to Great*[9], revisits this story also.

It goes like this:

> One day, a time management expert was speaking to a group of business students and, to drive home a point, he used an illustration those students would never forget.
>
> As this man stood in front of the group of high-powered overachievers, he said, 'OK, time for a quiz.' Then, he pulled out a one-gallon, wide-mouthed mason jar and set it on a table in front of him.
>
> Then he produced about a dozen fist-sized rocks and carefully placed them, one at a time, into the jar.
>
> When the jar was filled to the top and no more rocks would fit inside, he asked, 'Is this jar full?'

Everyone in the class said, 'Yes.'

Then he said, 'Really?' He reached under the table and pulled out a bucket of gravel. Then he dumped some gravel in and shook the jar, causing pieces of gravel to work themselves down into the spaces between the big rocks.

Then, he asked the group once more, 'Is the jar full?' By this time, the class was onto him. 'Probably not,' one of them answered.

'Good!' he replied. He reached under the table and brought out a bucket of sand. He started dumping the sand in and it went into all the spaces left between the rocks and the gravel. Once more he asked the question, 'Is this jar full?'

'No!' the class shouted. Once again, he said, 'Good!' Then, he grabbed a pitcher of water and began to pour it in until the jar was filled to the brim. Then, he looked up at the class and asked, 'What is the point of this illustration?'

One eager beaver raised his hand and said, 'The point is, no matter how full your schedule is, if you try really hard, you can always fit some more things into it!'

'No,' the speaker replied, 'that's not the point. The truth this illustration teaches us is: If you don't put the big rocks in first, you'll never get them in at all.'

What are the 'big rocks' in your life? A project that you want to accomplish? Time with your loved ones? Your faith, your education, your finances? A cause? Teaching or mentoring others? Remember to put the big rocks in first or you'll never get them in at all.

So, when you are reflecting on this short story, ask yourself this question: What are the 'big rocks' in my life or business? Put those into your jar first.

Many of us have a daily practice of filling the jar with pebbles and sand…and we are busy doing just that. How often do you greet people and ask them how they are and get the answer, 'I'm really busy!' But busy doing what?

As we so often hear today: *busy* is the new *stupid*.

The 'sand' in our working lives is all the low priority tasks that constantly demand our attention such as emails, social media, phone calls. Many people I know commence the day by opening their inbox. So often we want the quick wins to tick off in our to-do-list that we keep focussing on the sand and pebbles. Before you know it, its mid-afternoon, mid-week or mid-month and the big rocks are still out of the picture.

The 'pebbles' represent the higher value tasks that are not critical strategic drivers of your business or career (meetings, reports, quotes, social interaction and so on).

Focussing on the 'big rocks' accelerates your progress towards your long-term goals and vision.

Taking time out midway through last year to review, refocus, readjust and reset my goals, it became clear that one of my 'big rocks' had disappeared. While I still had focus on the other important strategic drivers, I experienced a nagging and sometime depressing frustration that one of my big, meaningful and important goals had been ignored. I wonder if you ever feel like that too.

On reflection, I think there were several reasons for this. Firstly, I believe my vision was unrealistic. Secondly, my daily/weekly jar was full of pebbles and sand. Thirdly, I had taken my eye off the big rocks. And fourthly, I am guilty of 'bright shiny syndrome'. Often my fascination is with new projects and the temptation to chase the next bright shiny thing means my energy will always go towards the newest and exciting project, and consequently, away from my key goals and projects. Finally, I did not review my top priorities or 'big rocks' frequently or consistently.

We cannot focus on everything at once. As the saying goes: 'When *everything* is important, *nothing* is important.' By laser focussing on our three to five most impactful strategies, we declutter our minds (and to-do lists) and our progress improves exponentially. As William James stated many years ago: 'What holds attention determines action.'[10]

We set unrealistic time frames

In a desperate attempt to overcome or make up for shortfalls or failures in our businesses, careers or personal lives we fall into the trap of setting unrealistic time frames. It's easy to understand why we do this with our goals. We get to a point of being 'sick and tired of being sick and tired'. At this point the fear of change is less than the fear of staying the same, so we are desperate to change. Our minds scream out: 'I'm over it', 'I've had enough', and 'I can't stand this anymore.'

In your personal life you might be experiencing poor health, a lack of energy, a feeling of stagnation and meaninglessness, a toxic relationship, or feeling empty and being in a spiritual vacuum.

In business you may have a website that really 'sucks' and has done for years. Your marketing strategy is just not working, your cash flow is shaky, you are overstretched and need to build a team or outsource but you can't break the catch 22. Or your boss may be leaning on you to achieve certain targets and you are frightened of the consequences if you fail.

In our desperation we want results and change now! So, our goals have unrealistic time frames and we miss the mark. We reinforce the history and cycle of failure and we give up rather than reset and re-evaluate. The timeframe to achieve our goal has been unrealistic and unsustainable.

We set the wrong goals in the expectation that: 'I'll be happy when...'

Have you heard people (and maybe you are one of them) say things like 'I'll be happy when...', or 'I can't be happy until...I get my new boat...house...car...degree...achieve my ideal weight...get my bonus...new position... marketing strategy ...or boss.' The list is endless. Based on this way of thinking, happiness is conditional.

We miss the step that recognises that 'I can be happy while reaching my goal. My perfect position... the correct diet... the new house... getting my book written,' and so on. Sometimes we set the wrong goals in the false belief that we can't be happy in life or business *until* we have achieved a certain goal. This belief is unhealthy and untrue and often leads to disappointment and a lack of fulfillment. When we set goals with this mindset, we fail to realise that *ultimately happiness is a choice at the level of the spirit coming from a core motive of Love, not a decision of the mind or dependent on external factors.* Happiness is unconditional.

This mindset is purely a form of avoidance and procrastination. It is keeping you attached to fear and preventing you from achieving meaningful goals.

We try to make up for our weaknesses

Have you noticed if any of your goals were targeting a deficit in your life or business? Often, we try to make up for a perceived shortcoming or failure in the goals we set. Working on our weaknesses is not necessarily a bad thing, but if this becomes our focus of attention we unconsciously hold ourselves back from working with our strengths.

Interestingly, when my clients do a personal or business SWOT analysis (Strengths, Weaknesses, Opportunities, Threats), and are asked to choose three to five points which have the greatest implications for the success of their lives or businesses, invariably they ignore the strengths list and focus on weaknesses instead. Both represent internal factors and forces in their lives or businesses.

My point is that if you set too many goals which focus on a deficit or weakness, you will be disappointed. Your energy levels will be depleted. Often goals like these are associated with negative emotions. There may better ways to deal with the weakness.

It's more important to be recognised and known for our strengths and to do more of what we do best – and do it more profitably. This way we will build authority and trust and become the first person to be called as the expert in a field.

We aim for perfection

Many of us aim for perfection, which is one of the silent killers of achieving our goals. We fear making a mistake and producing work that is *not good enough.* Or we worry that we won't be liked and accepted if we produce work that is not perfect. The result is that our productivity is stifled, our time frames blow out and we end up feeling anxious, depressed and like failures.

Perfectionism is also a silent killer of our dreams and lives. It is *fear disguised,* presenting itself in a more acceptable form. Putting this even more strongly, perfectionism is self-abuse and it keeps us stuck and unproductive. Perfectionism has little to do with being meticulous but everything to do with fear – the fear of making a mistake, of not being liked, and also of success and failure.

Our biological and social histories have a lot to answer for. You may have learnt to try to be perfect as a child and been punished for your mistakes. Being perfect may seem an honourable and worthy ambition, but it often hampers success and can lead to depression, anxiety and addiction.

Anne Lamott[11] put it this way:

> Perfectionism is the voice of the oppressor, the enemy of the people. It will keep you cramped and insane your whole life... and it is the main obstacle between you and a shitty first draft. I think perfectionism is based on the obsessive belief that if you run carefully enough, hitting each stepping-stone just right, you won't have to die. The truth is that you will die anyway and that a lot of people who aren't even looking at their feet are going to do a whole lot better than you and have a lot more fun while they're doing it.

As Brené Brown[12] points out, there is a difference between healthy striving and perfectionism. Healthy striving is self-focused: 'How can I improve?' Perfectionism is other-focused: 'What will they think?'

The bottom line is that *perfectionism is procrastination dressed up as excellence.* It forms a huge part in the 'I'm not good enough' story. It's time to recognise that it's keeping you firmly stuck on the procrastination nail. Becoming aware of this will help to release this handbrake from your life. I know it has for me.

We get stuck in the procrastination cycle

As noted, perfectionism usually leads to procrastination. We get stuck in the procrastination cycle and keep waiting for the right mood before acting. Often we end up using 'treats' such as alcohol and chocolate or activities including work or shopping to try to overcome the mood which keeps us stuck in the cycle. We wait until we 'feel like it' and use activities and substances to avoid positive action.

Ask yourself some questions like:

- How much is procrastination costing me generally in my life?
- What is it costing me in my business in terms of deals, customers, promotions, trade and cash flow?
- What is the cost in floundering relationships?

Perhaps you have wanted to break or strengthen a relationship for some time, but you hope it will just happen by magic or that the issue(s) will go away.

Procrastination is a major negative force that stops us achieving growth in our lives and businesses and prevents us from setting and keeping goals. Think about what it's doing to your health, happiness, finances and dreams. Because we neglect acting on our heart's desires and the things that matter most, our self-worth takes a battering. Have you gone down in your own estimation because you haven't done what you wanted to do or achieved the goals you've set?

Procrastination is also about avoidance and attachment to learned unhelpful thoughts and behaviours. By not acting on our goals we avoid the fear of failure, and also the fear of success and all the uncomfortable feelings that go with these. The frustration we experience is that neither avoidance nor 'me time' delivers the result we want. We end up trading small failures with big failures long term. I believe persistence trumps perfectionism and procrastination every time.

We set goals that are not in alignment with our Purpose, Vision and Values

An essential aspect of every goal I set is to test it against the question: 'Is this goal in alignment with my Purpose and Values?' Goals often fail for this reason alone. If there is a disconnect or a lack of alignment with our Purpose and Values, we can get sidetracked, lose heart and give up. We may also procrastinate because we have lost the conviction that the goal is worth the effort, particularly if there is little energy or emotion around the goal. Our heart and gut clearly tell us whether the change, habit or goal we are seeking or making is meaningful and in alignment with our True or Higher Self.

Not knowing our Why? (Purpose), Where? (Vision), How? (Missions) and What? (Values) makes us rudderless and directionless. How can we set goals if we don't know why we exist, where we are headed and how we are going to get there, or even the daily values by which we choose to operate?

Goals that are not in alignment with our personal, career or business vision also run out of steam very quickly. A clear vision is inspiring, energising and motivating. I know many people find it difficult to develop and articulate a picture of what they want their life or business to look like. If that's the case with you, it will be difficult to set and keep goals that are meaningful and growth-inspired.

I think nearly everyone has developed a vision board some time in their life. Your vision board graphically depicts the things that inspire and motivate you and includes pictures, illustrations and graphics of your dreams, hearts desires and goals. You can develop one for your business, career, personal life or a combination of these. An engaging vision board should be part of every success plan as it helps you bring to life what is encapsulated on it. The subconscious mind remembers and acts on pictures more than words. And because our brain is malleable and trainable and can 'rewire' and 'refire' itself – a function referred to as neuroplasticity – it allows you to train your brain for success and visualisation is a powerful way to do this. There is so much information and help available on how to develop and use a vision board on the net and I strongly recommend you research and use the templates that suit you.

For me this is an energising process, but your vision board needs to be placed somewhere it can be seen every day.

Linked closely with this practice is the skill of being able to visualise your goal completed. What will your life look, sound and feel like when you have completed the goal? Also important is visualising the process by which this will occur.

I vividly recall visualising winning the 800 metres track and field race when I was in Year 12 in the Western Australian PSA Interschool Athletics. I ran that race a thousand times in my mind, knowing exactly where I wanted to be in the pack, when I would make my move at the 200 metre mark and seeing myself crossing the line first. Winning by some 30 metres was a surprise but winning wasn't. Of course, I had a plan, undertook consistent training, and met milestones and put in persistent effort. This was in the days before formal coaching in sport.

We fail to understand what season of life we are in and the implication that this has for achieving our goals

For many of you, this chapter so far may have provided some understanding as to why only about 3% to 5% of us are 'goal keepers'. Given that there are so many hurdles for us to jump over, it's little wonder that many of us give up. There are yet more reasons we find it so hard to stick with our goals and no doubt you can think of some yourself.

We set goals that fail to acknowledge or don't align with our current 'season of life'. For example, the constant combined pressures of raising a young family and work commitments may deplete your energy, placing severe time pressure on you and resulting in you eventually giving up on your goals as it all just gets 'too hard'. We need to ensure that our goals are in alignment with and relevant to our current season of life or growth phase in our business. With this in mind, should our goals focus on growth or glory, success or significance?

To answer these questions, we need to understand that our lives typically play out in two halves. Just like in team sports, you can't 'play the second half before playing the first'.

Our first half of life is often about success. It is a journey of ascent. It is natural to try and 'conquer our Everest'. We want to test ourselves, see how far we can go in our chosen careers, push ourselves to the next level and be the best we can be at what we have chosen to do.

This is consistent with the egoic journey. During this first half of life many of us are strongly motivated by power, prestige, position, high performance and material pleasures. So, having goals for success and 'glory' in this season of life is perfectly natural. Witness all the sportspeople who are pursuing their goals with hard work and singular focus to achieve success (and sometimes the glory of a gold medal).

But something happens around halftime.[13] We begin to feel a sense of restlessness and lack of fulfilment. Something seems to be missing, even though we should be feeling that we have made it. We begin to question the importance of what we are doing and start to explore who we are *being* and *becoming*. Is the payoff worth the effort? Something inside us says we cannot keep doing what we do. Halftime is a good place to go but not a good place to stay.

If the first half of life is about *success*, then the second half is about *significance*. It is in this transition phase of our lives, moving into the second half, that we need to refocus our goal setting to On-Purpose® SMART Goals. In other words, if the first half of life has to do with getting and gaining, learning and earning, the second half has to do with yearning.

Just as the first half of our lives is about ascent and success, it is normal for many to see their second half as a journey of descent. We start looking inside of ourselves for meaning and purpose. We want our lives to count for something and we want to make a difference. We are no longer content to exchange our lives for a pay cheque or do meaningless work. If this were not the case, why would so many of our workforce be looking to 'downshift' – to take less pay and have less power and prestige in favour of more meaningful work?

We fail to develop an action plan and build in accountability and commitment

There's something highly motivating about having a supportive accountability partner to help you achieve your goals. Try as we might to coach ourselves and have self-accountability, this is rarely successful.

While this is not an academic book, you only need to do a quick search on the internet to discover the plethora of articles given to goal-setting and accountability. An accountability partner can be paid or unpaid; a work colleague; a supportive manager; a mentor or coach (either internal or external) or a friend.

In the research previously referred to by Dr Gail Matthews undertaken at Dominican University of California,[4] those who sent commitments and weekly progress reports to their friend accomplished significantly more than those who wrote their goals down and had an action plan.

The important thing is that you need to give permission to your accountability partner to hold you accountable and to discuss exactly how the relationship will work.

This must be a two-way relationship where there is mutual trust, respect, commitment, a good rapport and mutual benefit. Confidentiality should also be built into the relationship. An accountability partner is not there to tell you what to do but rather to support and encourage you as well as being prepared to ask you the tough and deep questions.

In my experience, the best accountability partner is a trained mentor or coach or a person who knows what it is to be On Purpose and can share your journey with you. In a lot of the work I do, we have an On Purpose Partner who has been trained to work alongside others as an accountability buddy.

You also need to set and commit to regular time frames. From experience it seems that such sessions need to be formalised at least fortnightly. Part of the accountability sessions will involve reviewing the action plan, action steps and your milestones. Having a goal without clear markers, milestones and time frames is setting you up for failure.

We fail to implement our plan

As I always explain to my clients, we can have the best career goals, life goals, business goals and business plan but without action, they remain just goals and plans. Success comes through taking action. And action comes from implementing many of the points discussed in this chapter: setting goals that are meaningful and for the right reasons, building in accountability and commitment, having milestones with associated dates, understanding and mastering procrastination, learning how to proactively manage your time, and so on.

Fear of success

Sometimes people give up because of the fear of success. 'Tall poppy syndrome' or the fear of standing out from the crowd is still alive and well in Australian culture. The fear of losing friends, and being the recipient of personal criticism is too much to handle for some.

We hit barriers and distractions and give in to them

Barriers and distractions come in many different forms and disguises and prevent us from achieving our goals. Life never pans out exactly the way we would like it to as we are not in control of the stimuli that come our way. As we saw in the previous chapter, we can't control or choose what happens to us (stimuli) but we can choose how we respond to what happens (response).

Often our distractions and barriers will have a pattern. They could be environmental, physical, psychological, emotional, and spiritual and so on. Commonly, as already mentioned, the combined pressures of raising a young family and work commitments may deplete your energy and place severe time pressure upon you. Eventually, you may give up on your goals. Another failure!

Or, it could be that you have been working on your goal consistently for a long time with little evidence of progress or success. For example, you may be striving for a certain weight but no matter how carefully you eat and how consistently you exercise, it's not happening for you...you just seem to hit a wall and plateau. You listen to and believe that voice which says: 'This is stupid and too hard. I just want to get a life!'

Often, the barrier may be the noise and chatter of your unhelpful self-talk, which fuels the confidence gap and the 'I'm not good enough' story that may have been with you throughout your life. Part of this may be that you are buying in to the negative or confidence-sapping words of others.

From the extensive exploration of why most people don't achieve their goals above, it's easy to see that the odds are stacked against us. It is no wonder that so few people achieve their goals, their resolutions or their heart's desires.

I want to encourage you not to give up on your heart's desires and the things that matter most to you in your life, career or business. Thankfully goal setting is not confined to January and not limited to a calendar month in the year, and the rewards of fully engaging in the process extend well beyond the calendar year.

Summary and Personal Reflections

In the Table below, is a summary of what I consider to be the top reasons why we fail to attain our goals. Complete this to home in on what is holding you back from achieving your goals and heart's desires.

I have drawn on the work of Russ Harris[14] who suggested that FEAR lies behind all the reasons we fail to achieve our goals. His acronym for FEAR is as follows:

- **F**usion with unhelpful thoughts
- **E**xpectations that are unrealistic and excessive goals
- **A**voidance of uncomfortable feelings
- **R**emoteness from your Purpose or Values

Using this acronym helps summarise and clarifies the reasons we fail to achieve our goals.

Complete the exercise. What are your three top reasons for you not achieving your goals?

Main reasons for not achieving goals:
(Tick the box to indicate the strength of this reason for you not achieving your goals).

1. Not at all
2. A small degree or sometimes
3. A moderate amount
4. Quite often
5. Very often

What's stopping me from achieving my goals?	1	2	3	4	5
Fusion with unhelpful thoughts.					
1. I find myself fusing or buying into negative thoughts and beliefs such as 'I'm not good enough' or 'what if I fail'? 'I'm going to fail anyway', 'I never meet deadlines', 'I seldom complete what I set out to do' and so on.					
2. I have the belief that I can't be happy unless I achieve a particular goal. i.e. 'I'll be happy when… I get my new boat…house…car…degree… achieve my ideal weight…bonus… new position… marketing strategy …boss', etc.					
3. My perfectionist tendencies often prevent me from getting started with implementing my goals.					
4. I have the belief that I must 'do it all' regardless of what season of life I'm in and my current circumstances.					
5. My goals are not really my goals, but I set them to please others.					
Expectations that are unrealistic. I expect to achieve my goals regardless of the following:					
6. I set too many goals at a time and get overwhelmed, anxious and often give up.					

What's stopping me from achieving my goals?	1	2	3	4	5
7. My goals and New Year's resolutions are not specific and measurable.					
8. The time frames I set to achieve my goals are unrealistic or unsustainable.					
9. I often set goals to overcome a weakness or to make up for shortfalls or failures in my business, career or personal life.					
10. I don't write my goals down.					
11. I don't develop action steps and clear milestones with completion dates for each step.					
12. I don't manage, track and adjust my goals implementation plan along the way.					
Avoidance of uncomfortable feelings					
13. I want to avoid the negative feelings, such as feeling inadequate, embarrassed or anxious, that come with the thought of failure.					
14. The thought of failure and the uncomfortable feelings that come with those thoughts often prevent me from starting or completing my goal(s).					
15. When I hit barriers and distractions or feel overwhelmed, I give up.					

What's stopping me from achieving my goals?	1	2	3	4	5
16. I haven't explored my emotional reasons for wanting to achieve my goals deeply enough.					
17. I don't build sufficient accountability into my goal-setting for fear of letting myself down or feeling shame if I don't fulfil my commitments.					
18. I'm a procrastinator and I don't know how to overcome procrastination. I keep waiting for the right mood before taking action.					
19. I feel uncomfortable about being seen as successful or being a 'tall poppy'.					
Remoteness from your Purpose, Vision and Values					
20. I don't consciously consider setting goals that are in alignment with my Purpose.					
21. I don't consciously consider setting goals that are in alignment with my Vision(s).					
22. I don't consciously consider setting goals that are in alignment with my Values.					

What's stopping me from achieving my goals?	1	2	3	4	5
23. I tend to set goals for material gain rather than for personal, or business growth.					
24. When I set a goal, I don't write down the reasons why it is meaningful and why I really want to achieve it.					
25. I don't consider the emotional benefits of the goals I set.					
26. When setting goals, I'm unclear about how the achieving the goals will contribute to the growth of others as well as myself.					

Eyeballing your responses, what do you consider to be the top three reasons for you not achieving your goals?

1. _____

2. _____

3. _____

Reflections

When I reflect on why I haven't succeeded in achieving some of my goals, I have identified several key reasons. The uppermost of these has been the fear of failure and the fear of success simultaneously at work deep within me.

The fear of failure has to do with what others will think and say of and about me, my disappointment in myself, and the overwhelming belief that I'm not good enough. Attaching to and buying into these negative beliefs and unhelpful thought patterns has held me back in so many ways and for many years. These, together with the silent killer of success and perfectionism, have been negative influences on my feelings around self-worth, productivity and my general well-being.

This has often resulted in procrastination. It's almost counter-intuitive and contradictory isn't it? How can someone who believes in and has been a successful goal-setter admit procrastination as a compelling reason for failure? Learning about procrastination and how to deal with it has been a big learning curve for me – so much so that I have devoted a full chapter to this later in the book.

The fear of success has been real for me. This is for two reasons. It's not about being frightened of standing out from the crowd or being a 'tall poppy'. I love to see people gain success in their meaningful chosen endeavours. In fact, success is one of my chosen values.

The fear of success for me centres around wondering how I would possibly cope if the vision I have had for my business became a reality. Age is not on my side. Would I have the physical, human, spiritual and emotional resources to lead it? I can easily coach others to develop an inspiring vision and implement it but doing it for myself is another matter entirely.

This book suggests I have been successful and that my life is flourishing – and so it is. To lose my career, experience years of depression and reinvent myself from an academic into an owner of a consulting business that has sustained my wife and me for nearly 20 years, certainly counts as success.

Goal-setting is very much a Western cultural construct and failure to achieve our goals produces anxiety in many people brought up in such a culture. I know it does with me. Some days, the fire in my belly to achieve a goal is all-consuming and burns deep within me. I don't know where that comes from or why I have it. However I've come to realise that all anxiety is future-orientated. We worry about the future when we only have today, this moment, now!

I'm reminded of the biblical phrase '*...so don't worry (or be anxious) about tomorrow, for tomorrow will bring its own worries. Today's trouble is enough for today*'.[15]

There is a real tension here for me and for many others too. Setting goals and achieving growth while simultaneously learning to live mindfully in the present is difficult. Learning to live with peace of mind in the moment while working on our goals and heart's desires is an invitation we may all accept. What I'm learning and practising is to live mindfully at whatever stage of the goal journey I might be on. For example, I have a strong goal to complete this book by a certain date, but all I have is this moment – writing this sentence – concentrating on and enjoying the gift of time to write this chapter. Being anxious about the finishing date and dwelling on that is counterproductive.

The other reason for fearing success for me has to do with my feelings around self-worth. This is a huge subject for many people and was present in my life even before I got *Mack-Trucked*! There are many reasons why some of us feel that we don't deserve to be successful and if that's the case for you, I strongly encourage you to speak to an experienced and qualified professional to assist you.

I now know about goal-setting and goal-keeping, and the vital importance of building in accountability and commitment into the process. Like me, you may be good at setting goals but not good at following through. Life gets in the way. Where I have failed to achieve my goals, I have neglected to use an accountability partner to keep me on track with my implementation plan, action steps or milestones. I have neglected to send my action commitments and weekly reports to a supportive friend. Telling someone what you are going to accomplish this week and promising to send them a weekly report is a powerful accountability process.

For the past two years I have been a member of a personal development group under the mentorship of Paul Blackburn from Global Success Academy. In one of our group sessions he asked who was having difficulty in accomplishing an important goal. I responded instantly. My difficulty was with completing this book. He asked me if I had something material that was important on my person. The only thing I could think of was my wedding ring.

He asked: 'How about you give it to me, and I'll give it back when you have your book draft completed?'

I stood up in front of the group and the camera (the workshop was being live streamed) and gave him my ring. It was a hard, dare I say it, courageous thing to do. That was some six months ago, and he still has it. But not for much longer. My wife and I have a 50th wedding anniversary coming up in just over a month's time. I'm determined to be wearing my wedding ring on the 20th December!

Where I have failed in my goals, I have failed to have powerful enough reasons for achieving them. The reasons must be strong, deep and emotional…and written down. It's normal for some of our goals to be materialistic and to amount to a search for glory; especially in the season of life I referred to as the first half where we are on the egoic journey of ascent. As I am well into the second half of life, I now seek goals that are significant in a different way.

I also need to be very clear in my mind about what success really means. From a worldly perspective it's more about power, position, prestige, pleasure and prosperity.[16] All of these have a place at some time in our lives. They are also amoral – neither good nor bad – and not usually given as the answer to the question: 'At the end of my life, how will I know that I've been successful?'

If I want to an authentic answer to that question, I need to ask my spouse, children, friends, colleagues and neighbours. For me, success increasingly has to do with having a rich, full and meaningful life; how I'm positively changing lives and making a difference; living out my Purpose and living in alignment with my values, building strong and lasting relationships; helping and supporting my kids and loving my wife. It's also about having success across all of my life areas – Spiritual, Mental, Physical, Family, Relationships, Work, Social and Financial.

We can set goals in order to make a lot of money, travel extensively, reach the top of our profession and so on, which for some may seem insignificant and meaningless as we ponder our mortality. Our lives can feel like a small pebble thrown into a pond: a small splash, a few ripples and then it's gone as it sinks quickly to the bottom. Your life has more significance than that!

Now I set goals that will help keep me physically, mentally and spiritually fit so that I can contribute meaningfully in the years I have left… and have some fun along the way! I'm amazed at how long it's taken me to learn to smell the roses!

References and Notes – Chapter 3

1. Morrison, M. (2017). *Harvard Yale written goals study – fact or fiction?* Retrieved from https://rapidbi.com/harvard-yale-written-goals-study-fact-or-fiction/

2. Ephenus, P. (2007). *Goal setting – the power of writing down your goals.* Retrieved from https://ezinearticles.com/?Goal-Setting---The-Power-Of-Writing-Down-Your-Goal&id=655551

3. Morrison, M. (2017). *Harvard Yale written goals study – fact or fiction?* Retrieved from https://rapidbi.com/harvard-yale-written-goals-study-fact-or-fiction/

4. Matthews, G. (2007): *Goals research summary.* Retrieved from http://www.goalband.co.uk/the-research.html & gail_matthews_research_summary.pdf

5. Sasson, R. Retrieved from http://www.goalband.co.uk/the-research.html; Davis, B. Retrieved from https://www.huffpost.com/entry/healthy-relationships_b_3307916; https://subliminalpro.com/thoughts/

6. In 2005, the National Science Foundation published an article regarding research about human thoughts per day. The average person has about **12,000 to 60,000 thoughts per day**. Of those, 80% are negative and 95% are exactly the same repetitive thoughts as the day before and about 80% are negative. Retrieved from https://faithhopeandpsychology.wordpress.com/2012/03/02/80-of-thoughts-are-negative-95-are-repetitive/
According to *Psychology Today* it has been estimated that an average brain has anywhere from 25,000 to 50,000 thoughts per day and 70% of them are believed to be negative. Retrieved from http://www.messagetoeagle.com/average-brain-has-up-to-50000-daily-thoughts/

7. Lahey, L., & Kegan, R. (2009*). Immunity to change: How to overcome it and unlock the potential in yourself and your organisation.* Boston, Massachusetts: Harvard Business School Publishing Corporation.

8. Covey, S., Merrill, A.R., & Merrill, R.R. (1994). *First things first.* New York NY: Free Press

9. Collins, J.C. (2001). *Good to great.* London: Random House.

10. James, W. (1950). *The Principles of psychology,* Vol.1.: Mineola, New York: Dover.

11. Lamott, A. (1995). *Bird by bird: Some instructions on writing and life.* Harpswell, ME: Anchor.

12. Brown, B. (2010). *The gifts of imperfection: Let go of who you think you're supposed to be and embrace who you are.* Minnesota: Hazelden Publishing.

13. Buford, B. (2015). *Half time: Moving from success to significance.* Grand Rapids, Michigan: Zondervan.

14. Harris, R. Workshop participation hand out which complements Chapter Thirty of his book *The happiness trap.* Retrieved from http://thehappinesstrap.com/upimages/Overcoming_FEAR.pdf

15. Matthew 6.34 RSV

16. Jenson, R. (2001). *Achieving authentic success.* San Diego, CA: Future Achievement International.

Humpty Dumpty had a great fall,
Contrary to success and standing tall,
Setting goals for growth, not for glory,
Meant letting go of failed old stories.

Chapter 4 – Optimising Growth

'The greater danger for most of us isn't that our aim is too high and we miss it, but that it is too low and we reach it'.

Michelangelo

'If you don't design your own life plan, chances are you'll fall into someone else's plan. And guess what they have planned for you? Not much.'

Jim Rohn

'Knowing is not enough; we must apply.
Willing is not enough; we must do.'

Johann Wolfgang von Goethe

In the previous chapter, I explained why goals are important, the key reasons we fail to achieve our goals and reflections on my own disappointments and successes with goals.

It stands to reason that by doing the opposite to all the reasons why we fail to achieve our goals, we will be in a much stronger position to achieve our goals.

This means that if you want to be unstoppable and achieve your goals, you must ensure that they are:

1. Written down using a tested and successful goal-setting formula.
2. Very specific and measurable with realistic and achievable time frames.

3. Accompanied by a clearly written implementation or action plan for their attainment with milestones and dates for each.
4. Targeting the key areas of growth you desire for your life, career or business. (I strongly suggest a maximum of five areas).
5. Emotionally charged. You need to articulate strong emotion around your goal. What will be the emotional consequences of you achieving your goal or of not achieving your goal?
6. Meaningful and reflecting what matters most in your life, business or career.
7. Relevant to your season of life, your career path or business growth phase.
8. Implemented with the weekly support of one or two accountability partners or buddies to help keep you on track with your commitments.
9. In alignment with your Purpose, Vision and Values to be relevant and meaningful.
10. Not in conflict with other goals you have set.
11. Visualised several times daily accompanied by the practice of self-awareness.
12. Observable and noticeable. Where and when are your unhelpful thought patterns including procrastination and perfectionist tendencies slowing you down, holding you back or preventing you from achieving your goal?

In this chapter I will outline six secret strategies for setting and achieving goals that will also address many of the reasons we typically fail in implementing them.

First, I want to encourage you to take stock of your life and look at your goals within a broader context including the current season of your life. This will require honest self-reflection.

I will then help you to systematically explore what you really want for all areas of your life...I mean *really* want. The tools I use here will help you dig deep to uncover what matters most for you now and in the near future and to prioritise your most important goals – goals that give your life purpose, meaning and momentum. This process will help you move from confusion to clarity and with clarity comes confidence and commitment.

I conclude this chapter by sharing with you two successful goal writing formulas, explaining how to write and achieve goals through habit formation, and demonstrating this, using examples of successful goals with milestones, a summary checklist and reflections.

Step 1 – Taking stock of where you are and what you want

Deep down, we know what is not working for us and what we want and need to do to grow and change. I would like to give you two strategies to help you take stock of your life: one qualitative and intuitive, the other more quantitative and objective. I elaborate on these in my reflections at the end of this chapter.

Taking Stock – Strategy One: Are you like the dog on the nail?

Years ago, I felt a bit like 'The dog on the nail' in the story below:

> One day a man was walking down the street on his way to work. As he walked, all the dogs in the street would bark at him as he passed by. However, there was one dog that remained on the front porch whimpering and whining – the sort of sounds dogs make when they are in pain. The next day as he walked to work, the same thing happened. All the other dogs would run to the gate and give their usual bark except that one dog. The man couldn't figure it out. After a week of the same daily occurrence, he decided to find out what was going on. So he went and knocked on the door and asked the guy, 'Sir, is this your dog?' The owner said, 'Yes, that's my dog, why do you ask?' 'I just wondered what was wrong with him,' replied the man. 'He's been sitting here whimpering and whining all week.' The owner replied, 'Well, he's actually sitting on a nail.' The man, incredulous, responded, 'What, your dog is sitting on a nail! Why doesn't he get off?' 'Well, it just doesn't hurt him enough.'

Like the dog in this story, there may be 'nails' you are sitting on right now from which you need to get unstuck. You can think of these nails as concerns, problems, issues, unhelpful thinking, behaviours and habits you want to break, negative feelings, frustration, and so on.

Maybe, like the dog, you **are** sitting on a nail, but it's not hurting enough, or you are too frightened to get off. In fact, it is terribly painful, and you moan and groan about your situation and lack of personal growth to yourself and others, but maybe the fear of change is too great for you. It doesn't really matter what the nail is – a personal, career or business-related nail; the reality is that it is preventing you from moving on with your life productively and proactively. You get stuck and procrastinate. And in this process, your dreams get lost.

So, what 'nails' are you sitting on right now? Where are you 'stuck'?

Personal 'nails'

In what areas of your life do you feel a sense of frustration and that you want to change?

Perhaps you are tired of being tired…of not having the energy you really want to have in order to be productive. You know you are not physically fit, and you've tried so many exercise and weight loss programs. But it all seems such a battle and despite your best efforts, you have made little progress.

Maybe you have been sitting on a relationship 'nail'. You have been secretly sharing your concerns, disappointments, frustration and perhaps even anger with a close friend or family member. You want to change the situation and have even made a goal around this but the fear of change is holding you back.

Sometimes I have had people tell me they are lonely. They don't have any friends and get to a point where they see themselves as victims. Is your social life empty and unfulfilled? Like the dog on the nail story, do you whimper and whine about this but just can't seem to get traction for change in this aspect of your life?

One of the big issues most of us face, is coping financially. I've certainly been there myself when both my wife and I had to quit our professions for health reasons. Costs are going up and incomes seem to be plateauing or declining. How many times have you set goals to get your finances sorted, develop a budget, increase your income, get rid of the credit cards or to develop a financial buffer or cushion in case of lean times? Yet each year rolls into the next and nothing changes.

We do the same today as we did yesterday and hope tomorrow will be different! As another old saying goes: 'Nothing changes if nothing changes.'

You may notice that you are stagnating intellectually. In the deep recesses of your heart and mind you feel and think it's time to learn new skills or knowledge. Perhaps there has been a course of study you have wanted to undertake or some important books you know you should read but never get around to. Somehow the 'busyness' of life just takes over and the goals get shelved.

Is there a habit you are trying to make or break? Often our personal goals are about changing our habits. For example, a friend said to me: 'I'm off the grog this year Edward.' Others have stated: 'My New Year's resolution is only to have a drink on weekends'. I've heard of several great success stories about habit changes but mostly these good intentions only last for a month or two at best. You may identify with this yourself.

What about your search for meaning and happiness? How many years have you been struggling with your spiritual growth? You set goals in order to commit to daily contemplation, meditation, mindfulness, prayer, reading the Bible, or other spiritual literature, yet you can't seem to get a routine going and soon you realise that another aspiration and goal has slipped away.

Most tragically of all, you may no longer dare to dream. Life has thrown you so many curve balls that you have lost hope of ever achieving your dreams. As a result, you have lost your mojo and energy, you feel Off Purpose and observe yourself marking time each day instead of moving forward intentionally with your dreams and goals.

Business 'nails'

What 'nails' are you currently sitting on with respect to your business right now? If you are like most business owners I know or work with, the demands of keeping your head above water just to survive the day-to-day running of your business occupies all your energy, thoughts and time.

Digital disruption, the rate of technological change, the constant challenges of learning and implementing new marketing techniques and strategies, managing new systems, employing and keeping good staff members all seem to keep you stuck on working in your business. Any thought, desire or need to work on your business can get swamped by daily operations and reacting to whatever comes up during the day.

The most frustrating part of this is that you probably have some very important business goals which, if implemented, would take you on the growth path you really want and envision. You know where you want to be within the next six months, one year and two years from now. You may have even set goals to achieve your growth plan but 'busyness' has got in the way (yet again!) and you regretfully find yourself like the dog on the nail.

Perhaps you have been thinking about starting your own business but don't have the confidence to have a go. Fear has wrapped its tentacles around your heart and mind, strangling the entrepreneurial spirit that is struggling for breath and life.

Career 'nails'

I have been deeply saddened to see so many people 'stuck' in their careers and jobs and seemingly powerless to get off the 'nail' they have been enduring for so long. For some it's the silent but nagging voice that keeps saying: 'I don't want to be here anymore,' or 'Is this what I want to do for the rest of my life?' The lack of alignment of personal purpose and values with those of the organisation seems to be tolerated because of the fear and uncertainty that goes with trying to make a change.

I know of people who have been physically sick every day prior to going to work. Or maybe they are really good at what they do but have lost their mojo. What's your situation? Perhaps your energy levels are depleted for a number of reasons and its time you reignited your career, but you feel powerless to change your life.

The scenarios above are just the tip of the iceberg. You may find resonance in some of them or you may have another story. The reality is that you are probably complaining about your situation or bemoaning the fact that you want to make changes in your personal life, career or business but you don't or won't. **Rarely is it a case of whether we can or we can't. More often it's whether we will or we won't!**

What 'nails' are you sitting on now in your life? Without agonising, use your intuitive self-reflection to jot down those things that are holding you back, slowing you down or getting in the way of living a purposeful, rich and full life.

My personal nails are: _____

My business nails are: _____

My career nails are: _____

What I intend to do next is not actual goal-setting. But it will give you clues and assist you in translating those 'nails' into a goal matrix.

For example some of the personal 'nails' you are sitting on might include you being overweight, feeling tired all the time, being in a toxic relationship, feeling lonely or experiencing aloneness, being trapped in the cycle of debt, lacking any fun or adventure or having no mental stimulation, and so on.

Turning these around, you may identify areas for goal-setting to include some of the following: being a certain weight, having a medical check-up and developing better sleep habits, healing or ending a certain relationship, joining social groups or entertaining more, or developing a budget.

Your personal goal matrix could look something like this. You will notice that not all the life areas are filled in. From experience, trying to set goals in too many areas leads to overwhelm, failure and disappointment. A small trim of the sail can often make a huge difference.

You will also notice that I have used six-monthly time frames. I could have just as easily set the top line with headings reading: End of June, End of year, Five years, and Lifetime. How you do this will depend upon your personal style and preference.

Personal Nails	Next 6 months	Next 12 months
Physical & Health & Fitness	Revitalise and increase energy	
Spiritual & Mental Health	Walk 5 days, 15 mins Meditation-prayer, yoga twice a week	
Learning/Intellectual		Complete course on _____
Vocation/ Work, Career		Start my own business
Family & Relationships	Heal a relationship with _____	
Finances/Wealth		
Fun, Adventure / Recreation, Hobbies		
Social		
Contribution/Giving		

Taking Stock – Strategy 2: Rate your 'Life Accounts'

Another way of taking stock in your personal life is to give a score to each of your life areas.

Ask yourself how well you are going now? Socrates remarked long ago that: 'The unexamined life is not worth living.' Whether you agree with him or not, take the opportunity to put the different areas of your life under the microscope. It will also give you a strong clue as to where you need to set your goals.

It may be helpful to think of these life areas as 'Life Accounts'[1] because just like a bank account, you can fill them up or deplete them with 'deposits' or 'withdrawals' which are the choices that you have made or will make in your life.

To get you started, you could categorise your life accounts as Family, Social, Mental, Intellectual, Physical, Vocational/Career, Business, Spiritual and Financial. These areas are not set in stone. You can categorise these in different ways as I have done further into this chapter.

Take a moment now to reflect on how well you are going in these different life areas. Rate yourself intuitively. Don't agonise!

Rate where you see yourself and how satisfied you are right now in each of your life areas by circling a figure in each of the two right hand columns.

Complete the table on the next page.

My life bank account

Name: _____

1. How empty or full is each of your life accounts?
    In the first column rate yourself:
    E meaning empty
    5 meaning neutral
    F meaning a full life account
2. How fulfilled or satisfied are you in each of your life accounts?
    In the second column rate yourself on a scale of 0 -10, with 10 being the highest level of satisfaction:

Account Name	Current Amount (after deposits and withdrawals)	Level of Satisfaction/ Fulfilment
Health/Physical	E 1 2 3 4 5 6 7 8 9 F	0 1 2 3 4 5 6 7 8 9 10
Family	E 1 2 3 4 5 6 7 8 9 F	0 1 2 3 4 5 6 7 8 9 10
Spiritual	E 1 2 3 4 5 6 7 8 9 F	0 1 2 3 4 5 6 7 8 9 10

Social	E 1 2 3 4 5 6 7 8 9 F	0 1 2 3 4 5 6 7 8 9 10
Career/ Vocation	E 1 2 3 4 5 6 7 8 9 F	0 1 2 3 4 5 6 7 8 9 10
Financial	E 1 2 3 4 5 6 7 8 9 F	0 1 2 3 4 5 6 7 8 9 10
Intellectual	E 1 2 3 4 5 6 7 8 9 F	0 1 2 3 4 5 6 7 8 9 10
Other	E 1 2 3 4 5 6 7 8 9 F	0 1 2 3 4 5 6 7 8 9 10

Now add up the scores and just out of interest, work out your average. Most people that I have worked with tend to sit on an average of between 5 and 6.

With the big picture of your life in mind, you can now start to be proactive in an area in which you wish to change and grow. Change for you right now may seem overwhelming because of the magnitude of what you see in front of you. It's a bit like the question, 'How do you eat an elephant?' The answer is 'One bite at a time.'

From your ratings in each of your life areas, you can select which one is going to be your first 'bite' and work on that. It is amazing how often small changes in one area affect other areas as well.

Completing the second column is important. For example, if you were just recovering from a serious operation which had you hospitalised for some time, you may score yourself low on physical health and fitness, but you might be quite satisfied with the score you have given yourself because you are simply glad to be alive and on the road to recovery.

Or, you may have rated yourself high in terms of your ability in business or career but low in terms of fulfilment and satisfaction. That's a strong clue for you. You may no longer wish to exchange your life for a pay cheque and consider it is time to get more mojo and meaning back into your work life. This may be an important area in which to set a goal.

Step Two: Identifying your WOWs

One of the mistakes people make in goal-setting is to set too many goals. I think this may be related to our personality style or FOMO (Fear Of Missing Out). As Leon Blum noted last century, 'Life does not give itself to one who tries to keep all its advantages at once. I have often thought morality may perhaps consist solely in the courage of making a choice.'

Sometimes in life we have to 'give up in order to get up'.

Whether in your business, career or personal life, setting your goals within a context is also helpful. This ensures that your goals are integrated across the whole of your business or life and not just in one area. For example, notice in the lefthand column in the table below that you could include goals in three to five of your life accounts or areas. The idea here is to integrate these different areas into your life or business. In the righthand column, I have included some prompters which may stimulate your thinking. But you yourself know your heart's desires.

I have provided you with WOW lists for your personal life, career or business. You will know what is relevant for you and most likely you will need to add your own points.

Personal Wows (Wants or Wishes) prompters

The table below provides a list of prompters for your personal life.

Goals for Life Accounts	Personal WOWs: Wants or Wishes Prompters
Physical Health	Well-being, Energy Levels, Learn about food and nutrition, Diet, Eating habits, Recovery, Aerobics, Exercise, Fitness, Pilates, Gym, Superior nutrition, Weight loss, Weight gain, Improve sleep, Regular medical check-ups, Habit formation, Have a blood test, Reduce alcohol consumption, Find a compatible exercise buddy, Regular massage, Cook for myself, Walk the dog daily, etc.

Goals for Life Accounts	Personal WOWs: Wants or Wishes Prompters
Mental Health	Mindset issues that hold you back, Anxiety, Depression, Aim to be medication free, Dealing with unhelpful thinking, Daily success routine, Habit-formation, Keep a journal, Personality profile, Changing self-belief, Developing self-awareness, Mindfulness, Meditation, etc.
Learning/Intellectual	Courses to take, Courses to develop, Write a book, Skills to develop, Books to read, People to meet, Conversations with relevant people, Find a mentor or coach, Join a class, Personal growth, Listen to stories, Keep up to date with technology, Visit Museums and Galleries, etc.
Vocation/ Work, Career	Start a business, Sell a business, Re-enter the workforce, Job satisfaction, Change careers or jobs, Personal Growth, Meaningful work, Travel, Working conditions, Become a mentor-coach, Promotion, Build leadership capacity and capability, Take on more responsibility, Reclaim mojo, Retrain, Improve performance, Know your career anchors, Undertake a personality profile assessment, Improve workplace relationships, Develop Emotional Intelligence, Move locations, Clarify Values, Being Valued, Manage emotions, Work part-time, Flexibility, Be your own boss, etc.

Goals for Life Accounts	Personal WOWs: Wants or Wishes Prompters
Relationships	Higher power, Family, Friends, Partner or spouse, Children, Work colleagues, Neighbours, Connection, New friends, Ending relationships, Brothers, Sisters, Apologise to_____ , Forgive_____, Show loving kindness to_____ , Renew friendship with_____, etc.
Family	Do things together, Future plans, Travel, Communication, Holidays, Children, Grandparents, Siblings, Meals, Gratitude, One-on-one time, Extended family, Quality time, Contribute to family relationships, Reconnect with_____, Apologise to_____ , Find a life partner, Be a friend to brother, Help sister with_____ , Restore marriage, Leave marriage, Renew wedding vows, Communicate feelings, Be home for meals, Help prepare meals, Deal with anger towards_____ , Learn to be a better parent, Do something special with partner, etc.
Finances/Wealth	Investments, Debt/Debt free, Income, Retirement, Savings, Special needs, Education, Things wanted, Things needed, Prepare a budget, Home renovations, Travel, Save for_____, Education fund, Learn about shares, Track spending, Increase cash flow, Pay off credit card, Bookkeeper, Accountant, Financial Advisor, Plan for bills, Discretionary income, Learn about tax, Prepare for tax, Change attitude towards money, Buy a new car etc.

Goals for Life Accounts	Personal WOWs: Wants or Wishes Prompters
Faith/Spiritual	Clarify beliefs, Implement spiritual practices, Mindfulness, Prayer, Meditation, Personal purpose, Unconditional love, Forgiveness, Loving kindness, Self-awareness, Peace of mind, Dealing with guilt, Face fears, Ask people about their beliefs, Find answers to spiritual questions, Have time of quiet reflection each day, Read spiritual and religious literature, Learn how to be still, Listen to your inner voice, Find a church that is meaningful, Rediscover or define values, Reclaim life, Experience peace of mind, Spread happiness, Create harmony, Strengthen inner core, Love unconditionally, Identify passion, What energises me? What depletes my energy? What motivates me? Learn how to make good life choices, Be joyful, Learn how to express gratitude, Who am I? What choices do I have? etc.
Fun, Adventure/ Recreation, Hobbies	Recreation, Sport, Travel, Camping, Walking trails, Hot air ballooning, Parachute jump, Holidays, Join a cooking class, Go dancing, Go fishing, Go camping, Go ice-skating, Play tennis, Join a golf club, Plan to participate in a fun run, Go to the movies, Plan a trip, Get some fun back into life, Take up _____? Plan a visit to _____ etc.

Goals for Life Accounts	Personal WOWs: Wants or Wishes Prompters
Social	Entertaining, Clubs, Events, Fun, Friends (current, old, new), Neighbours, Parties, Meeting new people, Networking, Dinners, Make new safe friends, Leave 'unsafe' friends, Join a volunteer group, sporting club or church, Dinner parties with friends, Fishing with kids or friends, Have lunch with_____, Get away for a weekend with_____, Get to know neighbours better, Do something nice for someone, Plan a surprise for someone, Renew an old, safe neglected friendship.
Contribution/Giving	Volunteer organisations, Small acts of kindness such as buying coffee for the person behind you, Pay it forward, Courtesy, Sharing skills and abilities, Not for profit organisations, Money, donations and gifts, Material possessions, Environment, Write to someone, Find a social justice group to support, Visit an old people's home and chat, Plan a surprise for someone, Help a neighbour with a job.

Career WOW List

Career Goals	Career WOWs - Wants or Wishes Prompters
Personal Growth Opportunities	Courses, Emotional Intelligence, Resilience, Conflict resolution, Develop my leadership, coaching and mentoring skills, Learn new technical skills and new technology, Personality profiling, Travel including overseas, Facilitating and presenting, Work-life integration, Strengthen relationships, Promotion, etc.

Career Goals	Career WOWs - Wants or Wishes Prompters
Leadership/ management role	New leadership role, Mentoring and coaching a team, Developing leadership capability and capacity, Relationship building, Strategic thinking, Implementing, Influencing skills, Engagement, Improving organisational culture, etc.
Career Goal	SMART Goal: Role, Location, Culture, Position/Role, Salary, Purpose and Values alignment, Workplace culture, Ability to use strengths, Workplace conditions, Time frame, Career move, Promotion, New role, Research, Career map, etc.
Work-Life Integration	Flexible working hours, Downshifting, Working from home, Family, Physical health, Spiritual and emotional health, Financial resilience, Social, Study and courses, etc.
Personal & Professional Awareness	Values clarification, Knowing my Purpose, Purpose and values alignment, Career Vision, Career goal, Knowing my top three career anchors, Understanding my personal style, Knowing my transferable skills, Career strengths and weaknesses, etc.
Career Move	e.g. Update resume, Achievement statements for all previous roles, Research careers of choice, Improve interview skills, Career move goal, Alignment with Purpose, Season of life, Redundancy package, Find a Career consultant/ coach/mentor, Career anchors (non-negotiables in your career move), etc.

Business WOW's – Wants or Wishes Prompters

Goals for the different areas or layers of your business	Your business goals could include the following:
Why? Goals Significance/Purpose	Writing your business Purpose Statement, Team members' personal Purpose Statements, Alignment of Purpose, How the organisation provides opportunities to be On Purpose, Organisational values, Personal values, Why our Values and beliefs are important to the business, Decision-making, etc.
Where? Goals Strategy/Planning	Vision, Positioning within the market, Time and energy, Resources, Products, Services, Financial targets, Business plan, Marketing plan, Strategic plan, Operational plan, Financial management plan, Working on the business etc.
Who? Goals Staff/Team/People/ Stakeholders	Present and future target market, Customer personas/avatars, Internal and external customers, Competitors, Suppliers, Roles and responsibilities, Team development, Work-life integration, Self-responsibility, Ownership, Accountability, Leadership role, Management role, etc.
How? Goals Strategy and Implementation	Vision implementation, Break even, Profitability, Marketing, Decision-making matrix, Time management, Gain and maintain customers, Manage finances, Planning for innovation and disruption, Staying competitive, Sales, Team meetings, Board meetings, Implementation of action plan, etc.

Goals for the different areas or layers of your business	Your business goals could include the following:
What? Goals Systems/Processes	Customer journey, Marketing processes, Marketing score card, Financial management processes, Cash flow forecasting, Budgeting, Pricing, New website, Social media, Processes to gain and maintain customers, Effective communication systems, Staff performance processes (training, coaching, mentoring, reviews), Technology, Efficiency, Effectiveness, New process to include, Existing processes to discontinue, Procedures manual, Onboarding process, Induction process, Product and service innovation, etc.
So What? Goals Success/Performance	Organisational On Purpose 'batting average', Implementation of vision and goals, Implementation of business plan, Personal growth of team members, Purpose and values alignment, Work-life integration, Increase in profit, Customer retention, Processes being both effective and efficient, Time management and productivity of people, Customer satisfaction, Best part about doing business with us, Why our customers are loyal, etc.

Step Three: How to Identify and Prioritise your WOWs

Now I would like to take you back to your Personal WOW prompters. What we will explore here is the skill of developing your WOW lists. These are your **W**ants **O**r **W**ishes (including your passions, heart's desires, visions, missions and values for each of your life areas).

A WOW List is a practical way of articulating the things you want or desire in an area of your life and getting these down on paper. I also suggest you review your responses to the 'dog on the nail' story as well as the page where you reviewed how full or empty your various life areas currently are and how fulfilled you are in each life 'account'. Now comes the fun part as your move to increase that score around the areas you have chosen to change or improve through setting and actioning goals.

Let's take, for example, your Family Life Account. The first step is to brainstorm! Let your thoughts flow freely as you jot down all the ideas and thoughts that come to you as you think about family. Write them down without judgement. If you *think it, write it*. It is your list and nothing in it is right or wrong. You can refer to the list of prompters provided in the Personal WOWs under Family, or you can simply write your ideas all over a blank page in a random way. The refining of your thoughts will come later. Dream BIG!

If you are having trouble with this exercise, refer to the list of prompters below. Adjust the wording to suit yourself.

Finding my #one family WOW

❑ Things to do together	❑ End my marriage
❑ Strengthen communication	❑ Pray or meditate with my partner
❑ Contribute to family relationships	❑ Release a relationship with _____
❑ Develop more respect between family members	❑ Form a relationship with _____
❑ Have more fun and spontaneity	❑ Reach out to _____
❑ Apologise to _____	❑ Be home for meals
❑ Reconnect with _____	❑ Help prepare meals

❑ Find a life partner	❑ Organise a family retreat
❑ Be a friend to my brother	❑ Provide for my family
❑ Help my sister with _____	❑ Communicate my feelings
❑ Heal my relationship with _____	❑ Listen to other family members
❑ Strengthen trust relationships within the family	❑ Be more accepting
❑ Have _____ trust me	❑ Deal with my anger towards _____
❑ Feel family support	❑ Go on a family holiday
❑ Preserve my family	❑ Learn to be a better parent
❑ Leave my family	❑ Do something special with my partner
❑ Restore my marriage	❑ Have fun and adventure as a family
❑ Renew my wedding vows	❑ Create a plan for the future
❑ Pay maintenance	❑ Stop fighting at home
❑ Spend time with each child	❑ Remove alcohol from the home
❑ Show my kids I love them	❑ Be a peacemaker
❑ Hug my wife/ partner/ husband	❑ Stick up for myself
❑ Tell my wife/partner/ husband I love her /him	❑ Take responsibility
❑ Be more caring	❑ Be trustworthy
❑ Stop swearing at home	❑ Other
❑ Dare to be more intimate	
❑ Share with my partner	

Does anything here ring true for you?

You can see that the list can be extensive. The important thing is that your list is created from your heart's desires and the things that matter most to you and not from the expectations of others. Goals set in accordance with the 'beat of other drummers' rather than those set in accordance with the voice within you do not work and, in your desire to please others, you compromise your self-worth and integrity.

Step Four: How to Prioritise your WOWs

The next step is to determine which one of these is really your most important WOW from those that you have brainstormed. I have adapted a tool called a TOURNAMENT for this, which I first came across when reading the book, *The On-Purpose Person* by Kevin W. McCarthy.[2]

In effect it is like a formatted sheet that tennis administrators use to write up the names of the players in a tournament. You are going to use the same format, but instead of writing in names, you will write in your brainstorm ideas. If you happen to have had 16 ideas or WOWs, list these randomly. Or, place your first WOW at the top and the second at the bottom and so on. Do this until all spaces are filled.

Now take the first two items and ask yourself which one is the more important of the two for you *at this point in time*. If you could only have one of these two WOWs, which would it be? Write that one down and continue down the list, playing the items off against each other just as would happen in a tennis tournament. Eventually you will come to the semi-finalist WOWs and then you will have to make the big decision of what is going to be your core family WOW at this time. Remember you have not eliminated ideas; you have simply advanced the most important one for you right now. The others are still on the list. They have not gone away, and they may resurface at another time.

Go ahead and have some fun with the template below. Make your decisions based on what is most meaningful for you. Decide from the heart and gut and not from logic. Feel the emotion as you decide on each combination. What do you REALLY want? You know that people buy on emotion and unless you end up with your number one Heart's Desire, I guarantee that it is not your number one!

I know that when some of my clients use this process, they get stuck in their heads. They reason that 'if I have this one then I will automatically get the others.' Where that may be true is because many of the WOWs may be action steps to achieve a bigger WOW. But always default to the one you are most passionate about, the one that engenders the greatest emotion and the one that will lead to both growth and transformation.

My family WOW list tournament

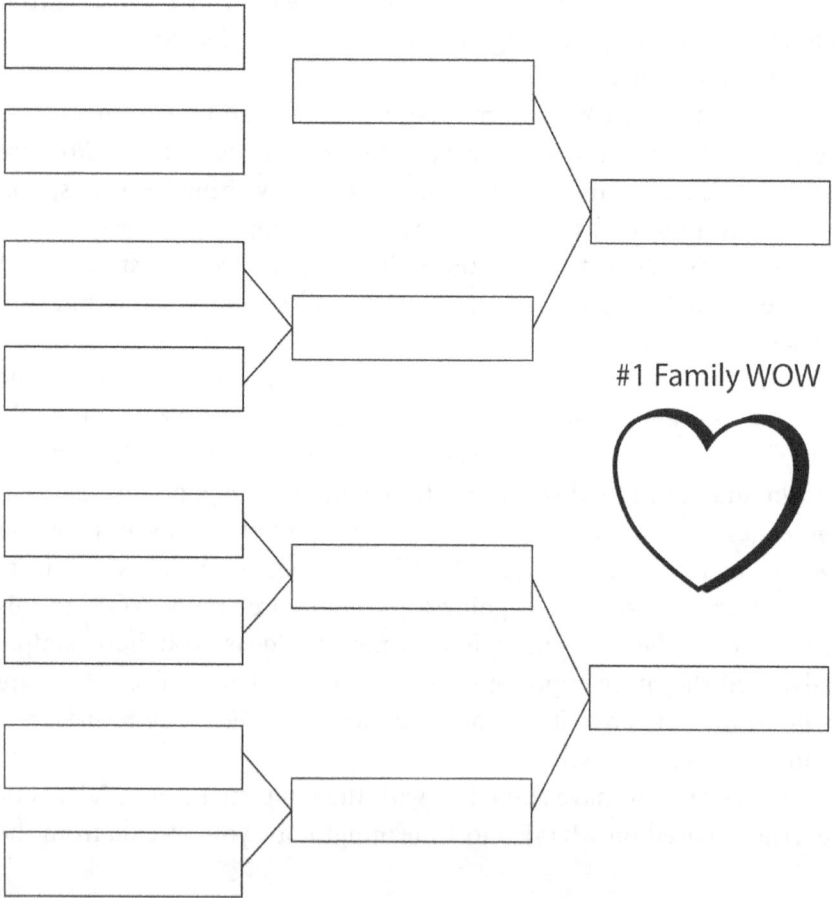

#1 Family WOW

Congratulations! You have your number one WOW for your Family Life Account. I would like you to test this out by answering the following questions.

- On a scale of 1 – 10 how passionate are you about achieving this Core WOW?
- How might you feel once you have attained this goal?
- What makes this such an important goal/issue for you?
- How did you choose that one?
- How is it meaningful for you?
- What would be the consequences of not achieving this goal?
- Would that worry you?

At this stage you have not written a goal but identified your number one Core WOW for your Family Life.

Now go ahead and use this same process to arrive at your number one WOW for up to five other areas of your life.

Place the winners in this template and on a scale of 1-10 rate how passionate you are about achieving this. On the right hand side, substantiate or justify why these are important and meaningful for you. Use the questions at the bottom to help you.

Life Accounts	Justifications/Substantiations Why are these important and meaningful? (See questions below to assist you)
Financial/Wealth #1. WOW_____ 1----2----3----4----5---- 6----7----8----9----10	
Spiritual/Faith #1. WOW_____ 1----2----3----4----5---- 6----7----8----9----10	

Life Accounts	Justifications/Substantiations Why are these important and meaningful? (See questions below to assist you)
Family #1. WOW_____ 1----2----3----4----5---- 6----7----8----9----10	
Physical/Health/Fitness #1. WOW_____ 1----2----3----4----5---- 6----7----8----9----10	
Social/Recreational/ Fun/Adventure #1. WOW_____ 1----2----3----4----5---- 6----7----8----9----10	
Intellectual/Learning #1. WOW_____ 1----2----3----4----5---- 6----7----8----9----10	
Vocational/Career/Business #1. WOW_____ 1----2----3----4----5---- 6----7----8----9----10	
Other #1. WOW_____ 1----2----3----4----5---- 6----7----8----9----10	

Key questions to ask when substantiating your core WOW's

1. What made me choose that one?
2. Why is that important to me?

3. Who else will this affect, positively and/or negatively?
4. How will my life be changed positively as a result of implementing this into my life?
5. Who benefits from this WOW and how do they benefit?
6. If I could only choose one of these WOWs from my Life Accounts, which one would it be?

To help you answer this last question, play a tournament starting with each of your WOW winners. This will give you your number one core WOW, top priority or your number one Big Rock!

Step Five: Turning your core WOWs to goals

Goal writing formula one: SMART goals

Once you have targeted the growth areas in your life, career or business through the tournament process, you can commence writing your goals. A widely used method is to write SMART goals.

This is a useful way for getting started as at least they are very specific, have a time frame and can be measured. Giving thought to whether the goal is achievable is extremely important as we don't want to set ourselves up for failure. SMART goals are also relevant to our season of life; where we are in our careers or at what stage of growth our business is in. The 'R' also means that our goals are recorded or written down. And importantly SMART

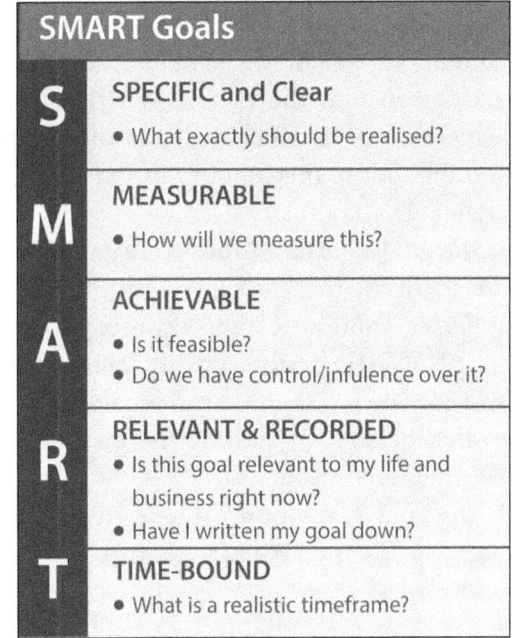

SMART Goals

S	**SPECIFIC and Clear** • What exactly should be realised?
M	**MEASURABLE** • How will we measure this?
A	**ACHIEVABLE** • Is it feasible? • Do we have control/infulence over it?
R	**RELEVANT & RECORDED** • Is this goal relevant to my life and business right now? • Have I written my goal down?
T	**TIME-BOUND** • What is a realistic timeframe?

goals are time bound so they always have a date by which the goal will be attained or completed.

For example, as a result of undertaking the tournament process for each area of your life, career or business, (or a New Year's resolution) a core WOW in your Physical/Health/Fitness might be 'lose weight and get fitter'. That is not a SMART goal but rather a wish, hope or number one WOW.

Written as a SMART goal it would read something like this:

Example 1 – Personal goal

I will lose 7kgs and measure 97cm around the waist by 30th March 2020 (or whatever the date might be).

So, let's test this against the SMART acronym.

Is the goal Specific? – Yes, as it clearly specifies weight loss rather than feeling fitter or having more energy.

Is the goal Measurable? – Yes, as it gives both the amount to lose, (7kgs) and the waist reduction measurement.

Is the goal Achievable? – Based on the fact that the maximum amount of weight we should lose is no more than 1kg per week, and, given that the person is writing the goal in January, then it's achievable or attainable. If on the other hand, if the person were seeking to lose this amount in four weeks, it may be neither wise nor attainable.

Is the goal Relevant (and Recordable)? – We don't know for sure. We are assuming that the person setting the goal is of sound mind, is not suffering from an eating disorder or other medical problems. If the goal is to help restore vitality, energy, focus and improve self-worth and confidence, then we can assume it is relevant to what is important to that person. By writing the goal rather than thinking the goal, it becomes recordable.

Is the goal Timebound (i.e. to be attained or achieved by a certain date)? – Yes, the 30th March 2020.

Example 2 – Business Goal

Perhaps you are a business owner and you say: 'I really want to improve my revenue or cash flow this year.' Again, this is a hope, desire or wish but certainly not a SMART goal. Here is how it could read as a SMART goal based on the assumption that current annual revenue is around $400K:

To increase my cash flow by 20% by end of the financial year 2020. Or:
To generate revenue of $500K with a profit margin of 15% by 30th
June 2020.

Is the goal Specific? – Yes, it specifies revenue or cash flow.
Is the goal Measurable? – Yes, 20% increase or a revenue of $500K.
Is it Achievable? – We don't know for certain. This would need further investigation.
Is the goal, Relevant and recordable? – Based on the assumption that the business is in its growth phase, it is relevant and has been written down.
Is the goal Timebound (attained or achieved by a certain date)? - Yes, 30th June 2020.

Example 3 – Career goal

I have worked with many professionals and executives who are seeking a career move. Sometimes this is the result of a redundancy and more frequently it's because they have outgrown their current position or lost their mojo.

Expressing the desire: 'I want to find another position' or 'It's time for a career move' are not goals but simply hopes, dreams, wishes or desires to get 'unblocked'. A career move SMART goal will need to consider criteria such as the role/position being sought, career strengths, Purpose and Value alignment, workplace culture, working conditions and opportunities for growth, location, commencement date and salary.

Specific - Has the actual position/role or field been identified? Have I specified the income level I am looking for?

Measurable – Are the criteria (work conditions, my strengths, personal and professional alignment of Purpose and Values, workplace environment) being met?

Achievable and **A**ctionable – Do I have the strengths, skills, experience and qualifications to get this job? Is it realistic? Is it achievable within the time frame I have set? Can I take specific actions steps from today to take me towards my career goal?

Relevant and **R**ecordable – Is this relevant and consistent with my career goals and my season of life? Have I written my career goal down and displayed it where I can view it several times each day?

Timebound– By when do I want to have this new role?

A career move SMART goal may read something like this.

To be appointed General Manager of a water utilities company with an annual salary package of $250K leading a team of 90+ in regional New South Wales by January 2020.

Specific? – Yes, General Manager of a water utilities company.

Measurable? – Yes, it states the location, salary package and team size.

Achievable? – We don't know for certain. This would need further investigation. If the applicant were already in a similar leadership position or an operational manager, then yes.

Relevant and Recordable? – Based on the assumption that this is a natural career path progression and that the candidate is seeking to find a challenging and meaningful role at the next level, then the answer would be affirmative.

Timebound (to be attained or achieved by a certain date)? – Yes, January 2020

Goal writing formula two – On Purpose SMART goals

I have noticed in my coaching and facilitating, that there comes a time in the seasons of our lives where goals also need to involve our Purpose and values direction. This led me to re-examine the traditional SMART Goal framework in order to reflect this.

I have used this common acronym quite differently in the context of clients building onto traditional SMART goals and developing goals and priorities that are meaningful and in alignment with their Life (and Business) Purpose. They may run in parallel with traditional SMART goals, but I have a different intention for them. Here is my new take on SMART goals and I have called them On Purpose Smart Goals.

ON-PURPOSE® SMART GOALS

S	Is my goal SIGNIFICANT and how will it help me live out my purpose? Does it have any SPIRITUAL basis to it? How will it provide SERVICE to myself, others and a higher power as I understand that to be? Is this goal in alignment with chosen values and what I want my life to STAND for?
M	How is this goal MEANINGFUL to me? How will this goal ensure that I will be MAKING A DIFFERENCE to my own life and the lives of others? To what extent does my goal ensure that I MAXIMISE my strengths, skills, abilities, experiences, personality and passion?
A	How is this goal in ALIGNMENT with my Purpose? How will it help me to live out my Purpose and is it in alignment with my Visions, Missions and Values and Core Wants?
R	How will this goal help RELEASE me from meaningless "busy-ness" and REFOCUS me on the things that matter most in my life? Have I RECORDED this goal in writing or visually?
T	Is this really a TOP PRIORITY for me? To what extent is this bound up with what others expect of me or is it TRULY important and meaningful for me? What makes this goal THE most important priority for me in terms of my life, business or career?

© *EDWARD GIFFORD, On-Purpose Partners®*

Example of an On Purpose SMART goal

If we were to rewrite the above example of the Career SMART goal as an On Purpose SMART goal it may look something like this:

To be appointed General Manager of a proactive water utilities company with clear alignment of purpose & values, leading a dedicated team of 90+ that is open to developing a coaching culture, in Regional New South Wales by January 2020.

This is still a SMART goal, but it is obvious that the candidate is seeking a leadership role where they can make a difference, know that the organisation operates or has the potential to operate from their core 'Why' and lived values. Implied shared values of sustainability, personal growth and responsibility, an openness to develop a supportive and coaching culture with people engaged in meaningful work, are also evident.

What is noticeable here is that most professionals get to a point in their career or a particular season of life where they are not interested in exchanging their time for money only. Other factors become more important such as significance, meaning, fulfilment and sense of Purpose. Knowing why and how they make a difference to their internal and external customers becomes a paramount consideration.

To bring this point into sharper focus, I share this case study:

After 12 months of being unemployed, a senior executive was offered a position that paid her the $300K salary she was looking for. Her savings had run out, her debts were beginning to mount, and the situation was now serious. In the course of her due diligence and through anecdotal evidence, she discovered her employer had a reputation for behaving unethically and that as a new member of the leadership team, she would be asked to make decisions which violated some of her core values. She took the job.

How long do you think she lasted in this position? The answer was: less than twelve months! What would you have done if you found yourself in a similar situation?

I have explained and demonstrated that SMART goals are helpful in taking the first step of turning your desires and wishes into something more tangible.

SMART goals focus you on five essential questions:

S = What do you want?
M = How will you know when you have reached it?
A = Is it in your power to accomplish it?
R = Is this goal relevant to my life or business?
T = When exactly do you want to accomplish it.

For some people, this is enough. For others who are seeking to achieve more meaningful goals, the On Purpose SMART goals process may be preferred because of the deeper spiritual and emotional significance of the goal.

Whatever the case, SMART goals ensure that you get clear on what you want and writing them down focusses the way you gather information and direct your actions. This in turn helps you organise your time and resources in order to maximise your desired outcome. More importantly, as you achieve your goals, your sense of mastery and self-worth are heightened and the motivation of experiencing growth in the different dimensions of your life is energising. Your competence, sense of mastery, and self-worth increase also.

Goal writing formula three: First person emotional goals

One of the main reasons that goals don't work is that we fail to build in emotion around the goal. My preferred way of incorporating emotion is using this formula. I first came across this in a workshop facilitated by life coach and mentor Paul Blackburn from Global Success Academy.[3]

It is (date) and I'm (target/goal). I feel/am (emotion/result).

If we apply the weight loss goal using this formula, it would read like this:

It is the 30th March 2020 and I have lost 7kg and measure 97cm around the waist. I have so much more energy and vitality and can't wait to get going every morning. I am very proud of my success, my self-worth has soared, and I feel much more confident.

Strategy and process is the key to achieving your goals

As we have seen above, how we write goals is extremely important. But it's only part of the process of setting and attaining goals. We know that goal-setting contributes significantly to our success but the goal itself is not the central focus. The real gain comes from the process we implement and who we become in that process. From the previous chapter, we also know that goals are more likely to be achieved when we have strong reasons to achieve them, make public commitments, engage a weekly accountability partner, set an action plan with milestones, action steps and dates for each and monitor our implementation daily. We also need to develop healthy habits around the process.

Once you have written your goal, apply this process. This is the way I set goals now and for me, this is the real secret of successful goal-setting. Everything else that I have shared with you on goal-setting has brought us to this point.

Step six: How to successfully set and implement your goal through HABIT

Once you have written your three to five growth goals using one of the three methods outlined, you need to test these out, not only against the SMART formulae but to ensure all the factors that normally prevent us from goal achievement are addressed.

I have incorporated these under the mnemonic HABIT and draw from the work of Ron Jenson (2001).[4]

H – Have a meaningful goal
A – Attach emotion
B – Build accountability
I – Internalise beliefs and behaviours
T – Train with milestones and timelines

I have developed the template below to assist you to set and keep your goals. I suggest you write the goal from the perspective that it has already been achieved using the third formula I demonstrated.

You will need to address each area of HABIT formation to ensure your goal is successful.

So, take one goal and apply each question to it.

Goal: It is [date] and I am [target/goal]. I feel /am [emotion/results].

H = Have a meaningful goal in alignment with your Purpose, Vision and Values.	
Why is this goal **meaningful and important** to me?	•
What is the **single most important reason** for this goal?	•
How is this goal in **alignment** with my Purpose?	•
How does this **complement** my values?	•
How does this goal **conflict** with my values?	•
Other goals affected by **reaching** this one + or -	•
Other goals affected by **missing** this one + or -	•
Strengths brought to this challenge/goal	•
Weaknesses brought to this challenge/goal	•
A = Attach emotion to the goal	
What emotion am I trying to **create** by reaching this goal?	•
What emotion am I trying to **prevent** by reaching this goal?	•
How will this goal **energise** me?	•
B = Build accountability	
Who will be my **accountability** buddy/buddies?	•
How will they help me?	•

I = Internalise beliefs and behaviours	
What **beliefs** do I need to change? Why?	•
What do I need to **stop** doing?	•
What do I need to **start** doing?	•
What **mindset** issue(s) need addressing?	•
What is my internalised **mantra?**	•
The only thing that would prevent my success with this goal is…	•
T = Training, milestones and timelines	
What is the completion date for this goal?	•
What are the milestones and dates for these?	•
What do I need to **focus** on doing?	•
What do I have to do to track and adjust my success along the way?	•

Example of goal implementation process using HABIT

To demonstrate this secret to successful goal setting template in action, I have given you my book goal as an example. (I have had to change the date of completion several times, but the rest has kept me on track and has shown up the 'red flags' that I've had to watch out for. I have shown these in bold.

Goal: It is [date] and I am [target/goal]. I feel /am [emotion/ results].

It's 20th December 2019 and I have completed my book *Broken to whole: How to put Humpty together again.* I have a strong sense of accomplishment, am proud of my achievement and profoundly relieved by its completion. I'm also energised by the anticipated impact my book will have on others, organisations and my business vision.

H = Have a meaningful goal in alignment with your Purpose and Values	
Why is this goal meaningful and important to me?	• I want to beat procrastination and 'get off the nail' that I've been sitting on for six years. • I want to inspire transformation in myself, others and the wider community. • I have a deep desire to help others get their lives back on track after they too have been *Mack-Trucked*. • I want to make a positive difference in the lives of others. • I want to help others achieve their dreams, visions and heart's desires. • I want to build trust and authority in order to further develop my online business.
What is the single most important reason for achieving this goal?	• I have a deep desire to help others get their lives back on track after they too have been *Mack-Trucked*.
How is this goal in alignment with my Purpose?	• My Purpose is *Igniting Enthusiasm* and my deepest desire is to inspire others to transform their lives, careers or businesses.
How does this **complement** my values?	My values that complement this goal include: • Transformation • Success • Personal Growth • Goals • Encouragement

H = Have a meaningful goal in alignment with your Purpose and Values	
How does this goal **conflict** with my values?	• I don't see any conflict with my values or Purpose other than time needed to ensure I exceed my clients' expectations while still writing this book. **Being OK with my progress when life and business get in the way.**
Other goals affected by **reaching** this one	By achieving this goal, the other goals impacted include: • Positively impact my goal to have my business fully online by 1st July, 2020. • Cash flow goals may be negatively affected in the short term while investing time in writing. • **This goal could be used as an excuse not to implement my goal of having a daily success routine every morning** (walking, meditation, planning).
Other goals affected by **missing** this one	If I miss this goal, the other goals impacted will be: • Goal to get business fully online by 1st July, 2020. • Being known as an expert and trusted authority in my area.
Strengths brought to this goal	• Written communication, perseverance, previous publications, past performance and success in achieving goals.

H = Have a meaningful goal in alignment with your Purpose and Values	
Weaknesses brought to this challenge/goal	• **I often get sidetracked with other projects and don't finish the one I've started.** (Following the next bright shiny thing.) • **I'm not always successful without accountability, encouragement and a buddy to help.** • **Buying into and attaching to the 'I'm not good enough' story.**
A = Attach emotion to the goal	
What emotion am I trying to **create** by reaching this goal?	• Sense of deep satisfaction, a sense of achievement…and relief. • Being On Purpose – being fulfilled, energetic and the pleasure of meaningful contribution. • Feeling successful and confident. • Being at peace with myself. • A feeling of yes! I've done it!
What emotion am I trying to **prevent** by reaching this goal?	• Failure and disappointment, frustration, anxiety. • Failing in my business. • Feeling lousy about myself.
B = Build accountability	
Who will be my accountability buddy/buddies?	• PB • AG
How will they help me?	• PB will contact me every two weeks to ask for a progress report and give me encouragement to keep going. • AG will read my drafts and provide feedback and encouragement.

I = Internalise beliefs and behaviours	
What **beliefs** do I need to change?	• I rarely complete goals that are not urgent. • **I can't write a book and generate cash flow at the same time.** • **It needs to be perfect and without 'holes' before I can publish it.** • I don't have the energy to do this while running a business full time.
Why?	• These are unhealthy thoughts and limiting beliefs which come from the egoic mind or the false self. Buying into these thoughts is a waste of time and energy.
What do I need to stop doing?	• Making excuses • Fusing to unhelpful mindset and thinking. • Trying to do too much. • **Worrying about money and the consequences of having insufficient.** • **Being a victim when it comes to the impact of the GFC.** • Placing unrealistic expectations on myself. • Drinking alcohol on weeknights. • Working after 8.00pm each night. • Giving into how I feel. • Setting unrealistic targets.

I = Internalise beliefs and behaviours	
What do I need to start doing?	• Be in bed by 10.00pm each night. • Rise at 6.00am every week morning. • Write a minimum of 750 words per day five days per week. • Place this goal where I can see it every day. • Practice self-observation constantly. • Accept the discomfort that comes from negative feelings. They will pass. • Even when I'm not feeling in the mood, just take some small action. • Walk 8,000 – 9,000 steps each day to ensure I stay mentally and physically fit. • Stand up and get going even when the 'black dog' is lurking.
What are the **mindset** issue(s) that need addressing?	• I'm not good enough. • It has to be perfect. • I rarely finish important projects like this as I need cash flow to survive. • Detach and defuse from unhelpful thoughts.
What is my internalised **Mantra?**	• I'm wide-eyed and electrified.

I = Internalise beliefs and behaviours	
The only thing that would prevent my success with this goal is…	• If I quit… • If I died… • If I got really sick…
T = Training, milestones and timelines	
What do I need to **focus** on doing?	• 80,000 words and 200 hours of writing. • Small daily steps that align with my milestones. • Getting up each day at 6.00am • Being accountable to myself and my accountability partners. • Writing four hours two days per week up until 30th June. • Write four hours per day, four days per week from 14th October. • Complete one of six modules each week commencing 23rd February of 'How to get your Transformational Book Done'.
What are the milestones?	• March 11-13: writing retreat, aim: 20,000 words. • Sept 8 hours: 2000 words. • October: 30 hours, 20,000 words • Nov: 64 hours, 40,000 words • Dec: 60 hours and editing • January 20th: publishing!

Here is a second example of how to set and achieve your goal using the HABIT goal-setting template. January is a typical time when we set New Year's resolutions and losing weight is often at the top of the list, especially after the eating excesses over the Christmas/New Year period.

Goal: It is [date] and I am [target/goal]. I feel /am [emotion/results].

It is the 1st of September, 2020 and I am 85kg. I feel wide-eyed and electrified: confident, full of energy and optimism. I have mastered self-discipline and am proud about achieving my goal and learning to live my life with intention.

H = Have a meaningful goal in alignment with your Purpose, Vision and Values.	
• Why is this goal **meaningful and important** to me?	• I want to wake up each day feeling energetic and have vitality.
	• I want to be able to continue working well into my third age and meaningfully contribute to the lives of others.
	• I want to fit into my clothes.
	• Apart from an unexpected medical condition, I want to stay medication free.
	• I want to be On Purpose every day.
	• I want to live a long, active and useful life.
	• I want to treat my body as a temple, have integrity with myself and 'walk the talk'.
	• It's a personal goal which has been nagging at me for years.
	• It is important for my well-being and energy levels to help me attain my other goals.
	• I need to set an example by being energetic, enthusiastic and passionate.

H = Have a meaningful goal in alignment with your Purpose, Vision and Values.	
What is the **single most import**ant reason for this goal?	• I want to wake up each day feeling energetic and have vitality.
How is this goal in alignment with my Purpose?	• For me to live my personal Purpose of Igniting Enthusiasm and my corporate Purpose of Inspiring Transformation, I need to stay physically fit, mentally sharp and spiritually empowered.
How does this goal **complement** my values?	• It is in alignment with my Values of personal growth and self-improvement, success, authenticity and integrity.
How does this goal **conflict** with my values?	• I don't see any conflict with my Values or Purpose.
Other goals affected by **reaching** this one + or -	• All my other goals will benefit from achieving this goal. Being fit and energetic will help me to get up each morning and work on my book. i.e. overall fitness and energy levels; ability to get more done; elevated self-worth.
Other goals affected by **missing** this one + or -	• My well-being is so important that my other goals will be negatively affected if I miss this goal. • Lack of energy and motivation to be more productive and purposeful.
Strengths brought to this challenge/goal	• Perseverance, tenacity and willingness to stick at the plan.

H = Have a meaningful goal in alignment with your Purpose, Vision and Values.	
Weaknesses brought to this challenge/goal	• I'm not great on my own and without accountability and will often cave in to wanting sweet foods including chocolate (if it's in the house). • If I don't sleep well, I feel too tired to exercise early in the mornings.
A = Attach emotion to the goal	
What emotion am I trying to **create** by reaching this goal?	• Feeling successful and confident. • Feeling fulfilled and joyful. • Feeling energised and On Purpose.
What emotion am I trying to **prevent** by reaching this goal?	• Failure, disappointment, frustration and anxiety.
B = Build Accountability	
Who will be my **accountability** buddy/buddies?	• AG
How will they help me?	• AG to help with daily routines, good eating and doing my daily step goal of 10K. • Ask tough questions when she can see me weakening with sweets and unhealthy foods. • Be encouraging when I reach my daily milestones.

I = Internalise beliefs and behaviours	
What **beliefs** do I need to change? Why?	• Food will give me pleasure. FOOD = LOVE • Food is a treat for working hard. • I won't have enough energy if I don't have a lot to eat. • I need to eat until I feel full. • I deserve and enjoy alcohol around dinner time to help me relax after working hard. • I need to think of my body as a temple rather than just form or matter and be respectful of it. • I need to thank my body for what it has done, what it is doing and for all the ways it helps me daily.
What do I need to **stop** doing?	• Giving in to how I feel. • Eating large portions. • Eating when not hungry. • Making excuses for overindulgences. • Fusing to these beliefs. • Drinking alcohol on weeknights. • Eating chocolate and sweet foods every day. • Having cheese and biscuits prior to dinner.

I = Internalise beliefs and behaviours	
What do I need to **start** doing?	<ul><li>Continue going to exercise class weekly.</li><li>Continue to go the gym at least twice per week.</li><li>Drink a glass of water when I feel hungry or have a craving for sweet things.</li><li>Learn and develop good sleep habits.</li><li>Be in bed by 9.30pm each night.</li><li>Rise at 6.00am every week morning.</li><li>Place this goal where I can see it every day.</li><li>Walk 8,000 – 10,000 steps each day to ensure I stay mentally and physically fit.</li><li>Start observing myself and my feelings more.</li></ul>
What are the **mindset** issues that need addressing?	<ul><li>I won't enjoy life if I don't eat chocolate or drink red wine.</li><li>FOOD = HAPPINESS</li></ul>
What is my internalised **Mantra?**	<ul><li>'I'm wide-eyed and electrified.'</li><li>My body is the temple for my soul – respect it.</li></ul>
The only thing that would prevent my success with this goal is…	<ul><li>If I do not practice self-discipline.</li></ul>

T = Training, Milestones and Timelines	
What do I need to focus on doing?	• Place my goal where I can view it several times each day. • Be in bed by 9.30pm and get up each day at 6.00am. • Being accountable. • Drink a glass of water when I feel hungry or have a craving for sweet food. • Dish out a portion of food on my plate and don't have seconds. • Four Alcohol Free Days Alcohol-Free Days (AFDs) each week. • Practice self-observation and mindfulness around this goal. • Walk my 10,000 steps each day and monitor this on my Garmin Watch.
What are the milestones?	• Lose 1kg every two weeks until I reach my goal of 85kg by May (This leaves me with a month up my sleeve.

Summary

I hope this chapter has been educational and informative. I wanted to inspire you and show you how to write goals that work for you – to make you unstoppable in achieving them.

Review of the barriers to successful goal setting

We commenced by reviewing strategies to help you overcome the barriers to successful goal setting. Take a moment to reflect on these statements. Just noting a true or false response will help you identify your gaps and what you need to focus on when you set your future goals.

Key strategies to successful goal setting

	My goals are:	Response
1	Written down using a successful goal setting formula.	True ❑ False ❑
2	Very specific and measurable with realistic and achievable time frames.	True ❑ False ❑
3	Accompanied by a clearly written implementation or action plan for their attainment with milestones and dates for each.	True ❑ False ❑
4	Targeting the key areas of growth that I desire for my life, career or business.	True ❑ False ❑
5	Really important and I have deep, strong emotional reasons for attaining them.	True ❑ False ❑
6	Meaningful and reflect what matters most in my life, business or career.	True ❑ False ❑
7	In alignment with my Purpose, Vision and Values.	True ❑ False ❑
8	Relevant to my season of life, personally, my career path or my business growth phase.	True ❑ False ❑
9	Implemented with the weekly support of one or two accountability partners or buddies to help keep me on track with my commitments.	True ❑ False ❑
10	Not in conflict with any other goals that I have set.	True ❑ False ❑
11	Captured visually and visualised internally and externally every day.	True ❑ False ❑
12	Emotionally charged both in terms of achieving and missing the goal.	True ❑ False ❑

How did you go? Are there some gaps you need to focus on?

Reflections

Sometimes goals evolve

In the previous chapter I stated that setting and achieving goals has been important for me as for as long as I can remember and certainly helped me get back on track after being *Mack-Trucked*. I also claimed that for me goals were the difference between floundering and flourishing.

Back in 2000 my academic career was over, I was unemployable, and I was told by one of my specialists that I would never work again. I could allow my new circumstances to define my future or I could recreate it. Finding and living my Purpose, understanding my true 'Identity, persistence, amazing support from family and friends, and goal setting were all massive factors in helping me recreate and reinvent myself.

But sometimes goals need time to incubate. In my case, having completed the training to conduct The Power of Your Purpose Workshops six years previously there was a latent desire to one day have my own business, but the training materials were gathering dust on the bookshelf in my home office! I dare say I was frightened to or not ready to ignite this latent flame.

While I was still working at university, and still well, out of the blue in November 1997, I received a phone call. It went something like this:

'Hi, my name's John – I hear that you are the guy in Australia who helps people find their Purpose in life – is that correct?'

I was momentarily speechless. When I tried to answer, I was coughing and spluttering. Finally I replied:

'Ah, yes, that's me.'

John went on to ask if he could do a program or attend a workshop to help him discover his Purpose. I was really caught out. I had been busy with my academic career, and life had just got in the way since 1994 when I first did the training in that program in the US with Kevin W. McCarthy. But right there and then I made a decision. I told him that I would get back to him in a few weeks with the details of my first workshop.

He said: 'Book me in, I want to be the first!'

It's hard to believe what came next. That same week, I received two similar calls – one from Perth in Western Australia, and the other from Melbourne in Victoria, asking me the same question. The universe was not whispering – it was beginning to shout!

Later that month I cobbled together 11 friends and associates who participated in my first ever Power of Your Purpose Workshop, including of course, 'John'.

At the end of the day I was exhausted but euphoric. It had worked!

All but one of the participants found their Purpose that day, or at least the seeds of their Purpose.

When they shared their thoughts at this point in the program, there was a depth of conversation that I had hitherto never experienced. I will never forget that day! My life changed forever as a result. Not immediately, but gradually. Little did I know then what life had in store for me and little did I know that the following year I would be *Mack-Trucked* and *Mucked Up*. Not by just a gentle poke or push, not even with a shove but by one huge big Mack Truck that bowled me over! I had a great fall and was emotionally smashed to pieces. Looking back, I understand that I *died* on that day – not in a physical sense but a spiritual one. It was the beginning of a journey where I died to my former self, my ego, and then became more alive to my True Self.

Back in 1999, in my second year of convalescence, I ran my second ever workshop on the Power of your Purpose. At the end of that workshop, one of the participants remarked during our closing conversation:

'Edward, there will always be someone to take your place at university, but you are the only person who can take this program to Australia. This is your destiny: helping Australia to get back On Purpose.'

That statement was powerful. It stopped me in my tracks. It was not a blowtorch but it certainly reignited the fire of enthusiasm which had been lying quietly dormant in me.

The point of this story is that sometimes goals evolve. Our circumstances can suddenly change. My goal of becoming a full professor faded while the goal of establishing my personal leadership business began to glow increasingly brighter. I didn't write the goal down, using the formulae and all the processes outlined in this chapter. But I did have incredibly strong emotional and pragmatic reasons to commence my own business.

Goal-setting: A work in progress

I also mentioned in the previous chapter that one of the biggest gaps for me in my goal-setting was not being consistent in my commitment and accountability with my buddy or accountability partner. Life gets in the way sometimes and you miss some of your milestones. Then you find your progress disappointing and even embarrassing, so your commitment levels drop off. I strongly suggest that you give your accountability partner permission to ring you if they have not heard from you each week. That way, there's no escape and no excuses. So, take massive responsibility for your milestones, your action steps and your commitments. To borrow a mantra from an old football coach: 'If it is to be, it is up to me.'

But be prepared! There will be curve balls; you will get Off Purpose and life will get in the way. The secret is to be realistic, keep your perspective, reset the dates where necessary and above all, be kind to yourself. This has been a big learning curve for me. My wife often remarks: 'You are so incredibly hard on yourself.' She is teaching me how to self-soothe, and not be so self-deprecating. I'm still learning how to love myself more. Observing my egoic mind at work, practising self-observation rather than self-absorption, knowing who I really am and understanding the one choice I truly have are helping me enormously.

Taking stock

Goals need to be set within a context if they are to be meaningful. In this chapter, I have suggested several ways of seeing your goals within the big picture of your life, career or business. As a reminder, here are several essential ways to do this.

1.   Alignment with Purpose, Vision and Values

Repeatedly, I have asked you if your goals are in alignment with your Purpose, Vision and Values. You will recall from Chapter One that your Purpose is your reason for being – Your *Why?* Your Values are very closely aligned with your Purpose. They are the ways you choose to behave while living it out. Vision is about clearly seeing the future picture you have for your life, career or business. Goals represent the content for the context of your life. They focus on what needs to be done to bring about your Vision and live your Purpose and Values.

I'm reminded of a wonderful illustration of the difference between context and content. If you Google *Rice Art in Japan*, you will find images of paddy fields. From an aerial view (Context), the rice paddy fields reveal incredibly detailed pictures and illustrations. You need this view to gain perspective of the art. On the ground level, we discover that the art is achieved through using different coloured rice (Content). Similarly, your goals represent the content while your Purpose, Vision and Values give your life a context. If you meandered through the rice fields, you would never see the beautiful artwork. You'd get stuck in the paddy fields, labouring away on your goals, not able to envisage the amazing difference you could make in your life or business as a result of achieving your vision and Purpose.

2.   What nails are you sitting on?

The *Dog on the nail* story is an invitation for you to be brutally honest with yourself. It's another way of taking stock of your life. It helps you to face up to what is holding you back, slowing you down, or getting in the way of your vision for your life, career or business. This is a time when you really can focus on your weaknesses and set a goal to turn your life around in the context of whatever 'nail' you are sitting on. It will be a defining moment for you.

Reflect upon these questions in relation to the 'nail(s) you are currently sitting on.

- How big, sharp and painful are they?
- How often do you notice them?
- What impact are they having on your life and business?
- Do you notice any regrets by being stuck?
- What impact are they having on others, especially your significant other, colleagues and clients?
- What makes getting off these 'nails' so hard for you?

- When you think about the 'nails' you are on, what do you notice about your energy?
- Do they deplete your energy or raise your energy?
- What is the biggest 'nail' you are on right now?
- How would your life or business be different if you got off the largest and deepest nail?

3. What season of life are you in?

Another way of setting a context for your goals is to be aware of the season of life you are in, where you are in your career path and what phase of the business growth path you are at.

This is where conflicting goals often emerge. Work or business is full on, demanding your energy, time and focus. Simultaneously you may be raising a young family, and you want to stay fit and healthy, be involved in sport or other interests and maintain a strong relationship with your partner or spouse, kids and wider family. You may also want to take another course or degree. The combined pressures are enormous. Yet it is tempting to set too many goals across work, family, physical health, children, study and so on.

I recall a conversation with a client many years ago. She had recently emigrated to Australia. She and her husband had two young children under four at the time. She had been used to servants, had had a very successful business prior to coming to Australia and was accustomed to a comfortable lifestyle. How different things had become since her move.

Two children had to be nurtured and cared for and food had to be prepared and cooked for the family, but these were things the servants always had done. On top of this, she had no business or work. To say she was discombobulated is an understatement. She felt unfulfilled, frustrated and anxious.

I invited her to consider this new situation as an invitation for her to learn new skills: to learn to be a homemaker and to learn to nurture and nourish her children. Rather than fight her new circumstances, I asked her what would happen if she embraced them. I also reminded her of a workshop of mine she had attended where I had played the Seekers' song *'Turn, Turn, Turn'* to the group.

I was asking her to be aware of the seasons of her life and invited her to consider how she might work with this new season to be more fulfilled. She was very moved by the words from the book of Ecclesiastes as we read through them together.[5] I have used capital letters and a new line for each point for emphasis and to facilitate ease of reading.

A time for everything

There is a time for everything, and a season for every activity under the heavens:

A time to be born, and a time to die,
A time to plant and a time to uproot,
A time to kill and a time to heal,
A time to tear down and a time to build,
A time to weep and a time to laugh,
A time to mourn and a time to dance,
A time to scatter stones and a time to gather them,
A time to embrace and a time to refrain from embracing,
A time to search and a time to give up,
A time to keep and a time to throw away,
I time to tear and a time to mend,
A time to be silent and a time to speak,
A time to love and a time to hate,
A time for war and a time for peace.

I asked her what season of life she was in prior to emigrating and what season she was in now. That was an 'Ah-ha!' moment for her and helped her to realign with her Purpose.

Previously she had developed her Life Purpose Statement, which was *Inspiring Greatness*. I asked her how she could live out her Purpose in this new season of her life.

My point in sharing this story is that we need perspective when setting goals and to be cognisant of the season of life we are in. This will help avoid goal conflict. More importantly, it will result in peace of mind – the Holy Grail that we all seek!

4.   Maintaining perspective

Closely linked to the above story, taking stock of how we 'do life', may also help us gain perspective when setting goals. I know it did for me.

In life you can be a 'floater', a 'fighter' or a 'navigator'[2]. Taking this metaphor further, the 'floaters 'just go with the flow, don't buck the system or the status quo, do anything to keep the peace and don't rock the boat. The tide takes them in whichever direction it is flowing at the time. These people don't generally set goals, or if they do, they certainly don't build in accountability and commitment to achieve them. I must say, I don't ever recall being a 'floater'.

The 'fighter' has goals and will achieve these at no matter what the cost. This has been me on previous occasions. This type swims upstream against the flow, and is smacked around by flotsam and jetsam, ending up exhausted and stressed. I was determined to achieve my goals and I persevered whatever the cost. I must emphasise that the long-term effects of being a 'fighter' will take its toll on your business, health, relationships, family and in every stream of your life. I know, I've been there!

Over time, I have learned to become a 'navigator'. My sincere recommendation and hope is that you do so also. On Purpose goal setters *know the flow then go with the flow.* They have a very good understanding of the currents, the hazards, the dangers and opportunities. This may mean fighting the 'elements' for a while, being determined, persevering even in tough times, but with a very clear understanding of the outcomes of the direction they are navigating. They are not fighting currents blindly upstream or drifting aimlessly downstream. They are well-informed, intentional and proactive.

5.   Honestly rate your life

At the beginning of this chapter, I shared with you a tool that put all your life areas under the microscope. You had to rate how you were progressing in each of your Life Accounts: Spiritual, Physical, Intellectual, Mental, Family, Work, Financial and Social.

When I first applied this strategy, my world nearly fell apart. It was a shocking wake-up call. The realisation that most of my life energy, time and focus was centred on work or my vocational life account was a revelation. This process was the beginning of my coming to understand the importance of work-life integration.

Today, I can honestly say that this in itself has been transformational in providing me a sense of wellbeing that hitherto I had never experienced. I was *running on empty* in so many areas of my life. I had bankrupted my health, key relationships and spirituality without being aware of it.

I should warn you that the consequences of making 'withdrawals' from all your other life accounts to 'deposit' into one or two only, may be catastrophic. Typically, for men, it is the huge deposits they make into work or business at the unconscious cost of everything else, and for women, I have observed they have deposited into their family account at the expense of their own spiritual, physical and mental well-being. It's so often others first and themselves last! I always remind women of the pre-flight instructions given by the crew prior to take off: 'In case of an emergency put on your oxygen mask first prior to placing them on your children.'

Taking stock of your life in this way is a great way of gaining perspective and will help you with your goal-setting. It will also give you clues as to where to avoid goal conflict.

What do you really want?

Playing the WOW tournaments for each of my life areas has been both challenging and enjoyable for me over the years. I hope they will be likewise for you as you prepare for personal transformation. They bring immense clarity and confidence and provide a foundational platform for setting meaningful goals.

The Tournaments need to be done at least once a year. I suggest you go away for a day or so to somewhere quiet, where you can set your Vision and Goals for the coming year that are in alignment with your Purpose and Values. Doing this will help you contemplate where you are heading, what's going on in your life, and the changes you need to make. This process will help you gain deep insights into what is important for you, what your big rocks are and how you make choices.

The apparently simple question of asking: 'What do I want for my life?' no longer remains simple. The process will also compel you to dig deep, reaching down into the depths of your soul and spirit. It will challenge your Values and your mindset in a new way and help you unlock the deepest desires of your heart. It will also make it so much easier to make decisions. You will be in a very strong position to know when to say 'yes' or 'no' to the myriad of demands placed upon you because you have already decided what is important and meaningful for you.

What the WOW lists and tournaments also do is get you to question your definition of success. I've worked with lots of men and women over the years and seen how their worldview has played out in their lives. Like the 'fighter' referred to in the earlier analogy, success for some people means winning at all costs or pursuing goals focussed on satisfying the ego. As I found out, this mostly leads to increased stress, relationship breakdown, and often physical, mental and emotional ailments.

Increasingly I see people living lives of quiet desperation. They are looking to exchange burnout and fatigue for balance, meaning and Purpose in their lives. 'Hurry sickness', too little time for family, fitness, and fun, and multiple roles are pulling people in many different directions with schedules out of control. Communities and families are collapsing under the strain of conflicting values and lifestyle pressures. Dreams are lost while people try to live up to others' expectations and they lose touch with what is most important to them often resulting in frustration, depression and anxiety. And all around me I see low self-worth, a lack of confidence and fear, impacting negatively on individuals and society. Is this the cost of seeking success? I think we need to set goals from a different paradigm.

Authentic success[4] is achieved across all areas of our lives: in self-awareness, our health, relationships, finances, careers or business, family as well as proactively having time for recreation, travel and hobbies, time consciously written into our schedules to smell the roses.

Having a growth mindset

Earlier this year I was participating at an exercise class that I took twice a week. This was and still is an important part of my personal success routine. There was a core group of people who attended the same session each week. We had fun together and there was usually quite a bit of banter and comradery.

One Friday, towards the end of the session, the instructor asked us, as she normally did, what we were planning for the weekend. When it was my turn to answer, I said that I was going to a personal development workshop on Saturday. There were groans from several of my classmates! One said, 'I'm over all that sort of stuff. I don't need any personal development. People will just have to accept me as I am. I'm not changing for anyone.' Another participant endorsed her comments, adding: 'Why even bother changing at this stage of my life?'

I responded by saying how much I enjoyed these days and that I tried to attend at least one every month and left it at that. I am very fond of both these people and am not telling this story to be critical, only to illustrate that we can decide to have a fixed or closed mindset, or a growth mindset.[6]

Reflecting on my life, I can see that I have always adopted a growth mindset. I love challenges, knowing that when I embrace them and come out the other side, I'm a stronger and improved version of myself. I have come to learn that our brain is like a muscle that can be trained and consequently, I can keep on improving – yes, right into my third age and hopefully into the fourth[7].

Having a growth mindset has meant that I was able to keep going in the face of setbacks. I could have easily given up on receiving the specialist's diagnosis that I would never work again in my life. That was never an option for me and I can't ever remember having that mindset. Perseverance and persistence are necessary predispositions for achieving a positive performance. They are also a part of having a growth mindset and an essential aspect of goal-setting.

In reinventing myself, I had not only to learn but to master a whole set of new skills to start up and run a business. I loved learning to be a coach and I loved the hundreds of hours I invested into acquiring and mastering these new skills.

Part of a growth mindset is being able to take on board criticism and negative feedback. My personality style makes this difficult for me, especially if my integrity is ever brought into question. But I've come to realise and learn that constructive feedback is just information that I can use to change and improve myself. It has taken me some time to understand that criticism is not a reflection of my essence and of who I am but rather a statement about my capabilities, and about something I know I can change.

I believe having a growth mindset, both consciously and unconsciously, is also an important ingredient for being a successful goal-setter. With this mindset, failure to achieve your goals becomes a setback, not a failure. With a growth mindset, failure becomes an important part of learning.

References and Notes – Chapter 4

1. 'Life Accounts' is a concept borrowed from *The on-purpose person: Making your life make sense* by Kevin W. McCarthy.
2. McCarthy, K.W. (1992). *The on-purpose person: Making your life make sense.* Colorado Springs CO: Pinon Press. Second Edition: McCarthy, K.W. (2009). Winter Park, Fl: On-Purpose Publishing.
3. Blackburn, P. Workshop participation, Global Success Academy. https://theglobalsuccessacademy.com
4. Jenson, R. (2001). *Achieving authentic success.* San Diego, California: Future Achievement International.
5. **Ecclesiastes 3:1-8 (RSV)**
6. The term 'growth mindset' was coined by Stanford University psychologist, Carol. S. Dweck (2007) – *Mindset: The new psychology of success.* New York: Random House.
7. The terms third age and fourth age in this context refer to the period after middle age. Since we are now living longer, more people between 55-75 are seeking active retirement with new opportunities and rewards including study, travel, paid and volunteer work and access to the latest medical advances. Arguably, this is the first time in human history that we have this active period of 'refirement', not retirement. The fourth age is what we traditionally refer to as retirement and for many, doesn't commence until around 75+.

Humpty Dumpty had a great fall,
Avoidance seems to plague us all,
Unhealthy thoughts hold us back,
Self-observation restores us on track.

Chapter 5 – Beating Procrastination

Never put off till tomorrow what you can do the day
after tomorrow just as well.

Mark Twain

Life always begins with one step outside of your comfort zone.

Shannon L. Alder

Understanding procrastination…now!

In the previous chapter, I explained that procrastination has had a significant negative impact on my life…and still does on occasions. This begs the question: How can someone who believes in goal-setting and who has been a successful goal-setter, admit procrastination as a compelling reason for failure or unfulfilled potential?

Since I got *Mack-Trucked*, learning about procrastination and how to deal with it has been a very big growth curve for me, so much so that I have devoted a full chapter to this. I don't think that I have beaten it completely, but I'm quietly grateful that this 'ball and chain' drags me down less often.

I'll explain how as we continue through this chapter.

The Procrastination Cycle

Procrastination is a common issue. Most of us have been in the procrastination cycle in our lives at one time or another (e.g. putting off cleaning the stove, repairing a leaky roof, seeing a doctor or dentist, submitting a

> **Everyone procrastinates but not everyone is a procrastinator.**

job report or academic assignment or broaching a stressful issue with a partner) and despite our best intentions, we fail to accomplish tasks and the gap between those intentions and actions widen. We know what we ought to do but we still just don't do it.

When this happens, our life seems to spiral downwards. Often we end up using treats such as alcohol and chocolate or activities including work or shopping to try to overcome the mood which keeps us stuck in the cycle. We wait until we 'feel like it', and use activities and substances to avoid positive action. We all assume that there will be more time tomorrow, thinking things like: 'I'll do better work if I wait longer', 'I'll start when I get all my ducks in a row', 'I need more willpower', 'I don't feel in the mood right now', or 'I'll do it when I feel better'. These are all classic avoidance stories that procrastinators buy into.

What has been helpful to me is to understand that everyone procrastinates, but not everyone is a procrastinator. Today I am confident in saying that I procrastinate rather than I am a procrastinator. But only those who are very close to me would be able to confirm that!

According to Joseph Ferrari[1], 'Procrastination is a tendency to delay the start or completion of a desired task to the point of experiencing discomfort. It leads to dysfunctional ways of being and a reduced quality of life. Procrastination is not the same as waiting, postponing or delaying.'

Ferrari claimed that as many as 20% of adults worldwide are true procrastinators, meaning that they procrastinate chronically in ways that negatively affect their daily lives and produce shame or guilt.

He also claims that this group of people makes procrastination their maladaptive lifestyle, postponing tasks at home, at work, at school, in relationships, and so on. This is their way of life. He also highlights the point that 'twenty percent is higher than the rates of many other diseases and conditions, yet we treat procrastination... as a funny topic, as just laziness, or as just poor time management'.

The Cost of Procrastination

I think we all are aware that procrastination always comes at a cost. It has for me.

What is procrastination costing you in your business in terms of relationships with customers, lost deals, promotions, trade, cash flow, or self-worth? What about relationships that have foundered? Maybe you have wanted to break or strengthen a relationship for some time, but you hope it will just happen by magic or that the issue(s) will go away. Maybe, like many, you have put off making a hard decision because you dislike conflict.

Clearly, procrastination is a major negative force in us not achieving growth in our lives and businesses and preventing us from setting and keeping goals. Health, happiness, finances and dreams are impacted when we take no action on our heart's desires and the things that matter most. Our self-worth takes a battering also. Procrastination is very real and certainly has consequences.

For example, I have worked with several people who were self-confessed procrastinators and were very frustrated at not being able to move forward with their goals and their 'Big Rocks'. I have been given permission by each of these people to share their comments and have changed their names for privacy.

For 'Tom', procrastination was costing him his reputation, self-respect and causing a loss of income. It was like 'living under a cloud', 'living with a false friend', 'living in a pseudo comfort zone' and avoiding confrontation or conflict. Naturally, his self-talk was negative too. Phrases like 'I should be… better, more organised, more action-orientated', all helped move him away from the person he wanted to be and the outcomes he wanted for his personal life and business.

'Jill' said: 'Procrastination is costing me progress, achievement, opportunity and income in my business and health, self-esteem, clarity, confidence and freedom in my personal life. Another cost, is not being able to connect meaningfully in important relationships.' Now, that's a high price to pay for procrastination isn't it?

And for 'Rob', being stuck in the procrastination cycle meant that he remained excessively overweight. In his words, this was 'costing me self-respect, energy, clarity, motivation, reputation in the marketplace and credibility.' Obviously and regrettably, all these factors meant his financial targets were negatively impacted and the procrastination cycle continued.

For me, in the past, procrastination has caused me to gain a reputation for not getting things done on time; cost me increased stress in trying to get things completed at the 'last minute' to preserve trust and my integrity; and impacted on my relationship with my spouse in that I continually put things off. Even little things never got done around my home and growth stagnated in my career and business. I wasn't implementing what was needed to enhance my reputation or grow my business.

> **Procrastination has been linked to higher stress levels.**

Continually putting things off and not completing what is in our best interests invariably results in us feeling bad about ourselves. We go down in our own estimation, we experience higher stress levels and lower levels of well-being, our health suffers, and even our income potential diminishes considerably. I think that is serious stuff, don't you?

The Psychology of Procrastination

> **Procrastination is a problem of emotional regulation, not time management. It's not the problem itself. Poor time management is a symptom of an emotional problem.**

It was when I first started out learning to be a coach after I was *Mack-Trucked* that I consciously thought about my own procrastination tendencies. I couldn't afford to procrastinate when I had to reinvent myself completely from a vocational perspective. When I first started becoming aware of what procrastination was costing me, I embarked on a journey of trying to understand why I did it.

I never thought I was lazy or unmotivated. Nor did others think that of me. Disorganised and often distracted? Yes, but never lazy. In fact, some would have seen me as highly driven (which is not a label I like). I also wondered if I were simply poor at time management. But deep down I knew that there were other things at play – emotional stuff for sure, but at the time, I didn't know what.

Now I do!

There is a growing body of knowledge that indicates procrastination is a problem of emotional dysregulation, not time management. It's not the problem itself. Poor time management is a symptom of an emotional problem.[2]

Timothy Pychyl[3] explains that procrastination is an irrational behaviour because it runs counter to our own idea of what will make us happy. He sees procrastination as an 'emotion-focused coping strategy to deal with negative emotions'. It goes something like this:

- We sit down to do a task.
- We project into the future about what the task will feel like.
- We predict that the task will not feel good (e.g. It will stress us out, make us feel bad, etc.).
- Our emotional coping strategy kicks in to keep us away from this bad feeling.
- We avoid the task.

This emotional avoidance technique that our brain employs, often subconsciously, is similar to that which underlies many types of anxiety. People with anxiety often do everything they can to avoid the perceived external threat and, in turn, shut off access to both good and bad feelings, often leading to depression.

I have had numerous conversations about this with my wife, Angela, a trained and experienced psychotherapist. It's generally understood that ongoing procrastination usually is a symptom or sign of an underlying, unresolved emotional problem. We know that people's emotional triggers influence how they feel and therefore how they behave. At a neuroscientific level, it could be seen as the brain's attempt to protect us from a perceived threat, or danger, always remembering that the brain cannot judge its appropriateness in a certain situation.

What we need to be careful of is not to incorrectly assume that procrastination is our only problem. Often, apart from being connected to an underlying emotional issue, it can also present itself in issues like ADHD, eating disorders, perfectionism, anxiety and depression.

In the case of 'Tom', procrastination had infused his whole life. Some of the presenting symptoms were being very disorganised, working in a cluttered office, not taking responsibility, having a schedule out of control, rarely keeping to deadlines, putting off important work that was central to his business success and avoiding conflict at all costs. He also could see the importance of a daily personal success routine including exercise and mindfulness, but implementing it was a bridge too far.

When we dug deeper to establish the reasons for his disorganisation, lack of planning, and inability to implement even a simple schedule or plan, we discovered that as a young person growing up and right up until he left home, his mother did everything and organised everything for him. He had never needed to take responsibility or learned positive behaviours and good habits. The brain neurons could never 'wire' or 'fire' together in the practice of developing positive organisational skills.

Initially we tried developing a daily and weekly planner but soon discovered that all the time management skills in the world were a waste of time. We had partial success through setting very small weekly actionable steps that he could commit to without fear of failing, weekly accountability through emails and phone calls, lots of encouraging feedback, constantly bringing attention back to his Purpose and Values and numerous searching conversations to uncover and discuss the reasons for his avoidance behaviours.

As with 'Tom', I have noticed that people procrastinate for a variety of reasons including aversion to a task, a fear of failure, frustration, self-doubt and anxiety.

From personal experience, I have realised that procrastination is largely about avoidance. By not starting or acting on our goals we avoid the fear of failure, the fear of success and all the uncomfortable or negative feelings that go with these. In order not to fail at a task and experience the disillusionment and rejection that we think might follow, we don't perform it at all. Some procrastinators would rather have other people think that they didn't make an effort than that they lacked ability.

In order not to fail at a task we don't perform it at all.

From a neurological perspective, when an activity is particularly challenging or overwhelming, the amygdala or emotional part of our brain activates a 'fight', 'flight', 'freeze' or 'flop' response to protect us from perceived danger – in this case, negative feelings. So, we seek short-term gratification and pleasure which dopamine provides as a temporary relief to the stress of the situation.

That is why in the face of overwhelm and feeling bad about our inaction, we look for rewards or short-term gratification to make us feel better about ourselves. We indulge in 'me time', rewarding ourselves with substances such as alcohol and chocolate, or we become workaholics or shopaholics. These negative substances and activities, whilst initially pleasurable and a distraction, in reality, eventually drain our energy and self-esteem and we remain stuck and unmotivated through inaction in the area that really matters.

The frustration is that neither avoidance nor 'me time' deliver the result we want. We end up trading small failures with big failures long term. We settle for short-term gain rather than run the risk of perceived long-term pain.

The Neuroscience of Procrastination

In the 1960s, Paul MacLean[4] proposed a theory that many have found helpful in understanding the basic functions of the human brain.

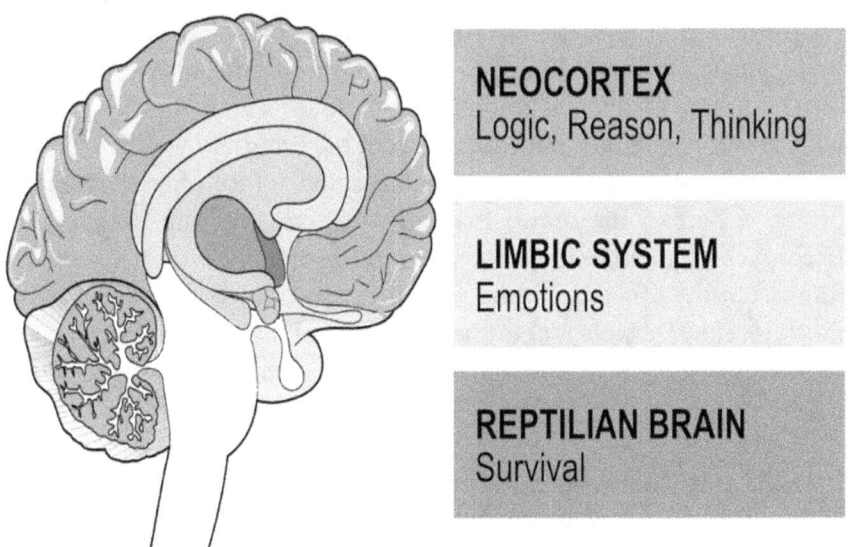

NEOCORTEX
Logic, Reason, Thinking

LIMBIC SYSTEM
Emotions

REPTILIAN BRAIN
Survival

This is sometimes referred to as the classical model, and as advances in Neuroscience have occurred, the model is falling out of favour as more is learnt about how the brain works, how humans learn, and consciousness. It is important to realise that MacLean's model is simplistic and provides an elementary understanding of the brain and the interaction especially between the limbic system (midbrain) and the neocortex (new cortex or 'smart' brain). It is now becoming more accepted that there is no such neat division; instead primal, emotional and rational mental activities are the product of neural activity in more than one of the three regions addressed in MacLean's model and their collective energy creates human experience[5].

For ease of understanding, with the above in mind, MacLean's model serves a useful purpose. The limbic system, sometimes referred to as the 'emotional brain', is the reactive part of us that initiates a 'fight', 'flight', 'freeze' or 'flop' response in the so-called Reptilian brain. Its primary function is to keep us safe. For example, the amygdala (part of the limbic system) is like an early warning mechanism with the motto 'safety first'. It immediately puts a safety plan into effect before consulting the executive brain (the neocortex). This explains why we jump instinctively to get away from a snake like object only to find it to be a hose in the grass once the pre-frontal cortex comes 'online' again.

The neocortex is our 'smart brain' or the executive part of our system that is responsible for all higher-order conscious activity such as language, abstract thought, creativity and imagination. It also houses much of our biographical and long-term memories (along with the hippocampus and other parts of the brain).

It is the super-fast reacting limbic system, (the older and more primitive part of the brain) that regulates cravings and desires and is concerned about immediate pleasure, not really caring about the future. On the other hand, the neocortex, (in evolutionary terms, the most recent decision-making centre located behind our forehead) uses a lot of energy, tires quickly, requires training to work more effectively, and is not as strong as the limbic system.

It is the clash between these two systems that lies at the basis of procrastination. Living in modern times where our personal safety is not constantly on the line, the ability of the neocortex to make rational decisions, to organise and to inhibit inappropriate behaviour is needed. In the past, it was the instinctual nature of the limbic system that promoted survival through immediate action without preoccupation for future consequences. Keeping us safe was the goal.

According to Piers Steel[6], Professor of Organisational Behaviour and Human Resources, University of Calgary, procrastination happens when the pleasure-seeking and pain-avoiding limbic system acts too quickly for the rational pre-frontal cortex to catch up. In this way, procrastination is described as the art of making intentions that get overridden, even if this is disadvantageous.

> **The amygdala, the fear centre of the limbic system, is not familiar with the modern world, and can't distinguish between an attacking bear and an unread email.**

In other words, according to Steel, when your brain wants to procrastinate on something important for you to do or achieve, it is trying to avoid a perceived threat. The amygdala, part of the emotional centre of the limbic system, is not familiar with the modern world, and can't distinguish between an attacking bear and an unread email.

As a result, it activates pretty much the same response in both cases, triggering the release of stress hormones necessary to cope with a 'fight' or 'flight' situation.

In addition, since the brain would very much prefer to be flooded with the pleasure hormone dopamine, instead of having to deal with stress neurotransmitters, it pushes us towards abandoning the stressful task in favour of a more rewarding one.

> **The instinctual part of the brain tries to keep you in bed.**

Furthermore, procrastinating saves energy. All jobs that are not evolutionarily essential like eating or having sex can be put off, thereby saving energy in case we experience threatening situations. So, while your modern, logical and goal-oriented neocortex understands that going for a run every morning can help you achieve long-term better health, the instinctual part of the brain tries to keep you in bed, so you can conserve energy.

One never knows what threats the day may bring!

To put it in the words of another psychology professor Timothy Pychyl[7], '...the second we stop actively controlling our urges with logical reasoning, our limbic system takes over and happily discount[s] future rewards in favour of immediate gratification'.

Summary of the Causes of Procrastination

As explained so far, procrastination is largely to do with avoidance especially of negative emotions. By way of summarising I have used the word AVOIDANCE as an acronym.

A = Attachment	• Mostly when we procrastinate, we attach or fuse to unhelpful thinking, self-labels and 'stories' of the past which result in us having a negative self-image. We avoid reality in the process.
V = Values Misalignment	• Procrastination often results in misalignment of Purpose and Values. When you notice yourself procrastinating, ask yourself if you are acting in alignment with your Purpose and Values? • It's hard to take action or continue life and business meaningfully when violating your Values and ignoring your spiritual DNA.
O = Off Purpose	• When we lose our way, when our life lacks significance and meaning, our mojo decreases, energy levels spiral downwards, and our confidence goes out the window. Life sucks and nothing really matters anymore. We avoid answering the questions like: 'Why do I exist?' and 'Why get out of bed anyway if I don't have a Purpose?'

I = Irrational beliefs	• We procrastinate when we consistently use 'should' and 'must' statements. We spend a lifetime 'shoulding' on ourselves and feel bad when we can't climb our mountain or face our 'Goliath'.
	• To avoid the negative feelings that come when we place unreasonable demands on ourselves, we take no action.
	• Our low frustration tolerance means we never get started. We are imagining the situation as bad as it can be, using statements such as: 'I can't stand doing this', 'It's so awful', 'It drives me nuts!'
D = Difficult, Doubt, Discomfort	• When people think something is too difficult, they won't do it. We are plagued with self-doubt, believing that if we start something and muck it up, we are a bad person or a failure.
	• We define ourselves based on one event or project, resulting in a negative self-image. Nothing is more demotivating than a negative self-image.
	• Often people procrastinate to avoid discomfort in the form of fear of failure, fear of what people will say about them, or fear of having difficult conversations. e.g. 'I know going to the gym is healthy habit but I'm so out of shape. I look terrible because I let myself go.'

A = Awfulising	• We avoid action or getting started because we imagine the task or project to be as bad as it could possibly be. • The task seems terrible and overwhelming and we dread it. • We don't confront this negative feeling of dread.
N = Neuroscience ignorance	• Neuroscience helps to explain why we procrastinate. • When your brain wants to procrastinate on something important for you to do or achieve, it is trying to avoid a perceived threat. • The amygdala, part of the emotional centre of the limbic system, is not familiar with the modern world, and can't distinguish between an attacking bear and an unread email. • As a result, it activates pretty much the same response in both cases, triggering the release of stress hormones necessary to cope with a 'fight' or 'flight' situation. • The brain would very much prefer to be flooded with the pleasure hormone dopamine, instead of having to deal with stress. neurotransmitters, it pushes us towards abandoning the stressful task in favour of a more rewarding one.

C = Consequences	• We procrastinate because we avoid the consequences of taking action. • These consequences include avoidance of pain, facing up to the truth, fear of failure and the uncomfortable feelings that come with it, increased stress and the fear of diminished wellbeing. • We avoid challenges that take us outside of our comfort zone such as confrontation, and a mountain load of 'what ifs'. Our avoidance paralyses our action, and our excuses foster self-sabotage.
E = EGO	• In order not to fail at a task and look and feel bad, we don't perform it at all. • The ego fuels self-doubt, self-judgement, self-deprecation, inferiority, self-pity, shame, and guilt, yet we will try to avoid these emotions at any cost – which often means not taking action at all.

It is evident that procrastination has been part of the human condition for thousands of years. Aristotle[8] and Socrates used the word *akrasia* to refer to procrastination, akrasia meaning 'the state of mind in which someone acts against their better judgment through weakness of will'. While they give different reasons for this, what is clear is that procrastination is certainly not a modern phenomenon.

Procrastination has been part of the human condition for thousands of years.

In 44 B.C., Cicero[9] condemned procrastination as 'hateful'. In the book of Romans in the New Testament, St Paul[10] wrote *'I do not understand what I do. For what I want to do I do not do, but what I hate, I do.'*

This human problem has survived all the way to the 21st century and is now further complicated by the wide range of distractions available 24/7, many of which are often just one click away.

Recognising that procrastination has been with us for thousands of years and that there is a perfectly logical reason for it means we don't need to beat ourselves up about being a procrastinator. However, we can implement strategies to calm or regulate our emotions thereby keeping the neocortex online, so we can take desired, intentional and meaningful action.

Many books and articles have been written on this topic. Strategies abound, including daily exercise, meditation, mindfulness, eating healthily, having meaningful, emotional and achievable goals and so on.

Overcoming Procrastination...now!

I have explored the psychology and neuroscience behind procrastination to help us understand why we procrastinate. I have also discussed the high cost that procrastination can have in our lives and businesses, especially in preventing us from setting and keeping goals.

Our health, happiness, finances, self-worth, relationships and dreams are all negatively impacted when we take little or no action on our heart's desires and the things that really give us meaning and fulfilment.

For the remainder of the chapter, I will share some strategies that I have found to work for my clients and me.

Gaining success from implementing these will be largely dependent on recognising that your brain is trying to 'protect' you. I suggest once you notice, acknowledge and accept this, you will be more capable of dealing with

> **The key is to become aware of and notice the urges and emotions initiated by your limbic system; thank the brain for wanting to protect you; acknowledge that you usually have nothing to be fearful about and wait for your neocortex to bring perspective and logic to the situation. This will enable you to MOVE and ACT.**

procrastination and able to move forward positively with those things that are important to you.

The key is to become aware of and notice the urges and emotions initiated by your limbic system; thank the brain for wanting to protect you; acknowledge that you usually have nothing to be fearful about and wait for your neocortex to bring perspective and logic to the situation. This will enable you to MOVE and ACT.

M = Move

So, the first step in overcoming procrastination is to stand up. Move! Although procrastination might not be life-threatening, the brain can misinterpret it as such. When you are procrastinating, you are usually sitting or lying down!

Taking action by standing up is your number one step.

For example, one of your goals might be to rise early to have an early morning daily success routine. This might consist of going for a walk, cycle, paddle or jog; investing time in mindfulness or meditation; reflecting on your goals (or 'Big Rocks') and planning your day. Accordingly, the alarm goes off, but your emotional brain warns you that you may fail, or that you haven't had sufficient sleep to cope with the busy day ahead, or you get a dose of irrational self-talk such as: 'I don't really enjoy this – it's too hard and a struggle to fit this into my day.' And so, you buy into the thought that you are 'not safe', are outside of your comfort zone, and consequently you stay in bed. It cannot imagine or assess the potential future rewards or positive habits which would keep you physically, mentally and spiritually fit. Instead, it favours safety and the immediate gratification of staying warm and safe in bed so you can conserve your energy for self-preservation, should it be required.

By taking meaningful action, you will experience renewed motivation.

Understanding what the brain is doing and why it is doing it will enable you to focus on the long-term gain for short-term pain. At this point, I suggest you put your alarm well away from the bed, so that you must 'move' (i.e. get up) to turn it off. You have just taken your first step to outwitting the amygdala! This first step could result in a regular early morning start, along with time to walk, meditate, reflect and plan for the day. Do whatever works for you and what you feel good about accomplishing.

By taking meaningful action, you will experience renewed motivation and begin feeling good about yourself. Action leads to motivation, which leads to more action, as seen in this diagram.

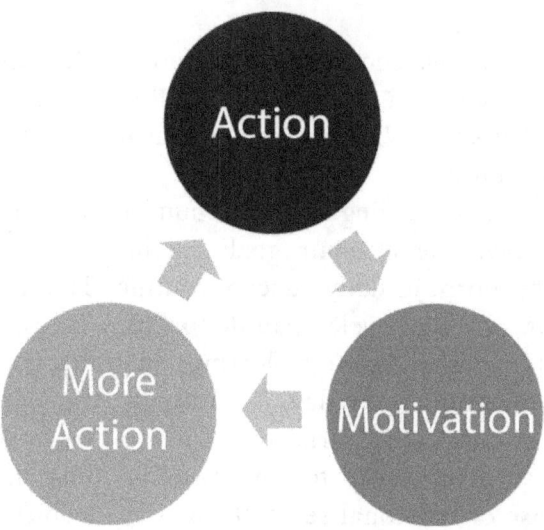

But moving means more than that. It involves a choice point. Basically, you either move away from the outcome you want and continue to procrastinate and behave *unlike* the person you want to be, or you move towards the outcome you want, acting effectively and behaving *like* the person you want to be. I discuss this in more detail under the E of MOVE.

This means that your goals are best broken down into small steps and then prioritised. Next, set up milestones or mileposts and organise an accountability partner or buddy. It also means having a very short 'to do' list and you jumping from lily pad to lily pad, instead of trying to take giant leaps. Taking 'baby steps' to begin with is critical to breaking the procrastination cycle.

What I encourage you to do is to take the half-double challenge to help you beat procrastination as well as assist you to get unstuck in other areas of your life. I first came across this helpful tool from Peter Barr, one of my coaching colleagues from Queensland.

He says we work too much on the 'all or nothing' principle and unfortunately, the brain does not like to change. Whether you agree or not, the brain is programmed to only do what it has to, no more. For example, we may decide we want to go to the gym or ride our bikes to work five days a week, spend daily time planning our business, set aside time to write each day and so on, but nothing changes.

As previously explained, we get more of a payoff for drinking (e.g. calm, confidence, control) or over-eating (control, endorphin rush etc.) or lack of exercise (e.g. escape time on Netflix or other screens) than we can by changing the behaviour or our mind sets, which is much more difficult.

Add to this a lack of a real, positive, compelling purpose or reason for the change, and we are caught in a loop that will ensure our success is limited or non-existent.

Here is a tool to help you make the change.

Halve the things that are keeping you stuck (moving away from)

If you are a procrastinator, you know that trying to eliminate what is causing the struggle, doesn't work. This process involves the challenge of halving it. You can still have that thing you crave, just less. Make that the challenge. Have just four pieces of chocolate, not eight. Have two glasses of wine, not four. Then, when you are ready, say in a month, halve this again. Then in another month halve this again, until you feel the amount you are having is OK or you choose to stop altogether. In the case of feeling safe by staying in bed each morning instead of having a personal success routine, try getting out of bed early once a week, then twice and so on until you start to feel good about the direction in which you are moving.

Double the things that will make you happy and healthy (Moving towards)

This might need to start with something very small first, as double zero exercise is still zero exercise. So, maybe start with five minutes of walking or riding. Then when you are ready, double this, and then double this again, until you are happy with the consistent level, intensity and impact of the exercise.

The challenge

Create two lists, one called 'My Half List', the other 'My Double List'. Pick the top three points in each list and assess what you would need to do to begin halving and doubling your achievements. Start small and be aware that you have the choice right now to be amazing by being a Half/Double Champion.

My Half List (Away)	My Double List (Towards)

What are you halving? What are you doubling?

O = Observation

The second letter in MOVE is to remind us about practicing *observation*. Procrastination involves **self-absorption** while successfully moving forward with your 'Big Rocks' involves the practice of **self-observation.**

As the diagram below shows, we 'appear' to have two minds: an 'observing mind' and a 'thinking mind'.

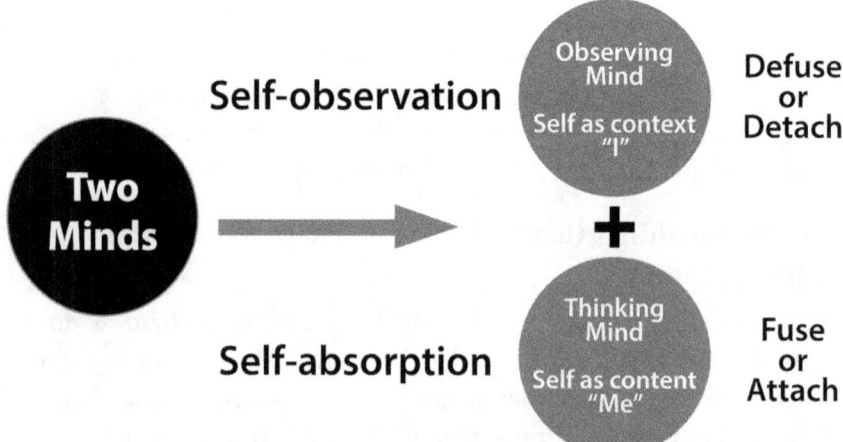

People who procrastinate typically attach to or 'fuse' to their negative thoughts and irrational beliefs. For example, if you were like me in earlier times, I used a lot of 'I should' and 'I must' statements such as I must walk five days a week or I'll...or I should go to the gym four days a week if I'm going to...I hear so many of my clients doing the same. I gently ask them how long they have been 'shoulding' on themselves and how is it serving them? Call it what you like – self-downing, being hard on yourself, or shoulding on yourself, – all will keep you stuck in the procrastination cycle.

The point is, we need to watch and observe these triggers, irrational beliefs and unhelpful thoughts. I think two of the main reasons I still procrastinate are fear of failure and not being good enough.

Following a discussion with my wife one morning over breakfast about fear of failure, she sent me a text later that day. It read as follows:

'But what if I fall? Oh, my darling, what if you fly?'

I also have low tolerance for and get very frustrated with some tasks, especially technical ones. My thinking mind says: 'I can't stand doing this...it drives me nuts'. I build up a huge monster in my mind, see the task as an unbearable struggle, and so I put it off!

Relevant to remember at this point is that the 'thinking mind' has an estimate of up to 60,000 thoughts per day and that 80% of these are negative.

Jennifer Read Hawthorn[11], author of *Change Your Thoughts, Change Your World*, claims that we are creatures of habit because as many as 98% of our thoughts are the same ones we had the day before. Whether these numbers are accurate or not, the point is that the 'thinking mind' produces an enormous number of thoughts each day and the majority of these are negative.

Negative thoughts are particularly draining and lead to procrastination. They diminish our self-worth, deplete our energy and produce corresponding neurotransmitters or chemicals that weaken our physiology, including our immune system. No wonder we feel exhausted at the end of the day! More than anything, they rob us of confidence and the belief that we can achieve our goals and heart's desires.

Sometimes, the difficult thoughts and feelings show up in response to a challenge or achieving a goal and go something like this; 'Life is hard and I don't want to do hard any more'; 'I don't have enough energy to achieve my goals'; 'I should be doing more'; 'I can't do this'; It's going to be difficult'; and 'I'm not productive unless there is a tangible way to measure productivity'.

You get the idea. When we fuse to these negative thoughts, we 'become' them, thereby blinding us to engaging purposefully, proactively and productively with life. With attachment or fusion to negative thoughts and unhelpful thinking come unpleasant feelings. These rob us of our confidence, fuel procrastination and prevent us from stepping outside of our comfort zones.

In contrast, by taking a 'helicopter' view and practising self-observation we can watch and observe what our thinking mind is doing. As humans, at any moment, we have the capacity to observe our thoughts and thinking patterns. Instead of fusing or attaching to them we can notice what is happening. Instead of fusing to the thought: 'I'm not good enough', we can notice the thought and detach. We can say: 'Ah, thank you thought, I know you. You are trying to protect me, but I don't need you right now.' You can decide which technique to use.

What we need to do is to watch, notice and detach from those unhelpful thoughts that fuel our procrastination. They'll come back again because that's what our thinking minds do – they have thoughts and you can't stop them. So, keep observing yourself as if you were watching someone else.

Freedom happens when you practice awareness. And freedom will also fuel action.

V=Values

The third letter in MOVE calls for us to embrace our **Values**. Moving in the direction of and being in alignment with our chosen values is another key to overcoming procrastination. Our values are what are important to us and they play a major role in governing our thoughts and behaviour (notwithstanding our personal styles). Values are our heart's deepest desires for how we want to behave as human beings. They are what we want to stand for in life, what sort of person we want to be and what sort of strengths and qualities we want to develop. Values are not goals. Goals have a start and a finish point, but Values are enduring and never end, like travelling 'west', for example. They are fundamental to our personal and business successes.

To use a metaphor, our Values, like our Purpose, are like a compass. A compass gives you direction and keeps you on track when you are travelling. Our Values (together with our Purpose) provide the same function in our business and life journey. We use them to choose the direction in which we want to move in and to keep us on track as we go.

If you have not revisited your Values recently or cannot state them effortlessly, then I strongly recommend that you do. For example, you might identify values such as: Quality, Growth, Trust and Fulfilment. If you are a self-confessed, habitual procrastinator you can clearly see that procrastinating takes you away from your Values. The disconnect will be a major source of frustration. Perhaps your values are: Nourishment, Growth, Possibilities, Belief, Responsibility and Persistence. In this case procrastination might cost you recognition and self-worth (contrary to Nourishment); achievement of your goals (contrary to Growth), no visible sign of change (contrary to Growth, Possibilities and Responsibility) and your freedom (contrary to Possibilities).

The solution is to know and connect with your Values (and your Purpose as I have written on many other occasions). Visit and review them daily when you rise and retire and ask the questions: 'How will I live out my Values today?' or 'How did I live out my values today?' and 'Is procrastinating moving me in the direction of my chosen Values?' I'm convinced that a person who is consciously aware of their Purpose and Values and lives in alignment with them every day, will not be a habitual procrastinator.

E = End in mind

The E in MOVE is inviting us to focus on the End Game. Many of my readers will be familiar with Stephen Covey's[12] call to develop the habit of: 'Beginning with the end in mind'. This is about actively and effectively moving towards the outcome you want and being like the person you want to be. It's about having a razor-sharp Vision.

Most people I work with find it exceptionally difficult to have a crystal-clear picture of where they want their business to be or what it might look like. While 'knowing' and 'being' your Purpose gives you meaning and fulfilment, your Vision should be so strong that it inspires you daily to move incrementally towards the picture you have so vividly painted. Somehow, without an energising Vision, we seem to shrivel into a meaningless existence. Our business becomes routine, boring, reactive, disorganised, and unfulfilling, and so too does our personal life. As the old Proverb says: 'Without vision the people will perish'.

Summary

As humans, we all have let ourselves become the victims of procrastination from time to time. But ultimately, unless we have a diagnosed medical issue which drains our energy and motivation or some other calamity, **to procrastinate or not, is a choice,** despite our amygdala saying otherwise.

Here is a summary of practical steps to help you **MOVE** from procrastination to purposeful progress.

Move

- Take action: stand up and **take the first step.**
- Make your first steps **'baby steps'**
- **Move away** from the thoughts and behaviour you want to avoid.
- **Move towards** the outcome you want, acting effectively and behaving like the person you want to be.
- Break down your goals into small steps, so you know you can take your first steps and not fail. Being able to take one small step is critical to breaking the procrastination cycle.
- Take the Double or Halve challenge in three things in your life…now!
- Understand that action leads to motivation which leads to more action.

Observe

- Practice self-observation. Watch yourself as if you were watching another person.
- Notice when you are procrastinating and the negative thoughts that are present.

- Let the thoughts pass and don't fuse or attach to them. Defuse and detach using self-observation.
- Remember that your thoughts are just that. They are not reality. They only have the meaning you give to them.
- You are not your thoughts.
- Self-Observation is the key to awareness.

Values

- Rewrite or revisit your Values.
- Recite them so you know them.
- Observe them in practice daily.
- When you notice yourself procrastinating, ask yourself: 'Am I acting in alignment with my Purpose and Values?'
- How important are your Values to you…really?
- Can you continue life and business meaningfully when violating your Values?

End in Mind

- Focus on your End Game.
- Draw or find inspiring graphics that represent your Vision (both for yourself and your business).
- Be able to visually see your vision board daily.
- Talk about your Vision to key stakeholders.
- Revisit it (together with your Values) at every team or management meeting.
- Celebrate your 'wins' and milestones daily and at team meetings that are moving you towards your Vision.

Even with just four strategies to help you overcome procrastination, there is a lot to think about and implement.

It's tough trying to get 'unstuck' on your own. Remember to exercise some self-compassion along the way.

While you need to MOVE, you will also need to ACT (Accountability, Commitment, Target). I strongly recommend that you have an accountability partner to whom you can make your commitments and who can powerfully assist you achieve your targets. I have explained this in detail in the chapter on goal-setting.

Bessel van der Kolk, a leading (trauma) psychiatrist supports the need to MOVE and ACT. He says: *'Taking action is the core issue...It's in action that people take back their power and words cannot substitute for action.'*

Reflections

Prior to being *Mack-Trucked*, I was aware that being a procrastinator negatively impacted so many areas of my life. It cost me in varying degrees my reputation in professional circles, income levels and relationships. This in turn impacted my health, diminished my confidence and lowered my self-worth.

Recognising that procrastination has been part of the human condition for thousands of years and knowing that there is a perfectly logical reason for it, has helped me in significantly overcoming this condition. Normalising procrastination in this way and understanding that there is a difference between procrastinating and being a habitual procrastinator also means that I don't need to beat myself up when I procrastinate.

More than anything else, learning about the neuroscience of procrastination was liberating. My limbic system's job is to keep me safe: it acts like an early warning system with the motto 'safety first'. From a neurological perspective, when an activity is particularly challenging or overwhelming, the amygdala or emotional part of my brain (and yours too) activates a 'fight', 'flight', 'freeze' or 'flop' response elsewhere in the brain to protect us from perceived danger – in my case, negative feelings.

Just knowing that means I can practice mindfulness and self-awareness to further understand what aspects of avoidance are at play.

Today, my self-image is one of being more of a proactivator than procrastinator. I'm sure you won't find proactivator in the dictionary, but I'll claim it!

I have applied many techniques to help me overcome procrastination. I will now highlight some which have helped me the most.

Understanding Who I Really Am

The 'True Self' doesn't experience procrastination, only the false self, the egoic self, or the conditioned mind does. Most of my limiting and irrational beliefs, including the stories represented by phrases or questions such as: 'I'm not good enough', 'What if I fail?', 'What will others think of me?', 'What if no one joins my Mastermind group?', What if people opt out?', 'What if no one reads my blog?', or 'I need to get this absolutely right', are all symptomatic of the ego at work.

The conditioned mind is doing its job, but I have learned to watch and observe these thoughts at play. They have held me back, prevented me from achieving my goals, and stopped me dead in my tracks in the past. Now I acknowledge my thinking mind and thank it for its many negative thoughts, and kindly tell it they have not helped me in the past and that there is no place for them right now. Developing self-awareness in this way has also helped me understand that my True Self or my Observing Mind – my Spirit – takes no part in procrastination. It watches, observes, notices, never judges or condemns and through all of that, continues to love. And this awareness has helped me to love myself more, something which has been a long, slow and painful journey for me.

When you understand your true identity, you see procrastination as another manifestation of fear at play; the ego hell-bent on protecting itself. Practice awareness and mindfulness continually. You will increasingly notice and be surprised by how the meaning you give to your stories and thoughts are deleteriously impacting your life.

Practicing mindfulness and self-awareness

This is an ongoing learning curve for me. Intellectually, I understand the importance of being present in the moment. I know that all anxiety is future-orientated. I know we only ever have *now*. I know who 'I' really am or who 'I' *really* is. All are vitally helpful in overcoming procrastination, but implementing mindfulness throughout each day has been a struggle. I'm getting much better at it. I'm learning to notice my triggers, the thoughts I fuse to, and recognise the 'stories' that I falsely have given truth and power to.

I must thank my wife Angela for helping me become more mindful. Even asking me 'noticing' questions has helped enormously: 'Did you notice what you ate for breakfast?', 'What did you notice on your walk this morning?', 'What are you feeling right now?', and so on.

My point is that by noticing my thoughts, feelings, behaviour, triggers, and attitudes to any given stimulus, I am more grounded and more aware of what is going on within and around me, and this has assisted me enormously when I apply mindfulness to helping me to understand and overcome procrastination.

Having the end in mind

This works powerfully for me. I do know that many people struggle to have clarity around their Vision and their Why. When I'm struggling to get started, I reset myself by keeping the end in mind[12]. Of course, the Vision must be meaningful, significant, and be in alignment with my Purpose and Values. It took some time to for me to articulate clearly why this book was important and why I wanted to write it, for example.

If you have an important project to complete, ask yourself why it is so important. Who will benefit, how will they benefit, what will be the consequences of you not completing the project or task, and would that worry you? I like to focus on the big picture, the *context* more than the *content*. Having a powerful reason is very motivating and I encourage you to uncover your big *Why* and crystalise your vision. It's hard to procrastinate when you continually 'feed' these.

Taking baby steps – 'just get started'

I used to really hate 'baby steps!' I wanted the big picture, the big results, the finished 'thing'…now! But I'm terrified of failing. Avoidance of the fear of failure and the negative feelings that accompany failure, have meant I procrastinated on the things that really mattered in my life.

It's like two opposing forces pulling with all their strength in opposite directions, one being the deep drive to succeed, the other the terror of failure. As I said above, learning to watch the ego at work has been liberating, freeing, but also alarming to see the power I give it.

I have learned to 'just get started' to great effect. I jot down about three points, making a few notes on the steps I need to do to finish the task. These are all baby steps of something I have been 'sitting on' or putting off. I think you can guess what happens. Yes! I have made progress, small though it might be, but still motivating. Action results in progress and progress is so amazingly motivating for me, and I dare say, I am not alone in this.

Understanding the power of small wins is relatively new for me. Making even modest progress on tasks I dislike, or projects I'm procrastinating on, even spending a minute or two at them helps me chip away at my perceived mountain. And the best part is that the huge anxiety that has built up worrying about the mountain when in fact it's just a mole hill, recedes almost instantly when I take baby steps towards my 'Goliath'. Getting started is where the war is really won. If taking baby steps is not working for you, try making them smaller, shorter or easier!

Commitment devices

In HABIT formation in the Chapter on Goal-setting, I mentioned that attaching pain and pleasure to outcomes can be effective in building good behaviour and habits. But at that stage, I had not formally been introduced to the concept of commitment devices.

In the same chapter, I told the story of my mentor inviting me to part with something worth a lot to me as a way of stopping me from making excuses as to why I was procrastinating in writing this book. He was to return my wedding ring once I had completed the draft of this book by Christmas this year. That is a commitment device. On top of that, I committed publicly, giving added weight to the commitment.

Note that this was not the other way around. The arrangement was not that I would give him the ring if I failed. Using a pre-commitment agreement device has certainly worked for me on this project. That is all I think about every day when I awake: getting that ring back for my 50th Anniversary, which is a few days before Christmas.

If you really want to get a project completed, lose weight, or whatever you are procrastinating on doing, send your friend that money or your most cherished possession and notice how motivating that is and how committed you become! If the commitment devices are not working for you, they are not meaningful or scary enough.

Building rituals and habits

Intuitively I have understood that building good habits can change behaviour. I have since uncovered multiple research data backing this up[13]. Even one good habit can be life-changing. Just as trimming the sails on a boat or changing course minutely can make significant difference to a boat's speed and direction, so too can one new habit impact on procrastination.

For example, by building a personal success routine into each day, the spin off has been huge for me. Walking, jogging, paddleboarding, meditating, daily planning, goal-setting and reviewing, swimming, exercise classes, gym attendance, or a combination of these, work differently for each of us. You will find what works for you and you might even find yourself enjoying it!

For me, an early morning walk followed by exercises, meditation and writing a daily 'to do' list is now habitual. If I miss this for any reason, I'm acutely aware of it. This might be where the Double or Halve challenge can work for you. Instead of wanting a personal success routine four days a week and failing dismally, try two. If you have been wanting to do it twice a week and it's not working, try once a week. Instead of doing it for 30 minutes, try 15. Instead of working on your business two hours a week, start with one hour. You get the idea. Keep doubling or halving until you get success.

When you experience success, even if it's small, you feel good about yourself and that is key. Don't forget to reward yourself in some way for your successes, either. Even the smallest change tends to set off a chain reaction that changes other habits as well. For me, exercising daily has meant I take more care of my eating habits. I proactively monitor what goes into my body and I have to thank my wife for ensuring that we eat correctly...and well...though I may eat too much sometimes!

The secret is to find a task that really makes you feel good about yourself, something that changes your self-image and that makes you feel like a person who can get things done. That should be your starting point. My personal success routine sets me up with a positive mindset for the day. I used to open emails first. Now I don't, as I don't want to start the day being reactive and marching to the beat of multiple drummers. If I do, I usually end up in a bad mood and frustrated because I haven't put the right things first.

Finally, enjoy considering the following metaphor and reflect on how it might apply or have applied to your life:

The bird's nest metaphor

I have found that writing this chapter on overcoming procrastination was not easy. In fact, this is my fourth attempt to do so. The other versions were informative but somehow lacked inspiration. My wife Angela, (always my best writing critic and editor) reminded me of a story which I believe gives an interesting end to this topic. I shall paraphrase it:

This story starts with a bird's nest with four eggs in the eaves of a front porch. A young boy and his family watched the birds hatch and grow feathers. Daddy bird came and fed the birds several times a day. The family could see that the four chicks were outgrowing the nest and were soon to fly the coop. 'Will they fly today?' was always the question in the family's mind.

Mum, Dad and the kids had all become deeply invested in this event.

After researching what they thought was a small finch of some kind they discovered that the birds were Red Head Finches.

After three days and evenings of watching and wondering when the big moment would come, the daughter discovered a dead baby bird on the ground beneath the nest on the porch as the family left to go to a restaurant. 'That was Orville,' she said as her brother gathered the remains.

It ended up being a sombre moment before dinner.

That evening after the family returned, all the family went to the patio to see what was happening.

It was a perfectly still evening, but the remaining three birds appeared restless. Perhaps they sensed the family was cheering them on.

Suddenly one of the birds, 'Wilbur', jumped to the edge of the nest, lifted a tentative wing to the breeze, and flew. A rise and a dive and a perfect landing in a nearby tree. There was, of course, loud cheer from the family (enough for the neighbours to probably think they were nuts).

Sister 'Amelia' soon followed, accompanied by more cheers and clapping. A swoop and an upswing and she landed safely in the tree next to her brother.

Now there was one left to encourage out into the wild. Right around dusk the next day, the last chick successfully flew the coop. That was a 75% success rate as minor and major miracles go.

The Daddy bird that fed those babies had an amazing bright red head, like a flaming Phoenix, red-tipped wings, seemingly dipped in ink and looking poised for flight as if ready to write the story of the world.

By contrast the babies were a drab brownish grey, the colour of earth and dirt that was not quite anything yet. And as they took that first dive into the open, all the family could think was: 'Do you have any idea how beautiful you're going to be, one of these days?'

It may appear that this story provides only a very loose metaphor for procrastination. But it describes the negative feelings of hesitancy that are often associated with risk-taking and the unknown; the fear of failure; the uncertainty associated with leaving our comfort zones; the fear of taking the first 'leap' or 'jumping the divide'; the negative consequences of rushing in headfirst without being prepared and the result of giving into negative memories associated with past experiences. These are all feelings and behaviours associated with procrastination which we know can lead to feelings of guilt, inadequacy, depression, and self-doubt. To procrastinate can hinder productivity.

This story teaches us what we can become when we do take the first step, how our brains are wired to survive and our potential for achieving extraordinary results when we do 'leave the nest' and explore the unknown. It also demonstrates the power of having support and encouragement from people who want the best for us and the benefits we receive from experienced mentors who can nurture and guide but who ultimately allow us to take personal responsibility for our success.

References and Notes – Chapter 5

1. Ferrari, J.R. (2010). *Still procrastinating: The no regrets guide to getting it done.* New Jersey: Hoboken.

2. Kemmis, S. (2019). *Procrastination isn't a time management problem, it's an emotional problem.* https://zapier.com/blog/procrastination-emotion/ Retrieved on 11 Nov 2019: Web.

3. Pychyl, T.A. (2013). *Solving the procrastination puzzle: A concise guide to strategies for change.* New York, NY: Penguin Group (USA) LLC.

4. Komninos, A. (2020). *The concept of the "Triune Brain."* Interaction Design Foundation. https://www.interaction-design.org/literature/article/the-concept-of-the-triune-brain. Retrieved June 2020:Web.

5. McKay, S. (2020). *Rethinking the reptilian brain.* Sarah McKay Blog. https://drsarahmckay.com/rethinking-the-reptilian-brain/. Retrieved June 2020:Web.

6. Steel, P. (2010). *The procrastination equation: how to stop putting things off and start getting stuff done.* Canada: Random House.

7. Pychyl, T.A. (2013). *Solving the procrastination puzzle: A concise guide to strategies for change.* New York, NY: Penguin Group (USA) LLC.

8. *How Socrates and Aristotle differ on akrasia essay.* https://www.paperdue.com/essay/how-socrates-and-aristotle-differ-on-akrasia-2160359. Retrieved 6 March 2020: Web.

9. Cicero, M.T. *Orations, the fourteen orations against Marcus Antonius* (Philippics) (C.D. Yonge, Ed.): Sourced from http://www.perseus.tufts.edu/hopper/text?doc=Perseus%3Atext%3A1999.02.0021%3Aspeech%3D6%3Asection%3D7. Retrieved 6 March 2020: Web.

10. Romans 7:15 New International Version

11. Hawthorn, J.R. (2014). *Change your thoughts, change your world.* https://jenniferhawthorne.com/articles/change_your_thoughts.html Retrieved 6 March 2020: Web.

12. Covey, Stephen R, 1989. *The 7 habits of highly effective people.* Simon and Shuster, New York.

13. *Seven steps to never procrastinating again.* https://www.bakadesuyo.com/2012/05/7-steps-to-never-procrastinating-again/. Retrieved 14 November 2019: Web.

Humpty Dumpty had a great fall,
Unmanaged stress destroys us all,
Living 'whole' from the inside out,
Brings peace of mind and not self-doubt.

Chapter 6 – Busting Stress

*'Stress is nothing more than a socially acceptable
form of mental illness.'*

Richard Carlson

*'I want to sing like the birds sing, not worrying who hears
or what they think.'*

Rumi

Prior to being *Mack-Trucked*, I lived uncomfortably with stress. Since that time, I have learned many helpful strategies to cope with it. We can't stop stress, transform it, or master it. Nor can we live stress-free lives. But we all can learn strategies to deal more proactively with stress.

This chapter is not a medical treatise on stress, but this book would not be complete without an explanation of how I have learnt and am still learning to live with both stress and anxiety. On reflection, these were big contributors to the major curve ball life threw at me some 20 years ago.

Good and Bad Stress

Shortly after being *mucked up*, one of my mentors at the time taught me the difference between good and bad stress – *eustress and distress*.

We all need and experience stress. It's a normal part of life and because we are wired for fight and flight, stress, which is a manifestation of fear, is part of the human condition. In fact, most of us live daily lives with our stress 'tank' or 'dam' nearly full of a combination of good and bad stress. But mostly we cope pretty well, and we think we are OK.

Since for most of us, our stress reservoir runs close to capacity, an added major event can cause the dam walls to break and overflow. We are tipped over the edge and our lives get flooded; catastrophically for some and less dramatically but still in a debilitating way for others. For me this resulted in the end of my academic career and many years of recovery.

As mentioned, a major event resulted in me being *Mack-Trucked*. I think that prior to this, my stress reservoir was consistently full to the point of overflowing – but not quite. At that time I was teaching 11 undergraduate subjects a year, working with Honours, Masters and PhD students, lecturing in course work and supervising dissertations and thesis writing, coordinating our small department, chairing a number of university committees, and conducting a major research project for the Board of Senior Secondary School Studies. I also convened a national conference for Australian Music Education Lecturers and was president of the State Chapter of the Australian Society for Music Education. I was busy...yes! Stressed... yes! But carrying out my responsibilities with a high work ethic and coping pretty well... or so I thought!

In reflection, I was a sitting duck for the *Mack Truck* that was coming!

I have found the following metaphor helpful in understanding what happens for most of us, and in understanding what happened to me. When we have more distress than we can handle or when a major event opens the stress floodgates we can be *Mack-Trucked*, Our stress is a result of our conditioned stories and learned but unhelpful thought patterns.

I was taught that one way to help deal with unhelpful thoughts is to visualise a stream. You take each negative thought and place it on a leaf in the stream and let it drift away. You watch it 'go with the flow'. We know that the thought will come back, and we can repeat the process. But over time, the leaves build up. There are only so many leaves you can place in the stream before it forms a dam. And then one gigantic leaf floats down and the dam bursts and overflows. That's what happened to me! I nearly drowned in the process. But some two years later I surfaced again!

I'd like to explore further the differences between good and bad stress. Learning about stress and techniques to better manage and live with stress has played a significant part in my transformational journey.

Understanding that some forms of stress are emotionally positive have meant I no longer demonise stress and get stressed out about being stressed! For example, gearing up for a sporting or artistic performance, a big occasion, going on an adventure, preparing for surgery, giving a talk, instances when we are moving outside of our comfort zone in order to grow and develop ourselves without being over stressed, are just a few occasions where stress is needed for peak performance.

We call this positive stress *eustress*. This word comes from the word 'euphoria', which means intense excitement or happiness. So, tensions produced by desire, eagerness, anticipation and so on are normal and necessary and help us to focus better. *Eustress* can motivate us to reach our daily challenges and goals and enables us to accomplish day-to-day tasks more efficiently. We also know that because stress produces the fight-flight response in dangerous situations, it works as an early warning system. In these situations, our bodies act with laser-like focus in ways that will keep us safe.

I have also learned that *eustress* brings health benefits such as strengthening our immune systems, improving heart function, and protecting the body from infection. It can also make us more resilient, boost our brain power and motivate us to succeed.[1]

More commonly, we think of stress as negative. It's no wonder we do because it's so ubiquitous, debilitating and costly.

I think we all know when we are over-stressed. Some particularly common symptoms are physical tension, poor sleep, a general emotional malaise or feeling of dissatisfaction with life, anxiety, irritability and depression.

This is called *distress* and is usually associated with mental or physical suffering such as extreme anxiety, sadness, pain or the state of being in danger. Some of our emotional responses when we experience *distress* are feelings of disappointment, inadequacy, despair, fear of missing out, jealousy and envy. For some people, their despair takes them to a point of committing violence against themselves or others.

According to one Mayo Clinic report[2], there are numerous common effects of stress on our body, mood and behaviour.

For example, check your physical early warning signs and notice things such as headaches, muscle tension or pain – especially a tightening of the throat and tension in the back and neck. Often this will accompany raised shoulders, an increased heart rate, chest pain, fatigue, changes in sex drive, stomach upsets and sleep problems. You may also notice cool but perspiring hands, a tight anus, tight leg muscles, clenched fists and become aware of your frowning face!

Be aware of your mood changes too. Are you experiencing increased anxiety, a feeling of restlessness, lack of motivation and focus, overwhelm, irritability, anger and sadness or depression?

You will also notice behavioural changes when you are overstressed. Over or under-eating, angry outbursts, drug or alcohol misuse, tobacco use, social withdrawal, and exercising less often are some of the more common behavioural effects of stress.

What we do know is that having too much distress over a long period, or chronic stress, can have a detrimental effect on our mental and physical wellbeing and can often be the trigger for an episode of depression or anxiety. Our preoccupation with our stress itself can reduce our focus on more positive and engaging areas of our life.

It seems that the connection between our health and our stress levels are undisputed. For example, air traffic controllers have one of the most stressful jobs possible, with continual responsibility for the lives of thousands of people; they also show levels of hypertension five times higher than the rest of the population.[3]

I have also learned that during times of stress our body releases hormones such as cortisol and adrenaline and that excess or chronic levels of cortisol can damage brain cells over time and lead to neurodegeneration. Stress is also associated with elevated inflammation and free radical production and lowers mood-supporting neurotransmitters such as serotonin and dopamine.[4]

The Cost of Stress

Learning to live with the stress epidemic is a challenge for us all. We only have to witness the huge increase in the use of antidepressants, the alarming impact stress has on the cause of illness and increased hospitalisations, the increasing sleep problems attributed to stress, the staggering rate of burnout amongst leaders, professionals wanting to downshift so as to have less stress at work, and increased suicide rates to realise some of the impacts stress is having in society. According to one report, stress is costing the Australian economy $12 billion a year.[5]

Mental health conditions cost Australian workplaces $4.7 billion in absenteeism, $6.1 billion in presenteeism and $145.9 million in compensation claims, according to a report by Price, Waterhouse Coopers.[6]

The causes of stress

One of the first steps in learning to live with stress is to know and understand what is causing your stress. This is especially true if you are experiencing high levels of chronic stress and you sense your tank is about to overflow.

Causes of stress in the workplace

My work in Careers Coaching including years in Outplacement as well as my own career, have enabled me to witness and experience firsthand the stress people encounter in the workplace.

While some stress is normal and most of us respond differently to different stressors, increasingly I have met and worked with many who are not coping. Long hours, job insecurity or fear of being laid off, difficult work relationships with the boss or colleagues, having to work longer hours because of cutbacks and pressure to perform to meet increased expectations all increase stress.

I have known people who are so stressed about work that they were physically sick daily prior to going to work. We only have to witness the increasing numbers of employees taking stress leave and being treated for anxiety and depression to know that stress is at epidemic proportions in the workplace.

Often, I see people highly stressed because they are the wrong fit for the position or the job exceeds their ability to meet the job requirements. They are stressed because of having to operate outside of their comfort zones. For others, Values misalignment or conflict is a huge stressor. I have also noticed that those who are bored or engaged in meaningless work also experience stress as a result of their work lacking meaning or purpose.

Alarmingly, there seems to be a silent increase in psychopathic behaviour in the corporate workplace. In my leadership coaching engagements, I have worked with several professionals and managers trying to cope with colleagues who demonstrated the characteristics of corporate psychopaths. Their resultant stress was enormous and like most chronic stress, led to a loss of performance and productivity. According to one report, 25% of all resignations are because of a corporate psychopath. Statistics show that the reasons 50% of all people taking stress leave, do so, are related to or caused directly or indirectly by a corporate psychopath. Each victim of a psychopath is out of pocket $10,000 and the community is out of pocket to the tune of $5000 per victim.[7]

I can confidently say that the unhappiest and most stressful period of my career was when I found myself, initially unknowingly, working with a psychopath as a direct report. The stress was enormous and debilitating. My productivity and performance diminished significantly, and I became sick. Being 'rescued' after enduring 18 months of hell in the workplace through another opportunity unexpectedly appearing, was an indescribable relief. It was as if the universe and all God's angels had felt my pain too and said: 'OK, you've had enough, you don't have to do this anymore.'

There's more to this story, of course, which happened well before being *Mack-Trucked*, but my point is that stress in the workplace is real. I have learned that we can't control the many stimuli that engender our stress in the workplace but we can learn to handle it in proactive ways.

Working with hundreds of small business owners, I continue to help them cope with the stress of keeping and engaging their teams, generating and maintaining cash flow, keeping up to date with and using new technology, being compliant with increasing legislative and legal requirements, coping with constant disruption in the market place...to name a just few! Stress coping strategies including mindfulness, self-awareness, coaching and mentoring, strategic planning and being proactive are clearly vital in today's unpredictable and rapidly changing business environment.

Stressing about the future has its roots in fear. We may be concerned with certain questions. Will I have enough money to live now and in my retirement? How will I continue my business when I move interstate? Do I have the physical, mental and financial resources to achieve my Vision and goals? Will my book be good enough, who will publish it and who will read it?

For others it can be worry over more macro issues like world climate change, saving for retirement, terrorism, paying off the mortgage or not being able to afford a home.

We spend time and energy imagining all the possible ways things *can* go wrong and the possible effects if things *do* go wrong. In these instances, our stress and anxiety are future-orientated, and we forget all about mindfully living in the present. The thoughts of tomorrow rob us of our peace in the present.

I have mentioned just a few of the more common causes of stress. There are certainly many others, including trying to control what you can't control, worrying about what others think of you, setting unrealistic goals, conflict and confrontation, being forced to go outside of your comfort zone, lack of preparation for a performance or for an important occasion and not having work/life integration. Others are living out of alignment with your Purpose, as well as fear shrouded in guilt, shame, anger, loss, sadness, remorse, embarrassment and stress associated with avoiding circumstances that exacerbate our fears.

What is certain is that the triggers or causes of stress are not the same for all of us. What is water off a duck's back for someone is a major stressor for another. I think that both personality and our biological and social histories have something to do with the individual ways we respond to stress. For example, Meyer Friedman[8] analysed the personalities of many heart patients and found that they showed a particular set of characteristics:

- An intense sustained ambition to achieve self-selected but poorly-defined goals
- A greatly pronounced tendency and eagerness to compete
- A persistent desire for recognition and advancement
- A continuous involvement in many different job aspects all of which are measured against time limits
- A marked tendency to work more quickly than necessary, both physically and mentally
- Constant mental and physical alertness

If you recognise yourself in the above descriptions, it may be wise to take steps to reduce stress, (although there are, of course, other factors involved in heart disease besides personality).

For the remainder of this chapter, I would like to share my journey in learning to live proactively with stress and anxiety and how developing these new skills has been hugely helpful for me in transitioning from experiencing post-traumatic stress to waking up to life.

Proactive strategies in learning to live with stress

Mindfulness

Being present in the moment is difficult for someone who has sleepless nights, worries a lot and exists in a constant state of anxiety. Mindfulness and learning to be mindful are popular philosophies and practices which Western cultures have increasingly adopted and adapted from Buddhist meditation principles. As I come from Judaean Christian roots, I was initially sceptical and wary about the practice when I first encountered it some 20 years ago. Looking back, I don't understand why I was so reticent. Apart from anything else, being mindfully aware of our thoughts, feelings, attitudes, behaviours, and our senses seems eminently sensible and helpful. But it's a difficult practice to master, and particularly difficult if your mind is anxious about the future and regretful about the past. It seems that 'when we are in our mind, we are hardly ever at peace, and when we're at peace, we're hardly ever in our mind.'[9]

Also, if you are in overload and overwhelm, why waste time noticing when all you can think about is the next project, job, new idea or 'fire' you need to put out! I have had some clients say that they haven't got time for that sort of stuff and state that 'that's just not me.' And I also know people who have said, 'I tried that once and it didn't work!'

I have to thank my wife Angela and two of my mentors for helping me become better at being more mindful. Learning to notice was my first step. Noticing what I was eating, the tastes, smell and textures of the food, my surroundings when walking, my thoughts and the triggers for my feelings, where negative feelings reside in my body, what's happening for me when I get anxious or experiencing suffering, noticing when my mind plays negative thoughts over and over again, noticing my stress and my triggers, and noticing my breathing. Doing something habitual in customary surroundings with our head caught up with and full of other thoughts is not being mindful, so we have to work at it throughout each day.

I keep reminding myself and others of the old saying: 'Tomorrow's a mystery, yesterday is history; we only have now and that's the present we give ourselves.' When tomorrow comes, it will be now! It's always only now! The future is the thief of the present.

Noticing, awareness, and self-observation are key to us learning to be present and to living in the moment. And this awareness comes from the True Self, which unlike the false or egoic self is non-judgemental, and is not self-condemning. When we come to realise who we really are, mindfulness instantly brings perspective. We have a helicopter view of life and living, we see the world through the eyes of love, and we are kind to ourselves.

Mindfulness is a *state of being* but because of our conditioning, the power of the ego, and the paralysing effect that fear can sometimes have, we need to train ourselves to be mindful. We might only take baby steps to start with, beginning with noticing, noticing everything… in us, outside of us, around us and even what is happening because of us!

Prayer and meditation

Nearly all the stress management literature cites the practice of meditation as an important strategy to help manage stress. At the time of being *Mack-Trucked* I used to pray daily, but I let go of that spiritual practice some years ago, until recently. I think that was because I was seeking a different, less fundamentalist spirituality which the church was not offering. I believe that everyone's spiritual journey is different, but meaningful for them at their particular stage of life. Looking back, I think then my prayer life was egocentric. I prayed to a God 'out there' essentially to make my life and that of others happier, easier and more fulfilling.

I'm now beginning to incorporate meditation again as one of my spiritual practices. My prayer, meditation and contemplation come from a core motive of Love which in turn comes from my conception of God, who is all, in all and through all, the ground of Being.

One of the key de-stressors for me is prayerfully and mindfully practicing gratitude. Years ago, my wife and I commenced incorporating the 'three good things' conversation each night at the dinner table. We encourage families to do this daily also. 'What three good things happened for you today?' It's easy to get so engulfed by negativity, the negative things that happened to us, or the negativity that is present on the News and in world affairs. Practicing the 'three good things' helps generate an attitude of gratitude. It takes us outside of ourselves so we can embody a more positive mindset and a heart full of thanks and it reminds us how lucky we really are.

In more recent years, we also practice and teach the opposite question: 'What three (or two or one) 'bad' or unhappy thing happened for you today'? If we only focus on all the good, the happy things, and are not brave enough to talk about the not so good or negative experiences which are also a part of daily life, we avoid learning how to deal with stress, unhelpful thinking and the uncomfortable feelings that come with these. Learning and developing resilience is key also to handling stress.

In the past few years I have benefited greatly from investing daily in meditation through using an App. This was hard at first for several reasons. Firstly, I thought I was too busy. There is never enough time to get the important things done, is there? Secondly, I was not used to sitting still and not doing anything! Thirdly, trying to let go of my hyperactive mind to concentrate on my breathing was incredibly difficult at first... and it still is. But I understand that this is normal and I'm certainly getting much better at it.

The meditation App I use also has a reflective theme which focuses on the greater good as well as a positive mindset. Strategies to manage stress, improve sleep, practice gratitude and forgiveness, develop self-worth, stay focussed, develop mindfulness in daily life, and deconstruct performance anxiety to collectively build resilience, and help me stay centred and focused and less stressed, have been most helpful.

The key is to do this daily...until it becomes a rich and consistent habit. 10-20 minutes is fine so long as you remain consistent. Some experts recommend you meditate twice a day or in multiple short bursts (two to five minutes) which is better than nothing. You can build up the amount of time until it feels right for you. Just start. Take regular baby steps at first!

For some of you reading this, I can hear your question loud and clear. 'If I'm going to invest my valuable time in meditating and prayerful reflection, what's the return on my investment? What results can I expect and how quickly will I see and feel the benefits?'

My answer is that it depends what you are seeking. Many meditate seeking peace and happiness and for others meditating provides an avenue for finding answers to deeper questions. For me, I have used the practices of meditation, mindfulness, prayer and contemplation to help me deal with stress and anxiety, to express gratitude, to intercede on the behalf of others, build resilience and to improve my feeling of physical, mental and spiritual wellbeing. Above all, I seek inner peace. Learning to still my mind and body through the practice of square breathing and other breathing techniques such as 'four, seven, eight,' (breathe in for four counts, hold for seven and exhale for eight) has also been key. For me the breath is both symbol and reality. It helps me live from the inside out.

Like any art or science, implementation of the knowledge and practice is key. For most of the people I talk with and in my own experience, results are both tangible and intangible – immediate and gradual. Be patient as the benefits will come, for some of you, right away, but for others it might take weeks or months depending on your histories, cultures and personality types.

Over time, I think I have become a kinder, more relaxed and a more patient person. I'm also learning to be more patient and compassionate with myself, understanding that for forgiveness and compassion to be complete, they must include me. I'm also more aware of and connected to the Oneness of life in which we all share.

Forgiveness

I'm convinced that the act of forgiveness reduces stress and suffering. From my experience, not forgiving is corrosive, debilitating, exhausting and distressing.

Researchers at John Hopkins University (John Hopkins Medicine, 2019)[10] have found that the act of forgiveness can reduce the risk of heart attack, lower cholesterol levels, improve sleep, reduce pain, lower your blood pressure, and decrease levels of anxiety, depression, and stress. And forgiveness provides greater benefits as we age. Sadly, the converse is also true: failing to forgive undermines our wellbeing, emotionally as well as physically, and it chips away at any possibility of restoring relationships.

I have pondered the nature of forgiveness in my own life as I unknowingly and ignorantly attributed so much of my stress to the behaviour of others. Back then, I didn't understand that I had a Choice in terms of my response to the perceived stressors, or the divine and spiritual nature of that Choice. Without this profound understanding, it was so easy to adopt a victim mindset and blame others for my state of mind and circumstances.

I think forgiveness is multilayered. I'm not a psychotherapist but from my understanding and experience, 'letting go' of the negative thoughts and feelings associated with the behaviour of the 'perpetrator' is essential. But that's easier said than done for many of us. We all unconsciously or consciously hold grudges and I dare say, we want to get even! What is important to remember is that 'letting go' does not mean condoning.

There is a process in letting go… or in forgiving. Being aware and getting in touch with the feelings that are within us is so important. We can't deny them, push them away, stop them or even change them. And we must understand that these negative and uncomfortable feelings are ours and no one else's. The same behaviour that produces certain feelings in us most likely will not affect another. These thoughts are 'not out there' but are our internal creations.

There is another crucial step in the process of letting go. Once we understand that it is our ego at work here, and that it is trying desperately to seek comfort, revenge, and payback, we understand that this suffering and stress is the result of our natural mind at work. The ego is that part of our mind that knows only fear. Its every thought and action has grown out of fear. The ego behaves the same way in all of us. It is not evil. It's just that some of us choose at some point to see reality through a different lens, and to let go of the ego's power. At this point, we can allow our True Self to observe the ego at work, and to watch what is really going on. By observing our hurt and stress from a place of detachment, we can acknowledge the hurt, which is to the egoic self only, and let it go.

Our True Self never gets stressed, never seeks revenge, is never unforgiving but always loving. And don't we want to be true to our True Self? As the words from the musical 'Aspects of Love[11]' so beautifully say: 'Love changes everything... And nothing in the world will ever be the same.'

> **When you tap into your higher self, and decide to 'let go and let God', the burning coals of unforgiveness get left to smoulder in the corner of illusion... and finally die out.**

This might be a bridge too far for some people for many different reasons, and I can understand that. But I also know that when you tap into your higher Self, and decide to 'let go and let God', the burning coals of unforgiveness get left to smoulder in the corner of illusion... and finally die out. I don't expect or think that we ever forget, but we can let go. Forgiveness changes everything too, for to Love is to forgive.

I think there is another step or aspect to the process of letting go and that is letting go of expectations. If we wait for or expect an apology and if forgiveness is conditional upon that apology, mostly we are going to be disappointed. Unless the apology is given freely and without expectation and from the very depth of our soul, it is worth little. If the only reason we forgive is to salvage a relationship or to regain something we have lost, it's likely that the relationship will never recover.

There's another dimension to forgiveness that I'm coming to understand. Forgiveness is not an act of generosity on the part of the forgiver to the forgiven. If we are doing anyone a favour, it is to ourselves, not to the other person. If the other person has not made the big Choice in life and tuned into the voice of their spiritual Being, they cannot be blamed for their behaviour. Anyone acting from a core motive of fear knows no other way. They have only ever identified with their separated, conditioned mind. They only hear one voice. They don't hear the voice of Love, only the voice of the ego demanding protection. They are trapped in their ignorance and doing their best, even when their best might be brutal, uncaring, destructive, and selfish. How can you not forgive someone trapped in their egoic state and who has lived their whole existence unconsciously through a core motive of fear? Who are we to judge and condemn? As Jesus said in the New Testament – *'Father forgive them, for they know not what they do.'*[12]

This paradigm of forgiveness is summarised so insightfully in the following poem by my friend Phil Harker.

Whadayamadat!
When you think someone has wronged you,
and you wish to 'pay them back'
When you look on them as guilty,
and say "thank God I'm not like that"
Remember that they never chose
their birth, 'twas merely chance
Like you, their motive's love or fear,
all else is circumstance
So, really, it's the motive that you're judging,
they don't choose the things they do
And the motive that you're mad at,
is the same one driving you!

Phil Harker
(Used with the permission of the author)

Seeing the perpetrator of your perceived stress and suffering through your spiritual eyes will change your seeing, change your being and change your life. While you may probably never forget, you will either gradually or perhaps even instantly be able to 'let go' and claim back your peace of mind. And what can possibly be more important in life?

> **Seeing the perpetrator of your perceived stress and suffering through your spiritual eyes will change your seeing, change your being and change your life.**

The other 'layer' of forgiveness is our lack of forgiveness towards ourselves. Learning to forgive ourselves for the world we have created and the mistakes we have made is a conceptually challenging paradigm. I think when we get to a point of understanding that what another has seemingly done is no different from what we have done, we can truly forgive. In this way, the act of forgiveness reverses how we think. We have no hope of forgiving another until we forgive ourselves. And this forgiveness must include the realisation that our initial condemnation of another was also driven by the same unconscious fear that motivated the behaviour of the other. Waking up to this realisation is an almost automatic pathway to a kind of forgiveness that sees no real guilt in the first place. Staying guilty and not forgiving ourselves doesn't serve us well in the short or long term.

> **When we get to a point of understanding that what another has seemingly done is no different to what we have done, we can truly forgive.**

One way of 'staying guilty' is expressed through the acronym SHAME – aka Should-Have-Always-Managed-Everything. I can add to this: and done everything perfectly. How we look at our experiences in the past and present will determine whether we add shame, guilt, resentment, and perfection to our list of 'I'm not good enough' stories. When we let go of our resistance to forgive ourselves, we can more easily forgive others. And forgiving others somehow mysteriously and unconsciously lessens our own self-condemnation.

We have opportunities daily to forgive ourselves and others. Living mindfully and in our prayers and meditation, we can continually ask God or a higher power as you understand that to be (which may well be your Higher Self) to help us practice Love. Make that your prayer or mantra throughout each day so that your response to everything is always the same: 'God, please let me feel, see and practice only Love in this moment.'

Diet

Much has and still is written about the importance of eating correctly. Indeed, hardly a week goes by without a new book or article on diet being published somewhere. Knowing about diet and implementing a healthy diet daily are two very different things.

But I really must reiterate how important this is if you are wanting to get your life unblocked, on track and flourishing. When you are stressed out of your brain or have a life schedule that is out of control, it's normal for people to overeat, consume excess alcohol and indulge in chocolate or other empty calories. I did for many years. I wish I could say 'not anymore' but that wouldn't be completely honest. Certainly, I have moderated the use of these to the point where I'm more disciplined and conscious of what and how much I eat and drink.

- Here a brief summary of how we eat:
- Five vegetables per day
- Lots of raw salads
- Fish at least once a week
- Small servings of red meat twice a week
- No or very little processed meat except an occasional indulgence in smoked bacon
- Cook fresh from scratch, without preservatives
- Consume unprocessed grains, organic cereals and porridge
- Fruit, nuts and yogurt daily
- Consume dark chocolate, with a few exceptions!
- Make our own dips and use rice and gluten-free crackers
- Cut down on potatoes (which is a bit sad but…sweet potatoes are great, right?)
- Never drink soft drinks or fruit juices. We use still or soda water with lemon

- Drastically reduce sugar consumption (though I still choose to have a pinch in coffee)
- Reduce alcohol consumption with the goal of five alcohol free days per week
- Try very hard to reduce my portions!

Don't take this as a nutritionist's guide to eating a correct diet. Seek professional advice. Paying attention to our diet has been hugely beneficial. It certainly has led to healthy weight loss (everyone I meet who knows me well comments on the weight I've lost), more energy (my mantra of being *wide-eyed and electrified* is mostly a reality), sharper focus and reduced inflammation. We still enjoy our food, and it's fun and easy to prepare, interesting and tasty, and it's very healthy!

You know my eating habits and I hope you have picked up on the importance of consciously monitoring what you put into your 'physical temple.' As the saying goes: garbage in – garbage out. If you put garbage food into your body, the fruits of your contribution to yourself and others will be diminished. You end up feeling disappointed and bad about yourself, resulting in procrastination, self-sabotage, low self-worth and depression. And so, the cycle continues!

Dietary supplements

Antidepressants were a mandatory part of my early recovery. I hated taking them, but I was locked into the allopathic medical model for two years through my employer's sick leave regimen and requirements. I was able to come off them when it was confirmed that there was no possibility of my returning to work, thus causing me to retire from my academic position. It was a torturous process and one I would never want to repeat.

Since that time, I have been fortunate to have been under the medical supervision of my good friend and integrated holistic practitioner, Dr John Ryan. Having quarterly check-ups, regular and ongoing blood tests, and taking prescribed dietary supplements, caused my health to return – gradually at first but very noticeably as time went on. These things have played such an important part in me getting my mojo back.

In the early stages after being *Mack-Trucked*, I had no energy, experienced constant brain fog, and my memory seemed to vanish into the cybersphere. I had the concentration span of a sparrow and had great difficulty sleeping. I didn't want to socialise either. But through persistence, and through developing myself in the ways shared in this book, I was able to reinvent my career and build a successful business.

I'm not knocking allopathic medicine or medical practitioners, but I am advocating a personalised integrative approach to treating depression and anxiety. We are physical, mental and spiritual beings from different socio-biological histories and our complete wellness depends upon each part being nurtured and treated. Research confirms that depression and anxiety can be caused by factors including psychological and coping skills; diet and nutrition; lifestyle and environment; social and spiritual; and biological and medical.[13]

For example, having a poor diet and consuming food with nutritional deficiencies or being intolerant or sensitive to different foods may be a potential cause of depression. Lifestyle and environment factors which also may contribute to depression include being physically inactive, having sleep problems, spending limited time outdoors and limited engagement with pleasurable activities, high stress, excess screen time, exposure to excess environmental toxins and not including enough relaxation activities. From a psychological perspective, your depression and anxiety may develop as a result of underdeveloped or ineffective coping skills and or unhelpful thoughts and beliefs that don't serve you well. In terms of social and spiritual causes exacerbating depression, these could include limited social support groups or networks, excess social strain and lack of purpose and meaning in your life. Adrian Lopresti[14] also suggests several possible biological and medical causes such as suffering from a medical condition, side effects from pharmaceutical medications, avoidance of potentially beneficial medications, sex or thyroid hormone imbalance, blood sugar imbalance and obesity or excess weight.

The point is that one size does not fit all. That was certainly the case for me.

Psychological and pharmacological interventions may form important components of treatment and work well for some, but they are not the only strategies used to enhance physical and mental wellbeing. What I have come to understand and appreciate is that rather than targeting one area or use only medication or psychological skills, a personalised multitargeted approach that treats the causes not just the symptoms, has worked for me. And the use of dietary supplements based on blood test results being well monitored, has been so very helpful.

Exercise and personal success routine

The benefits of exercise are also widely documented. Certainly, if you are suffering from stress, anxiety and depression, the first habit to put into place is daily exercise. But most of us don't do this, do we? We know we should, but the discipline and persistence required to get started is just not there. Our heads say one thing and our actions quite another. We procrastinate and I have explained why in the previous chapter.

Prior to being *Mack-Trucked* I was too busy; too busy to invest in anything really except work. It was as if being busy was a badge of honour. As previously mentioned, we now call it the *new stupid*.

For many years now, I have put into practice what I teach. Walking the talk does so much for your self-worth, integrity and confidence. I live a much more integrated life (I prefer that word to the commonly used 'balanced') by design and intention. This of course includes exercise.

Currently I walk for an hour five days a week with two buddies, participate in an exercise class with an exercise physiologist once a week and do a 45-minute workout in the gym two to three afternoons a week. I also love golf and try to play at least once a week.

It's so easy to make excuses and be in denial. If you don't invest into yourself, no one else will. Take ownership, responsibility and accountability for your wellbeing. The benefits, as you know, are both tangible and intangible.

The secret is to make exercise part of your daily success routine. I call this my Personal Success Routine (PSR) and implement this five mornings a week. For me, this includes a cup of tea, a one-hour walk, and 10-15 minutes of mindful meditation and contemplation.

Success literature indicates that people who are exceptionally productive and are leaders in their field all have a daily success routine. It doesn't have to occur in the early morning, but this is the most common time to set up your day for success. For some, their PSR includes exercise, meditation and daily planning – and definitely no viewing of emails unless their day depends on knowing what came in during the night.

I know that there are compelling reasons for setting up your day by joining the '5.00am club'. If, like some, you are not a naturally early morning person, then join the 9.00pm club! Getting to bed early and having a great night's sleep will make your PSR so much easier to implement.

> **When you develop and implement your personal success routine your energy and focus will increase, your mojo will soar, your confidence will radiate, and your sense of wellbeing will be massively elevated. You will feel On Purpose!**

If you want to manage your stress more proactively and live a life of productivity and no regrets, then I strongly, strongly encourage you to develop and implement your personal success routine. Your energy and focus will increase, your mojo will soar, your confidence will radiate, and your sense of wellbeing will be massively elevated. You will feel On Purpose. Your life will begin and continue to flourish! In the adapted words of one motor vehicle advertisement: 'Oh what a feeling!'…more mojo!

Proactively Living with Fear

Back when I was *Mack-Trucked*, I had so little understanding of the knowledge, paradigms and information that I have shared in this book. You will recall that in Chapter Two, I discussed the nature of fear and love and how we predominantly live our lives through a core motive of these: we are either full of love or full of fear. This discussion was more philosophical and spiritual rather than based on mainstream psychology.

Understanding the nature of fear on a biological and psychological level has helped me enormously. I think it will help you too in having a greater understanding of why fear plays such a major part of your

> **Fear holds us back, gets in the way, slows us down and prevents us from growth, personal transformation and living a rich, full and meaningful life.**

conditioning and your life. I have shared this information throughout the book and my hope is that you will understand why fear plays such a major role in your suffering, anxiety, depression and stress.

Fear holds us back, gets in the way, slows us down and prevents us from growth, personal transformation and living a rich, full and meaningful life. But fear is normal also and is not necessarily bad.

That's a big claim I know, but once we understand the nature and neuroscience of fear, how it prevents us from moving outside our comfort zones; and the nature of our true identities, we will be in a much stronger position to proactively and successfully live with stress and move forward with our life, careers and businesses.

Much of this information I have included in the Chapter on Procrastination and how we deal with it. Here is a brief summary of some of the content:

The Neuroscience of Fear

Fear manifests itself in many ways. We all know that the brain, particularly the 'emotional brain' (limbic system) is the reactive part of us that initiates a 'fight', 'flight', 'freeze' or 'flop' response. Its primary function is to keep us safe and acts as an early warning mechanism with the motto 'safety first'. For very early Homo sapiens, this function of the brain ensured physical survival from predators or other emergencies. It is lightning-fast and therefore processes information quicker than we can think. It immediately puts a safety plan into effect before consulting the executive brain (the neocortex). To reiterate, because its primary function is 'survival' it is reactive and completely unresponsive to logic.

At this level, fear could be equated with the saying 'Forget Everything And Run'.

Fastforward to eons later and our threat is not so much physical but psychological. Fear of failure, fear of success, fear of being embarrassed, fear of loneliness, fear of rejection, fear of having our feelings hurt, all play out in our lives daily. Fear also manifests itself as anger, guilt, envy, pride, jealousy, self-adulation, self-deprecation, blame, excuses, being a victim, being in denial and so on. Dig deep, and underneath all these states of mind, feelings and emotions, fear will be lurking.

It's not surprising, therefore, that the acronym of **False Expectations Appearing Real** seems an apt expression to define fear at the psychological level.

The point is that fear is multilayered, multifaceted and plays out in so many ways to keep us 'safe' and therefore, firmly stuck on the nails we would like to get off. But it also produces worry, stress and anxiety if left unchecked or unobserved.

In previous chapters I have explained how fear is exacerbated by us fusing or attaching to our unhelpful thinking patterns and limiting beliefs. When we fuse to these negative thoughts, we become them. There's a proverb which states: 'As a man thinks in his heart, so is he'[15]. So, you are or become what you think. When we fuse to these thoughts, they blind us to engaging purposefully, proactively and productively with life. All we can think see and feel are the limitations that the 'buying in' to these thoughts bring.

Learning to live with and manage stress requires us to defuse or detach from our negative thoughts. That's where mindfulness and awareness are so important. As so often discussed throughout this book, as humans, we have a 'thinking mind' and an 'observing mind' corresponding with our false self and True Self (or the self as context and the Self as content). When we understand who we really are, we realise that our stress always and only exists in our conditioned or thinking mind – our egoic self. The True Self never ever feels or identifies with stress; it can only observe and watch it. By knowing and understanding that, we simply observe and watch our suffering and realise how absurd it is. We can disidentify with our suffering and all the negative thoughts that come with our biological and sociological histories.

Because we are the creators of our thoughts, we can also change our thoughts. We know that many of our thoughts are not good for us and our negative thoughts come when we live with a core motive of fear. Negative thoughts about ourselves and others harms us, and the resultant accumulative guilt associated with our negative thinking hinders our relationships which in turn changes every experience we have.

> **When we understand that love is what we are born with and fear is our learned conditioning, we can tap back into our True Self.**

As you have read in a previous chapter, there is a space between stimulus and response and in that space, you have a spiritual choice. You can choose your response to any stimulus. That's the only real Choice you have in life. Don't get confused between choice and decisions. All decisions of the mind are made through our core motive of *Love* or *fear*.

When we understand that Love is what we are born with and fear is our learned conditioning, we can tap back into our True Self. We can choose our response. We can choose our thoughts. What is not *Love* is always *fear*. Fortunately, the ego is not the only voice we have access to. Like our thoughts, *Love* can be very subtle and varied. It can be expressed in laughter, silence and tears as well as all the more common manifestations including compassion, joy, forgiveness, peace and patience.

Knowing and practicing this, is living mindfully: living in and through awareness. I still experience stress and anxiety, but deep down, knowing that I'm the 'knower' not the 'known' and that my True Self is the unseen 'watcher' or 'observer', changes everything.

References and Notes – Chapter 6

1. *5 weird ways stress can actually be good for you*. https://www.health.com/condition/stress/5-weird-ways-stress-can-actually-be-good-for-you. Retrieved 11 March 2020: Web.

2. *Stress symptoms: Effects on your body and behaviour*. https://www.mayoclinic.org/healthy-lifestyle/stress-management/in-depth/stress-symptoms/art-20050987#. Retrieved 11 March 2020: Web.

3. *The physical effects of stress*. https://www.reduce-my-stress.com/stress-1.html. Retrieved 21 January 2020: Web.

4. *The physical effects of stress*. https://www.reduce-my-stress.com/stress-1.html. Retrieved 21 January 2020: Web

5. *Problem costing Australia $12 billion a year*. https://www.news.com.au/finance/work/at-work/problem-costing-australia-12-billion-a-year/news-story/f663da06efc18487bdbb3f2cc33d9ed5.Retrieved 20 January 2020: Web.

6. The Mentally Healthy Workplace Alliance: *Creating a mentally healthy workplace*. Final Report, March 2014. https://www.headsup.org.au/docs/default-source/resources/beyondblue_workplaceroi_finalreport_may-2014.pdf?sfvrsn=90e47a4d_6.. Retrieved 11 March 2020: Web.

7. Psychopath victim support community. http://www.psychopath-research.com/forum/ubbthreads.php/topics/1074/2/Corporate_Psychopaths.Retrieved 11 March 2020: Web.

8. *When stress becomes harmful*. https://www.reduce-my-stress.com/stress-2a.html. Retrieved 20 January 2020: Web.

9. Rohr, R. *The prayer of quiet*. Richard Rohr's Daily Meditation, Action and Contemplation: Part Three. Retrieved 21 January 2020 from: Mailing List.

10. John Hopkins Medicine, (2019). *Forgiveness: Your health depends on it*. Hopkinsmedicine.org. Retrieved 31 January 2020, from: Web.

11. *Love changes everything* is a song from the musical Aspects of Love, composed by Andrew Lloyd Webber, with lyric written by Charles Hart and Don Black. https://www.lyrics.com/track/17739125/

Andrew+Lloyd+Webber/Love+Changes+Everything+%28From+Aspe
cts+of+Love%29. Retrieved June 2020 from:Web.

12. Luke 23:34, New International Version.

13. Lopresti, A. (2019). *Integrative solutions to build a better mood.* Duncraig WA: Innovative Wellness Pty. Ltd.

14. Lopresti, A. (2019). *Integrative solutions to build a better mood.* Duncraig WA: Innovative Wellness Pty. Ltd.

15. Proverbs 23:7, New International Version.

Humpty Dumpty had a great fall,
Life throws challenges to us all,
We can break up or become whole,
Is it Spirit that conquers all?

Chapter 7 – Developing Resilience

In this chapter I would like to highlight the main themes that have enabled me to get my life back on track and in so doing, remind you of strategies, and give you encouragement and hope if you too have been *Mucked Up* or find yourself blocked or stuck.

Without doubt, all of us go through suffering and tough times and life can and does throw us curve balls when we least expect them. We all bear the scars of our wounds. It may be that your wounds have not yet healed. But, as I hope you have picked up from reading this book, whilst we have so little control over what happens to us, we do have control over our response.

My story is neither unique, nor do I consider it special. Countless people have endured hardships far greater than mine; the sudden, unexpected loss of a loved one or loved ones; being in a debilitating accident; suffering from an incurable disease; having to undergo emergency surgery; going bankrupt through tough economic times; experiencing a tumultuous relationship breakup; dealing with betrayal; and suffering unfathomable loss through drought, floods and fires are a few examples. Having said that, I'm glad that I have persevered and shared some of my experiences. It is said that writing a book is of most benefit to the author. I think that is true for me.

On reflection, at the time of being *Mack-Trucked*, my old paradigm had come to the end of its usefulness. Maybe it has for you too if you have 'hit a wall' or are still stuck living 'below the line' or 'sitting on a nail'. It's at this point for all of us in these situations that the universe or God extends us an invitation: an invitation to stay stuck or to transform through seeing the world and life through a different lens.

The final reflections that follow are built around the main themes woven throughout this book. These themes represent the process and strategies in my journey from post-traumatic stress to reawakening and wholeness. You may find other themes that stand out for you. Furthermore, what I think is important or central may not be so for you. Above all, I hope that you can implement some of these ideas and strategies. The biggest compliment would be to hear how you were able to turn your life around as a result of implementing even just one or two ideas from this book.

I have identified several main themes: resilience, spiritual re-awakening and transformation, self-awareness, Purpose, having a growth mindset and perseverance. These are all interwoven and interconnected.

Resilience

Years ago, I came across a book written by Robert H. Schuller entitled *Tough Times Never Last but Tough People Do.* I don't recall any of the content now but have never forgotten that title. While I think my journey demonstrates resilience, and that it could be an overarching theme of the book, I did not consciously choose to be resilient. However, on reflection, I found on getting to the end of my tether I needed a new paradigm for life and living. I could either 'break up' or 'wake up', staying stuck and continuing to experience post-traumatic stress, depression and anxiety or practicing acceptance and thereby choosing post-traumatic growth and transformation. To do the latter required resilience, which meant I had to search the depths of my spiritual being and be open to seeing the world differently. The themes of spiritual awakening and self-awareness were central to putting Humpty together again and demonstrating the core aspects and practices of resilience.

Spiritual re-awakening and transformation

While the seeds of spiritual re-awakening started with my journey of discovering and living my Purpose, it is in what I have shared in Chapter Two that the roots of resilience and my restoration lay.

The coffee shop conversation with my friend and spiritual mentor Phil Harker was a seminal moment. Although I was spiritually aware because of my religious roots and fundamentalist Christian upbringing, a fresher and deeper understanding of the nature of my true 'I'dentity, the difference between the True Self ('I') and the false self ('me') was life-changing. Through this developed a dimension of self-awareness and self-observation that I hitherto had not consciously thought about or practised.

The first part of Chapter Two explored how I applied this new awareness to detach and defuse from the unhelpful conditioning of my biological, social, and environmental history and circumstances. I was able to see how my 'stories' and unhelpful thoughts resulted in self-sabotage, paralysed me and kept me attached to an egocentric paradigm that was unworkable, useless and unsustainable.

Becoming alive and awake to our deepest and truest Self and in a sense, 'dying' to the old conditioned egoic self that constantly seeks reassurance and protection, was, and still is, part of the process of *waking up*. Understanding the paradox that our unseen all-seeing True Self is immortal and indestructible yet needs to be awakened and chosen gives further meaning and insight into the invitation for us to make this great Choice in life.

What I didn't fully understand years ago was that the 'I' or what I then referred to as the Holy Spirit, is given unconditionally to everyone equally, but it must be awakened, chosen and received to become a living presence. At that point, we unconsciously 'be Love' because the 'unseen, all seeing Being' is all, in all and through all and is the ground of Being-Itself.

As Richard Rohr[1] explains in one of his meditations, 'While none of us are psychologically or morally whole, we are all ontologically (in our very being) whole.' It has nothing to do with our personal or private 'me' or with anything we can do, earn or deserve. Our culture, conditioning and even religion, teaches us to identify and live through the false or separate self of reputation, self-image, role, possessions, money, appearance, and so on. It is only as these things fail us, as they always do eventually, that the True Self stands revealed and ready to be chosen.

Furthermore, I believe this 'choice' is often made in times of personal suffering when we realise our old paradigm: the one we were conditioned to believe was real, fails us. And the best part is that because our True Self naturally indwells us all, we don't need to try and create or improve it by our actions or behaviour. The True Self does not teach us love, compassion or peace because it is all these already. Being grounded, mindful and present in this place and space means that we naturally empathise, forgive, connect and love. Furthermore, this means that we are already what we are seeking. In the same meditation Richard Rohr says: 'We are made in love, for love, and unto love, and it is out of this love that we act.'

A further step in my transformation journey was the realisation and understanding that our peace of mind was not dependent on the behaviour of others. Just knowing that in the space between stimulus and response, we as humans, uniquely have a choice (our core choice) of how we respond to our thoughts, feelings attitudes and the behaviour of others was both challenging and liberating. Peace was a choice. My happiness, wellbeing and peace of mind was within my power, was my responsibility, and I could choose not to relinquish this power to anyone else.

That was big.

Prior to that realisation, I believed that my happiness and my material wellbeing was partly the responsibility of others and was dependent on how others treated me. I dare say it was more about receiving than giving! Looking back, I see how powerfully self-centred and selfish the personal self is.

The concept of living above or below the line became increasingly more significant and meaningful for me, especially as I understood that I could take responsibility and ownership for my life or live it as a victim. In the space between stimulus and response I could choose to be *bitter* or *better*, a *victim* or *victor*, *proactive* or *reactive*, Off Purpose or On Purpose. That was all in my power, no one else's. I could blame others for my circumstances; the loss of my career, being physically abused, having to reinvent myself and to claw back from potential physical, emotional and financial ruin, but ultimately, I chose not to let these events and circumstances define me.

It's for this reason I found the white wolf /black wolf story such a helpful reminder of where my thinking and behaviour was focussed and which 'wolf' I gave voice to. One represented the many faces of love: joy, peace, hope, kindness, generosity, empathy, faith, transparency, compassion, humility. The other encapsulated the numerous, and often unconscious faces of fear in its many manifestations of anger, sadness, pride, envy, jealousy, self-adulation, sorrow, regret, inferiority, self-centredness, self-pity, resentment, guilt, arrogance and superiority.

The 'wolf' story was a natural segue into the paradigm of understanding the nature of Choice and that we choose to live from a core motive of either Love or fear.

Understanding that we only ever have one Choice in life is a mind-boggling concept for most people. I know it was for me. Coming to grips with and understanding that the 'choice' between Love and fear is not in the decision itself but in the **motive** that such a decision serves was a fundamental paradigm shift for me.

Like most people, I believed that we make numerous choices every day. But the realisation that the single 'choice' at the core or ground of our being, provides the foundation criteria for all our subsequent decisions, actions and reactions took my understanding and self-awareness to another level. When I came to understand that although we make many conscious intellectual decisions with our body based mind, the one Choice for which we are ultimately responsible (our core motive) is always the same and answers the question: Are we acting to fulfil the purposes of Love (shared interests) or fear (separate interests). When we change our *seeing* we change our *being* and ultimately, our lives.

Questions for discussion and action

- If you were having a conversation in a coffee shop and someone asked you the question, 'Who are you…?' How would you answer them? (Try thinking about what answer you would have given prior to reading Chapter Two of this book).
- What is the difference between the True Self ('I') and the false self ('me')?
- How does knowing this difference impact on your life and how you live?
- What was your reaction to the white wolf, black wolf story?
- What ways would help you to live 'above the line?'

- How do you understand Einstein's quote: 'We are either full of love or full of fear?'
- What is the one Choice we are ultimately responsible for and why is this called our core motive? Why is this sometimes called the 'great choice of life'?
- What is the difference between the 'personal mind' and the 'observing mind'?
- How do you respond to the claim that your peace of mind and happiness is not dependant on your circumstances or the behaviour of others?

Developing Self-awareness

As already evident, intertwined with my personal and spiritual growth was developing my self-awareness. This, of course, is a key aspect of Emotional Intelligence.

Anthony de Mello's four-step process outlined in Chapter Two (identify your negative feelings; understand that the negative feelings are in you, not in the world, not in external reality; do not see the negative feelings as an essential part of 'I'; and understand that when you change, everything changes) was the beginning for me of becoming more mindful, noticing what was happening in me, around me, through me and because of me. Self-observation at a level hitherto not consciously practiced meant I could see 'me' from a helicopter perspective. I could watch and observe my thoughts, feelings and behaviour as if I were watching someone else. I could live from the new perspective of my 'higher Self'.

Learning to detach, defuse and disidentify with all aspects of my old thinking meant I no longer let these become a self-fulfilling prophecy. I could watch my inner critic at work and see it for what is really was – nothing more than a mechanism for falsely trying to keep me safe on the one hand and the source of self-sabotage on the other.

Learning about and practicing mindfulness and other strategies I used to manage my stress, were also examples of how I developed and demonstrated a heightened awareness of how I could enhance my spiritual, emotional and physical wellbeing. I hate to admit it, but when I first started hearing about this and trying it, I thought it was all a bit woo-woo. How wrong I was!

The blue sky metaphor gave another tool and dimension to expanding my self-awareness and understanding my dual identity, especially at a psychological level. The blue sky represents the 'self as context' while the wind, cloud, rain and storms represent the 'self as content'. Our 'self as context' is the 'observing mind' emanating from our True Self, while the 'self as content' is our 'thinking mind': the personal mind that has thousands of thoughts daily, the majority of which are unhelpful and negative. Being able to observe, watch and notice my thoughts, feelings, emotions and behaviour from my blue sky persona, as if I were watching someone else, was powerful. Knowing that my thoughts were like the wind, clouds and rain which come and go, I could watch them come and go – letting them be and not attaching or fusing to them. I found this simple act of self-observation to be freeing and through practising this, learnt a new way of seeing and being.

The chapter on procrastination could stand as a theme by itself. Essentially, learning about procrastination and why I procrastinated was a momentous revelation in my becoming more self-aware. Understanding that procrastination was a problem of emotional regulation, not of time management gave me freedom and confidence to dig deeper. By doing so I understood that there was a perfectly logical reason for it, and I didn't need to beat myself up so much when I did procrastinate.

By becoming more aware of my dual nature I have learned how the personal mind works and that most of my limiting and irrational beliefs including all my 'not good enough stories' are all symptomatic of the ego at work.

The personal mind is doing its job, but I have learned to watch and observe the thoughts it sends. They have held me back, prevented me from achieving my goals, and stopped me dead in my tracks in the past. Now I acknowledge my thinking mind and thank it for its many negative thoughts, kindly tell it they have not helped me in the past and that there is no place for them right now. Developing self-awareness in this way has also helped me understand that my True Self or my observing Mind – my Spirit, takes no part in procrastination. It watches, observes, notices, never judges or condemns and through all of that, continues to love. And this awareness has helped me to love myself more – something which has been a long, slow and painful journey for me.

Knowing my inner self better, including identifying and getting in touch with my feelings and emotions in the moment helped me to become more comfortable with my softer side. My behaviour began to change too. During this time, I led a men's leadership group for some six years. I can't tell you how hard it was for some men to give each other a hug and display their emotional sides. At first, it was as if they were touching someone with leprosy. I think this is exacerbated by the still prevalent Australian macho-male culture where not appearing strong, tough and in control is not accepted or respected and is often treated with suspicion.

Learning to understand my own moods, emotions and inner drives and how these impacted on others was not something I was always conscious of. Sometimes, I thought I was emotionally 'dead' and wondered why this was the case. I have searched for reasons and wonder if losing my mother when I was fourteen months of age had some impact on that.

My point is that by noticing my thoughts, feelings, behaviour, triggers, attitudes to any given stimulus, I am now more grounded, more aware of what is going on within and around me, and mindfulness has assisted me enormously in helping me to understand and overcome procrastination.

Self-awareness is a central component of Emotional Intelligence and much of this book has implicitly demonstrated how having a developed sense of self-awareness, being able to self-regulate, as well as becoming more empathetic and self-motivated, have been key components in my ongoing journey. Having to develop a business from scratch has also meant I have had to handle and positively influence the emotions of others, another important aspect of Emotional Intelligence.

Questions for discussion and action

- What are some strategies you can use to identify your negative emotions?
- What strategies would you use to quieten your inner critic?

- While some people are inherently more emotionally intelligent than others, we can all consciously improve our EQ. What is your response to this statement?
- How is understanding the real reasons as to why we procrastinate helpful in becoming more self-aware?
- What avoidance strategies do you notice yourself using when you procrastinate?

Purpose

The existential question of 'why am I here?' or 'why do I exist?' is one that we all confront at some point in our lives. Increasingly, I am finding that our search for meaning and purpose is beginning at an earlier age. Years ago, this was typically a question for people in mid-life, but through my work, I have found that young people in their 20's are searching for their Purpose. We all want our lives to make sense and to have a sense of meaning and continuity.

I don't want to regurgitate the content of Chapter One other than to re-emphasise that our Purpose is not what we do but who we are 'being' at our spiritual core. Finding and naming your Purpose in the manner that I have demonstrated is also an important process in the understanding of who we really are. As already inferred in my reflections above, arguably our macro Purpose in life is the Choice we make to either act out the Purpose of Love or fear. And because Purpose is the unique way in which we express love to ourselves and humanity at large, our reason for being is living our Purpose.

Our two-word Purpose Statement is the name we give to our spiritual DNA. It describes the unique way in which each of us serves ourselves and others. It becomes another expression of Love. For example, my Purpose of *Igniting Enthusiasm* or my wife Angela's Purpose of *Rejuvenating Spirit*, has become our state of Being. It's why we exist, moment by moment and always in the now.

Our visions change as do our missions and even our values. But we only ever have one single Purpose: to wake up and to 'be' our spiritual DNA regardless of our age, circumstances or history. When we are On Purpose, we are fully present in the moment, simply *being* our Purpose. When we name our Purpose, these two words are lived as an outward manifestation of an internal calling. What a difference two words can make to our lives and to humanity at large!

Being On Purpose or being 'one with our Purpose' also keeps us on track. Being consciously and unconsciously mindful of our Purpose means we are less likely to go off course when life throws us curve balls, when we are hit with unexpected challenges throughout each day or even when we get *Mack-Trucked*. Because Purpose is our True North, it becomes a 'plumb line' or 'homing beacon' and therefore keeps us from going astray. It keeps 'us above the line.' It keeps us fulfilled. It keeps us optimistic and offers us hope.

As Purpose has its roots in Love, our response to events, circumstances, the behaviour of others, is always proactive, positive and purposeful. Every aspect of our life, every role we perform, and every task we undertake is fused and infused with Purpose. Remember the example of the third stone cutter in Chapter One? He wasn't just laying stones or building a strong stone wall, he was building a magnificent cathedral – a place of worship for the community for the next thousand years. He infused his work with joy, meaning and purpose because he was able to envision a larger, more transcendent Purpose for what he was doing. He was *Building Magnificence!*

Being in alignment with our Purpose means decision making becomes so much easier. It ensures that our core wants, goals and priorities are in alignment with our Purpose and that we focus on what matters most in our lives and businesses. The decisions you make will be through the filter of your one Purpose.

When you are one with your Purpose you will be proactive and make things happen, rather than living your life reacting to events and circumstances. This is helped considerably by you knowing your core wants and top priorities for each of your life areas and by having developed clear goals and action plans to achieve these. As a result, there will be less stress and less clutter in your life, and you will be able to make decisions more confidently. By taking ownership and responsibility for your life in this way you will be in a much more powerful position to say *yes* to some things and *no* to others. Remember the adage and question: 'Whenever I say *yes* to something, what am I saying *no* to?' Living in alignment with our

Purpose also gives a greater depth of meaning and insight into the so-called work/life balance. It is not something you seek when you are one with your Purpose. Why?

Rather than trying to apportion equal importance and give equal time to all of your life 'accounts' (Spiritual, Physical, Mental, Intellectual, Family, Work, Social, Financial, Recreational, Relationships and so on) you see and live your life in terms of being holistic and integrated. I think this makes life more workable and sustainable.

It is evident that knowing our Purpose and being On Purpose means that we have clarity of direction in our life and that we live out our lives intentionally. We acknowledge that there will be occasions when we will be taken 'off course' but with a clear focus, a clear sense of direction and Purpose, as well as consciously and unconsciously *being* our Purpose in the now, we will keep returning to or being pulled back to the things that matter most in our lives. When we live through our Being, life is so much more freeing.

Questions for discussion and implementation

- What is life like for you when you sense you are Off Purpose?
- What does being On Purpose mean for you?
- How does the definition of Purpose explained here sit with you?
- Can you clearly explain the difference between your Purpose, Vision, Missions and Values?
- Why is it important to understand these distinctions?
- Why do you think Purpose comes from a place of goodness or Godness?
- How does your two-word Purpose Statement 'define' you in a special way?
- How is Purpose different from your Passion?

Having a growth mindset

Imagine yourself approaching the peak of your career when from out of nowhere, it suddenly ends. Your career vision is clear, you are doing the work you love, the years of training and experience are in full swing, you are making a difference and are respected by your colleagues nationally and internationally. And then it's all gone, snuffed out, just like that! That's what I have called being *Mack-Trucked*. And as you have read, that is what happened to me. You may have experienced something similar in your life.

Having a growth mindset meant that I was able to keep going after being *Mack-Trucked* and in the face of this and many other setbacks. I could have easily given up on receiving the specialist's diagnosis that I would never work again in my life. But, as I have described, that was never an option for me.

As I have inferred throughout this book, having a growth mindset has played such an important part in my journey from post-traumatic stress to growth. It is part of having a positive mental attitude, of wanting to be the best that I could possibly be.

Reinvention is challenging to say the least. But I have found that when you embrace your challenges you come out the other side stronger and an improved version of yourself.

In reinventing myself from a music educator to a business entrepreneur, I had to not only learn, but master a whole set of new skills to start up and run a business. Over the course of my recovery, and even now, I have invested a huge amount of time and money into retraining to be a personal, business and careers coach. As you can imagine, this involved acquiring vast amounts of knowledge and skills and, most challengingly, their successful implementation. Having highly developed skills and knowledge without implementation is like being a river without water. Thankfully, I had valuable transferrable skills including written and oral communication as well as presentation skills and these have been invaluable in the process.

Learning to be a coach and to be internationally accredited as a professional coach through the International Coach Federation has involved hundreds of hours invested into acquiring and mastering these new skills. It's one thing to train and be a great coach but it is quite another thing to operate a successful coaching business – to the point where it replaced two salaries!

For the past 20 years I have been regularly involved as a participant in short courses, workshops, seminars, weekend courses, networking meetings, webinars, podcasts and so on. I'm a lifelong learner and for the past two years I have been an active participant in a personal success program facilitated by Global Success Academy. I think having a growth mindset has been made easier by having a spouse who is also a lifelong learner – exemplified by being a daily researcher and completing a second master's degree in her early sixties.

As well as having a willingness to learn and grow, of being open and transparent, and letting go of your ego, I think it's essential to have people who can challenge you, keep you accountable and encourage you. Having several personal coaches and mentors over the past twenty years has been seminal in my personal and professional growth and transformation. Coaches (paid or unpaid) are supportive and encouraging on the one hand and challenge you on the other. They ask the searching and sometimes confronting questions which make you dig deep to uncover your 'personal truth'. They help develop self-awareness in a powerful and practical way and keep you accountable in the setting and implementation of your goals for growth. You can still have a growth mindset without having a coach or mentor, but sometimes in life, it is imperative to have someone look across at your mountain from their mountain. They see your journey differently, freshly objectively and from a new perspective.

While not directly linked to having a growth mindset, I can't begin to tell you how important it is to have a support network beyond mentors and coaches, not just in tough times but also in good times.

We are social beings and need each other for equanimity, well-being, advice, affection and for an opportunity to share and give. Having a small number of people including blood relations, who are mutually supportive, loving and caring, gives us pleasure, and 'influences our long-term health in ways every bit as powerful as adequate sleep, a good diet and not smoking'.[2]

Building a community that we want to be a part of isn't always easy. Observe how busy we are and how often we don't take the time to check in with our friends and loved ones. My point is that I could never have 'resurrected' myself on my own. You don't have to soldier on and be a hero on your own. When we are depressed, suffer from anxiety and recovering from post-traumatic stress, it is so easy and natural to want to self-isolate. As humans, we need and long for connection so having a growth mindset encourages us to include others in an expansive, generous and loving way.

Part of a growth mindset is being able to take on board criticism and negative feedback, which my personality style finds challenging. By reframing this, I now consider constructive feedback is just information to use to change and improve myself. As I heard once, 'feedback is the breakfast of champions.' It has taken me some time to understand that criticism is not a reflection of my essence, of who 'I' am but rather a statement of my capabilities, something I know I can change. With a growth mindset, failure becomes an inevitable part of learning.

Having a growth mindset, both consciously and unconsciously is also an important ingredient for being a successful goal setter. I have written two chapters on goal-setting and if you have not already done so, I invite you to read these if you really want to improve and change your life. When you learn to set goals for self-improvement and growth, relevant to the season of your life and in alignment with your Purpose and Values with strong emotion, accountability and commitment built into the implementation process, you automatically facilitate personal growth and transformation. Setting goals in this way will mean the difference between floundering and flourishing.

Questions for discussion and action

- What do you think is the meaning behind the old saying 'You can't pour from an empty cup?'
- What was your reaction to the anecdotes shared in the reflections on goal setting about my classmates' negative attitude to personal development?
- Can you recall when, in your life, you have had a 'fixed' mindset? How did that impact you?
- What positives can you take out of being a lifelong learner and having a growth mindset?
- Reflecting on my story, what are examples of having a growth mindset?
- What does have a growth mindset mean for you and what are some personal examples?
- What would be the benefits of having a coach or mentor in your life right now?

Perseverance and persistence

Whether you have noticed it or not, I think perseverance is an underlying theme throughout the book. This personal attribute helped considerably in my transformative journey of spiritual reawakening, Purpose and post-traumatic growth. It's throughout each chapter, mostly implicit, but nevertheless quietly but powerfully present.

Throughout this time when I was going through my journey, my wife and I would spend time together most mornings over a 'cuppa' meditating, reflecting and reading something that would inspire us for the day. Without this daily practice it would have been easy to get sucked into a vortex of negativity and self-pity.

On one of these occasions we came across a long-forgotten childhood story from the Bible, of Samson, not the one where he pushes the great pillars of the temple down, but where his enemy had bound him and, on breaking free, Samson found a fresh jawbone of a donkey and killed a thousand men with it…(so the story goes!)[3]

The story caught my attention and interest, so much so that I would like to share with you the interaction that followed. This is not to be self-indulgent, but to encourage you to become more aware of a special personal attribute that gives you strength when you most need it.

Drawing from one of my slightly edited old blogs, the interaction and subsequent reflections that morning went like this:

> I was still half asleep when Angela read the story, but I woke up quickly when she asked me what my 'jawbone' was. (As I was a professional coach and Angela a psychotherapist, we have given each other permission to ask tough questions). Instinctively, I gave her a cheeky (maybe pathetic) smile. 'No', she said, 'We had our children long ago – that is not what I meant.'

> She asked the question again but from a different angle. 'What have you been innately given (your 'jawbone') that has helped you 'win the day' when faced with your 'enemies?'

Now I was awake!

Like a good coach and counsellor, she remained quiet while I pondered this question. My first responses centred around my life Purpose of *Igniting Enthusiasm* and how I expressed love to others in this way. Still silence from the coach.

This was a significant moment. I began to enter a space of greater self-awareness as I started to think about that one most obvious, enduring, innate personal trait: my personal life 'jawbone'.

And then I had it – not a tentative, meek, maybe this is it, but a confident, all-knowing awareness. It was **perseverance!**

At this point, Angela shifted her role from *counsellor* to *wife*. She began to recall all the times I persevered in the face of adversity, criticism, false accusations, self-doubt, life threatening illness, financial struggles, relationship breakdowns and much more.

I tried to recall when I first became aware of this trait. At six years of age, I had polio (not severe as I only missed three months of school) and could not bear to stay in bed. I still hobbled around the farm and even milked the cows. Over three months off school was a challenge for an active young boy. Even now, I remember the excruciating pain of the slightest movement, but I persevered and persisted.

Have you ever had a disastrous public performance? My first 'penny concert' in primary school certainly was. I really muffed my first piano solo around the age of ten. It was a moment of sheer terror, shame and embarrassment when I froze and couldn't play another note. The next day we had to go to the infants' school and repeat the concert.

My teacher kindly asked if I wanted to play. At home, I found a new piece, practised it for four or five hours that evening, learned it off by heart and played it the next day without a mistake. What a relief! I felt better even when my teacher said, 'Well done!' Maybe then I learned the lesson of not giving up, of not being a quitter.

As you may recall in the chapter on goal setting, there were the times I attended the convent for after-school piano lessons. By now I was taking music seriously and wanted to do it for my Junior (now called Year Ten). As explained earlier in this book, we lived on a farm midway between two small towns. My transport home after the lesson was to hitch hike or walk – 12 kilometres! A heavy case, old shoes, and feeling tired from a full day at school made this quite a challenge. It was difficult but I wanted music for my Junior Certificate. I persevered even when I had to walk home in the rain, or in the cold dark winter and when no one would stop to give me a lift.

I know what you are thinking. Why didn't your parents come and pick you up? Mum didn't drive and farmers worked on the farm till dusk, didn't they? But that's another story! I passed my Junior music (and later my Leaving (Senior)) with Distinction. I persevered through adverse circumstances and often sacrificed cricket and footy for music practice. My 'jawbone' won the day!

Academic work didn't come easily for me when I was in school. In Year Ten (Junior as it was called in the 60's) my Maths B teacher was the Principal (Headmaster in those days). He said a terribly deflating thing to me one day: 'Gifford, you'll never pass your Junior.' I did pass, with eight subjects but failed one. Yes, you guessed it – Maths B! As Head Boy this really pricked my ego and I did hold a teenage resentment. If only I could have responded then, the way I know now!

Then, having failed my Leaving the first time due to an acute case of shingles just prior to and during exams, I had another go. Despite the humiliation of having to go back and mix with a different year group, I held onto my childhood goal of wanting to be a schoolteacher and passed all subjects.

At University the Professor talked to me about 'recognising my ceiling and limitations'. Another lecturer, fully aware that my wife had recently nearly died in childbirth and we had a very premature baby at home said, 'We will have to wheel you out in a wheelchair by the time *you* pass'. Not only did I pass my BA, then my Dip Ed while working full time but I went on to complete my MA and PhD from London University Institute of Education and along the way did a M.Ed. degree.

I had been given such a powerful 'jawbone'. Perseverance won the day again.

And then there was the sport! Overcoming the setback of polio and becoming captain of footy and cricket in Junior High and vice-captain of cricket and football (AFL) and captain of athletics in my final year as well as winning the PSA Schoolboy 800 metre race comes not only from talent but perseverance and determination.

I guess I was brought up to never give up. This inherited *Value* was nearly the death of me when I first went to the city from the country town to finish my final two years of schooling. My sporting reputation had gone before me. At the cross country trials, I was absolutely spent by less than the half-way mark. I just wanted to quit. The stitch in my side was killing me but I hung on to lead the race. With about two kilometres to go, I thought I would black out. Stupidly, (or was it an inbuilt determination or my Dad's 'tape' in my head?), I kept going. I led the runners back to the school oval for the final lap – lungs bursting, muscles stretched to breaking point, just willing myself to finish the race. About 20 metres from the tape, as the *new boy from the bush* running against the well-trained city kids, I became aware of something passing me. It must have been another runner – all was a blur. Apparently, I did finish second but woke up in the school's hospital hours later with a doctor hovering over me.

Writing that story some forty-five years after it happened, it seems almost as if I were there in the race again. In my perseverance, was I stupid, proud, courageous or determined?

Later, in my professional life, I came to understand that for my personality type (ENFP in Jungian terms) the questioning of my personal integrity is the worst thing anyone can do. On numerous occasions the 'jawbone' of perseverance combined with unconditional love and positive regard toward my 'false accusers' have become powerful weapons in winning the day.

Persevering in relationships and behaving in a way where others have to face themselves and not the ugly, fearful manifestation of my ego, has enabled me to maintain a peace of mind in adversity. For many, this is unfathomable, and they give up or quit relationships without persevering.

There are many more stories like these. And this is the one I tell here in this book. It's now many years since I *hit a wall,* as they say or when I was *Mucked Up.* The opinions of the many 'experts' that I would never work again, have been confounded. In fact, I have had one of the most productive and rewarding periods of my life. When I think back on this story and reflect on my 'jawbone' called perseverance and persistence, I'm reminded of what Churchill said in his famous speech to a group of schoolboys, 'Never, ever, ever give up!' I agree!

Angela's question was a fantastic catalyst for me to reflect upon and explore a great personal attribute that I have been given. Clearly, it has been my 'jawbone' throughout my life, was powerfully present throughout my transformative journey back to wholeness and will be for the rest of my earthly days.

Perhaps we could all benefit from seeing what we already have been given and put it to work, instead of searching in faraway places. Often the answer is right under our nose!

As with many people, what I had thought was secure in terms of work, health and finances was suddenly lost. We all go through tough times and bear the scars of our wounds.

As I close this piece of self-reflection, I am mindful of the *shadow side* of the 'jawbone of an ass'. The *shadow side* of perseverance is stubbornness. And to be stubborn is to be a silly ass!

And so, in all of this, I ask myself, 'What is the core motive for my perseverance?' Is it born out of a stubborn pursuit and need to protect and preserve the ego? Is it a blind determination to achieve goals, no matter what the cost? Perhaps once it was. Now, older and wiser, I test my reason for persevering in situations against these questions. How might I positively serve my character and humankind by persevering in this endeavour? How is it On Purpose for me?

Samson needed to see the potential in what he had already – just the jawbone of an ass. But it was sufficient for him to win the victory.

So, what is *your* 'jawbone' to help carry you through to success and significance? Once you realise what you have been given, recognise where it has come from and put it to work you will be amazed at your achievements and insights. Enjoy your discoveries!

I have always persevered in the face of adversity but I was interested to learn from research undertaken at Pennsylvania State University and published in 'The Journal of Abnormal Psychology[4]' that people who persevere and cultivate a sense of purposefulness can create resilience in the face of hardship, thereby lowering their risk of mental health disorders in the decades that follow that initial challenge. The researchers found that people who persisted in achieving their goals had much lower levels of mental health disorders like depression, anxiety, and panic attacks over the following 18 years. The study also found that people are likely to stay strong mentally and ward off depression, anxiety and panic if they find the strength to tackle setbacks and solider on.

Facing hardships is challenging. When we practice acceptance, self-awareness and self-observation, viewing life from the perspective of our True Self, living in alignment with our Purpose, staying connected with our family and friends, and doing something small, even when life seems dark and difficult, we will be in a much stronger position to overcome adversity.

To conclude this theme of perseverance and persistence I would like to leave you with a quote from Calvin Coolidge[5], 30th President of the United States: 'Press on. Nothing in this world can take the place of persistence. Talent will not; nothing is more common than unsuccessful men with talent. Genius will not; unrewarded genius is almost a proverb. Education will not; the world is full of educated derelicts. Persistence and determination alone are omnipotent. The slogan 'press on' has solved and will always solve the problems of the human race.'

Questions for discussion and action

- Do you persevere in the face of obstacles or do you throw in the towel?
- Reflect on the times that you have stuck at something – pushed through and overcome your challenges, fears and setbacks. How was that for you?
- Based on my example above, what do you consider to be your 'personal life jawbone' (your most obvious, enduring, innate

personal trait that you bring to bear to overcome obstacles and setbacks)?
- How has that worked for you? What is your most recent example of your 'jaw-bone' in action?
- Many of us learned a poem or were quoted a line by William Edward Hickson which says: 'It's a lesson you should heed, Try, try again. If at first you don't succeed, Try, try again.' How do you respond to this? If someone claimed that this childhood rhyme is one of life's greatest lessons, what would you say?
- The only way to learn perseverance is to fail. What do you say to that?

Thank you for reading this book about my journey from broken to whole and how I put Humpty together again. It means a lot to me and my sincere hope is that some of the content shared has relevance, meaning and application for you.

As you have read, and can no doubt imagine, to reinvent myself personally and professionally was not plain sailing. I admit there were numerous (and sometimes maybe too many) setbacks, disappointments and challenges. Sometimes it felt like the *Mack Truck* kept reversing back over me just to ensure the 'job' was done properly.

I have come to believe that overcoming adversity is often accompanied by an invitation and a gift, if only we realise it. The invitation in my case was to remain a victim or to have victory over my circumstances – to either break-up or wake-up! The gift was being able to see the world and life through a new paradigm when my old one had failed me. The content of this book shows how this new paradigm gradually unfolded for me. I knew none of this prior to 'having a great fall' other than having embarked on, (and then parked) my journey of Purpose, a few years prior to my life being turned upside down.

Finally, as I reflect on what has been shared here, several questions come to mind. The first is, what would I say now, so many years later to the specialist who told me I was totally fucked and wrote in his report that: 'This man will never be able to work again'?

The second question is, what do you think was the one factor that he didn't consider when he spoke and wrote those remarks?

I would love to hear your answers.

References and Notes – Chapter 7

1. Rohr, R. *Naturally indwelling.* Richard Rohr's Daily Meditation, From the Centre of Action and Contemplation: Friday, January 10, 2020. Retrieved 21 January 2020 from: Mailing List.

2. *Strengthening relationships for a longer healthier life.* Harvard Health publishing, Harvard Medical School: Retrieved from: https://www.health.harvard.edu/healthbeat/strengthen-relationships-for-longer-healthier-life.

3. This story comes from the book of Judges in the Old Testament – Judges 15:16

4. *Perseverance towards life goals can fend off depression, anxiety and panic disorders.* Story source: American Psychological Association, Retrieved from:
https://www.sciencedaily.com/releases/2019/05/190502100852.htm
Journal Reference: Nur Hani Zainal, Michelle G. Newman. Relation between cognitive and behavioural strategies and future change in common mental health problems across 18 years. *Journal of abnormal psychology*, 2019; 128 (4): 295 DOI: 10.1037/abn0000428

5. Quote by Calvin Coolidge. Retrieved 7 April 2020 from:
http://thinkexist.com/quotations/persistence/

Putting Humpty Together Again

Humpty Dumpty had a great fall,
Life's curve balls seem to hit us all,
Discovering our Purpose deep in our soul,
Starts our journey from broken to whole.

Humpty Dumpty had a great fall,
Our old life paradigm fails us all,
When the True Self rises from the ashes,
It's only Love that truly matters.

Humpty Dumpty had a great fall,
Being *Mack-Trucked* doesn't end it all,
Learning how to realise your goals,
Continues our journey from broken to whole.

Humpty Dumpty had a great fall,
Contrary to success and standing tall,
Setting goals for growth, not for glory,
Means letting go of failed old stories.

Humpty Dumpty had a great fall,
Avoidance seems to plague us all,
Unhealthy thoughts hold us back,
Self-observation restores us on track.

Humpty Dumpty had a great fall,
Unmanaged stress destroys us all,
Living 'whole' from the inside out,
Brings peace of mind and not self-doubt.

Humpty Dumpty had a great fall,
Life throws challenges to us all,
We can break up or become whole,
Is it Spirit that conquers all?

Acknowledgements and Special Thanks to:

Angela Gifford
Thank you for your love, support and patience and for the hundreds of conversations we have had about the content of this book. Thank you for your unconditional love over 50 years of marriage and for being my sounding board, encourager, editor and best friend. When I went through my darkest times, you were *always* there for me; when I had self-doubt, you encouraged me; when I saw the glass half-full, you challenged me to see it overflowing; when my Spirit was low, you lifted me up; when I got stuck, you showed me a way through.

Dr Phil Harker
Thank you, Phil, for being my mentor in most issues psychological and spiritual over the past 35 years. This book would not have been written if it were not for the countless conversations we have had over this period on 'what it means to be human,' the nature of Mind, and human choice. My transformational journey owes so much to your wisdom, spiritual insight and generosity. The positive impact you have had on my life has been immeasurable and profound.

Kevin W. McCarthy
Thank you for inspiring me to start On-Purpose Partners® Pty Ltd and for helping me find my life Purpose. Your Books, *The On-Purpose Person* and *The On-Purpose Business* were inspirational in getting our business started. Your training program came at a time when I was Off Purpose! Little did I understand back then, but knowing my Purpose was to become central to my transformational journey. Both Chapter One and Chapter Four have been informed and inspired by your work.

Paul Blackburn

Thank you for your support, mentoring and coaching over the past two years. Being a 'student' of Global Success Academy has been educational, inspiring and has taken me to another level in my personal growth. Thank you for your encouragement to get my book written, for being my accountability partner and motivating me to get my wedding ring back! The pre-commitment strategy was a winner!

Janine Gramshaw

Sincere thanks for your loyal and ongoing support and skilfully assisting me in the presentation and formatting of my drafts and with the final presentation of all of our Learning and Development Programs over the past 20 years. You are such an amazingly generous human being! I owe you so much gratitude.

My clients

Thank you all for teaching me so much and for giving me a sense of purpose and meaning over the past 20 years. You are such an important component of my Why!

Ted Scott

Thank you, Ted, for the many lunchtime conversations we have had over the years. I'm so grateful that we were introduced through our mutual friend Dr Phil. Your books and blogs are inspirational, informative and have helped me considerably in my transformational journey. Thank you also for being a keynote speaker at one of my major events.

Dr John Ryan

Thank you for your medical and personal support for the past 35 plus years. On several occasions when life threw me curve balls, some pretty massive, you gave me amazing support. Your daily phone calls checking in on me and the holistic medical treatment played such a significant part in restoring me to wholeness and good health. I will never forget and will always be grateful to you for your kindness, generosity, medical wisdom and care.

Susie Reeves

To my daughter Susie, thank you for helping me with my new title. Our 'walk and talk' together ended weeks of frustration. Coming up with the Humpty metaphor was creative, timely and just right! Thank you also for being such a support when 'I had a great fall'. I know you were doing it tough yourself at that time as you came to live with us with two small children. Despite your circumstances, you were brave, stood tall and refused to be a victim. You helped me every day in ways that you will never know.

David Gifford

To my son David, thank you for your sharing your generous spirit in so many loving and practical ways. I especially want to thank you for helping your mother and me when we were massively financially hit by the GFC. We will always be so appreciative of you supporting us in this and many other ways.

Dr Michalia Arathimos

I express enormous gratitude and thanks to you for editing this manuscript. It can be quite a daunting process but you made it seamless due to your expertise, professionalism and encouragement. I have had other editors prior to writing this book, but you were different. You bought a human and personal touch throughout the process and seemed to 'live' and share in my journey. Your helpful suggestions and encouraging annotations reignited my mojo when I felt like I was completely 'over it'. I count myself fortunate to have had the opportunity to work with you and also thank Andy McDermott from Publicious for recommending you.

Ryan McDonald - Smith

From Younique Creation for the cover design and the Humpty images. It was so easy to work with you and your intuition and creativity are inspiring.

Publicious Book Publishing (Andy McDermott)

You journeyed with me throughout the publication process with patience, generosity and helpful advice. Nothing ever seemed to be too much trouble and your knowledge and experience were invaluable.

Meet the Author

Dr Edward Gifford is a Director and the Chief Enthusiasm Officer of award winning On-Purpose Partners®, a professional coaching and training consultancy. Edward's coaching inspires and facilitates personal and organisational transformation in leadership, career transition, strategic thinking, team building, workplace engagement and work/life integration. Edward is a Professional Certified Coach with the International Coach Federation. Having assisted over 600 business entrepreneurs, he has also facilitated executives and senior professionals in transitioning to careers with greater meaning and purpose. An experienced public speaker, he is passionate about sharing key life and business transformational messages. Edward has authored several eBooks including *Resumés that Work* and *Interviews that Win*. His book, *Broken to Whole: How to put Humpty together again* is his first major work of creative non-fiction. Formerly, Edward was a Senior Lecturer in Education, his university career spanning some 20 years. With his wife Angela, Edward recently moved from Queensland to his family roots in Dunsborough Western Australia where he combines work with golf, walking, fishing, music and gardening.

Edward Gifford Ph.D.

www.ingramcontent.com/pod-product-compliance
Lightning Source LLC
Chambersburg PA
CBHW071827020726
47502CB00004B/1273